TRACEY BARSKI

Heart In Parallel

An Alternate Chronicles Prequel

First edition

ISBN: 978-1-961707-03-0

This book was professionally typeset on Reedsy.
Find out more at reedsy.com

To Lyssa. I hope I say enough that you are the very best. Okay, talk to you before bed tonight. And when we wake up tomorrow morning. And after lunch for our midday check-in. Love you.

Contents

Prologue

It tingled along his skin—the feeling that someone was following him in the growing darkness. And it pissed him off that it had come to this.

Twenty years had afforded him a stable, if not totally satisfying, life. And then it had happened.

The carefully crafted life he'd made for himself and his niece would come crumbling down, so he'd had to make a plan. He cursed himself for not having the pieces in place sooner.

Before pursuers had come knocking.

So now he was scrambling to put everything in place to keep himself alive and his niece from being found.

This was definitely the timeline he needed. But he'd have to come back, slip out for now and make his way back in to put it all together—once he'd lost the lackey he knew was tailing him.

He held the charm in his palm, the familiar buzz of energy like a hum through every cell in his body. It made him feel more alive, but it also put his senses on hyper-alert. And he knew the cretin following him was gaining.

He was too close to the bars and restaurants of downtown to jump. One percent was too high of a risk with that large of a sampling. So he walked faster, putting as much distance between himself and the crowded area as possible.

A thrill shot up his spine as the footsteps grew louder, the tail less concerned with going unnoticed.

He was far enough from the busier areas, and he needed to go before this guy caught up to him. He bared his teeth, starting to calculate the risk before the tail made it a now-or-never decision.

His thumb moved over the charm, sending the new and stronger buzz shooting up his arm and through his body, warping the view in front of him.

Pressure on the air, as if weights were being added to the atmosphere, made him grit his teeth. The ringing in his ears started, though that was something he'd long ago grown used to.

He heard the grunt of the person chasing him, and it was a distinctly female voice as she broke into a full sprint.

Just before the blackness stole his vision and comprehension, a man crying out from the closest parking lot echoed in his ears.

"*What* is *that?*"

1

Status Quo

LUKE

Luke stared into the depths of his empty glass, the last sip of beer listing as he tipped it, debating.

"Buy you another?" Ryan asked.

Luke looked over at his coworker. He'd been disappointed with the local brew, but he didn't have the time for a second, more enjoyable one. Even though he had that itch for another.

He clicked his tongue. "Nah, man. Gotta get home."

Ryan gave him a sly grin. "Don't want to upset the little woman?"

Luke snorted. "She's anything but little, and she'd kick your ass for calling her that. But, as a matter of fact, I still have some paperwork to go over for tomorrow. Some clients are coming in early."

Ryan sucked in a breath. "Always working harder than the rest of us. You make everyone else look bad."

Luke grinned, knowing it was his million-dollar smile. "That's why I get paid the big bucks."

He slapped Ryan on the shoulder as he got up, putting

enough force into it to make the other man wince. Which gave Luke a warm sense of satisfaction. Friendly competition and all that. Or maybe because of his comment about Erin, since he knew Ryan hadn't been as light-hearted as he'd intended. He always called her a "wet blanket" when they went out for drinks, which she often had an opinion about.

"Touché," Ryan said with a laugh, turning back to his own beer.

Luke shuffled through the after work drinking crowd toward the door. He didn't realize how loud it was in the pub until he got outside and the summer air enveloped him in jarring near-silence. A couple of guys stood a few feet away smoking, but their voices were a low murmur.

Luke started to pat his pockets for his keys before he remembered that he'd left his car at the office parking lot two blocks over. He tossed his blazer over his shoulder and checked the street in either direction before jaywalking.

A glance at his watch made him grimace, and he regretted the impulse to walk to the pub instead of drive. It was already seven forty-five.

But he remembered that Erin was out to dinner with her mother, so he had no reason to rush back other than going over the accounts for the Gillespies in the morning.

He forced himself to relax, to enjoy the twilight glow that settled over the buildings. The sun was no longer visible, but the last fingers of light still reached up to paint the sky in oranges and pinks.

"Hey man, got a buck?"

Luke looked over at the homeless man sitting against a stop sign on the corner. His cardboard sign was folded up beside him, but he rested one grubby hand on it.

Luke felt in his pockets for his wallet and found two wrinkled ones tucked inside. "It's all I got."

The guy smiled, his teeth in surprisingly good shape. "Appreciate it."

Luke continued on, riding the high of his good deed and the hum of alcohol in his blood, which carried him until he was close enough to spot the parking lot where his car was waiting, probably hot as an oven even with the sun down.

The lot was shared by a cluster of office buildings that huddled together like some secret clique, the architectural elite. During business hours, there were almost always people around. But at this time of the evening, everyone had either gone home or were tucked inside, burning the midnight oil.

He pulled out his keys, letting them dangle from his fingers until he got close enough to unlock the car. It was on hot summer days or freezing winter ones that he always found himself wishing for a remote start so he could at least get it to a reasonable temperature before he got in. Erin had warned him he'd regret getting a black car on these ninety degree days.

"Hey man, that's a pretty fancy car."

Luke jerked around at the voice. The homeless guy's eyes didn't leave the sleek sedan. The fact that the man had followed and cornered Luke made unease coil in his belly.

"Got anything else in there you could spare?"

Luke had mentally patted himself on the back for being as generous as he had been earlier, but now, only regret mingled with his tension.

"Nah, dude," Luke replied, hoping his casual tone wouldn't give away his rattled nerves. "I don't leave stuff like that in my car."

"Not even spare change?" The man's eyes flickered to him,

narrowing as he moved closer.

Luke instinctively stepped backward. The heat radiating off of his car warmed his back. Maybe if he gave the guy something else, he would leave Luke alone.

"I might have a few quarters or something, but that's it."

The man moved closer still, and his benign smile turned sour. Luke dropped his blazer as he pressed back against his car, ignoring the sting of the hot paint through his thin shirt.

"You fancy Suits never have much to spare for the likes of me, but I know you got more money than you know what to do with." His breath reeked of rancid alcohol, cigarette smoke, and what Luke could only assume was whatever the guy had last eaten.

"I gave you what I had. And you're right, I have money, but I did work for it so—"

"Then get some more out. You got your card. There's gotta be some ATM somewhere. Spread the wealth, man. I work hard too. Ain't got nothing to show for it."

Anger flamed through Luke, chasing out the fear. "No. I don't trust that you'll use it well. Some other time, I might consider buying you a hot meal or groceries. But I'm not just handing over cash because you demand it."

The man's grimy hand shot out, gripping the front of Luke's shirt before he could react. Luke made to shove him off when he felt the prick of a knife at his gut, just below his ribs. He froze, his hands suspended between them. Never once had this sort of scenario ever crossed his mind as a possibility.

"I watch you walk in and out of this building every day, watch you head over to the cafe to get yourself a nice, hot lunch. Every day!" The knife pricked at his side as the man spoke.

Luke jolted, praying the knife wouldn't break the skin.

Clearly, this was about more than just a need for money. This guy had some pent-up resentment, and Luke was a convenient scapegoat.

"You want to join me every day? I'll buy you lunch any time you need it. I have no problem with that." Luke's words tumbled out in quick succession, but his voice didn't shake. "This is not the way to fix the injustices you think you've experienced."

"*Think?*" the guy repeated through his teeth, the knife making another little jab into Luke's side.

He grunted. "Look, I don't know your story, so I can't speak to whether you've truly experienced some unfairness. I'll buy you dinner right now. You can tell me all about it." A drop of sweat trickled down Luke's left temple, and he fought the insane urge to swipe it away. It was crazy that he would even notice that sort of detail.

But he was noticing a lot of things. The fingernail he'd cut too short, which throbbed. The lack of cushion in his shoes that walking two blocks made more obvious. The buzzing in his ears that steadily grew louder.

"You don't want to hear it. You just want to placate me. With your empty words. That's all they've ever given me," the man muttered.

The buzzing in Luke's ears grew louder, rising to a point that he wondered if it wasn't only in his head. He grimaced. "I'm sorry you feel that way. But you've gotta make a decision right now. Am I really the guy you're mad at?"

The homeless man's gaze seemed to sharpen on him, un-certainty entering his eyes. Beads of sweat rolled in the grime coating his face too.

"Because I'll listen to what you have to say, but not like

this. Not because you forced me to—agh! Do you hear that?" The buzzing rose into a full-on ringing, like feedback from a microphone.

Confusion deepened the man's uncertainty.

The ringing grew louder, and Luke lost any sense of the situation as he reached up to cover his ears. "What *is* that?"

"You trying to trick me?" The muffled voice of the homeless man barely broke through the rising torturous sound stabbing into Luke's eardrums.

The streetlight above them burst, popping like a glass bubble. Luke didn't even hear the shards raining onto the hood of his car.

He buckled over, his head throbbing from the piercing noise, pressure mounting in his ears. He expected them to burst just like the light bulb at any moment. It was a quick, painful slide into unconsciousness.

* * *

He woke to distant voices, beeping, and quick footsteps. Even with his eyes still closed, he could tell the room he was in was dim but not dark. The antiseptic, sterile smell and the murmur of activity outside of the room he was in tickled at his memory—a flashback to getting his appendix removed in middle school.

His eyes flew open as the thought settled. He gripped the thin blanket under his hands. An oxygen monitor was clipped to the end of his left forefinger. Other monitors beeped out steady rhythms that jumped a little with his momentary panic.

Why am I in a hospital?

He moved his hands over his body, taking stock of every part.

Nothing hurt, other than a stinging at his side and a headache that pulsed behind his eyes.

"Oh, you're awake!" a woman's voice chirped.

He winced as the sound ricocheted in his head. "What's going on? What happened?" He wet his chapped lips with a sandpapery tongue.

The woman smiled, sympathy in the soft lines around her eyes. "Someone found you unconscious in a parking lot outside the Henderson building. We have a suspicion you were mugged. Couldn't find your wallet or cell phone. Lost your shoes too." She walked over to sign in on the computer beside his bed, then checked the readouts on the monitors and tapped them into the open fields on the screen.

"The homeless guy," Luke murmured, remembering. "He had a knife."

Her eyes widened, but she reined it in quickly. "That explains the small laceration on your abdomen. You'll want to file a report with the police. We can call them down or you can go once you're released."

Luke squeezed his eyes shut, bits of the night before blinking behind his eyelids. "I remember him pulling the knife. And this awful ringing sound in my ears." He looked to her as if she might have an answer for him on that one.

She pursed her lips, eyes narrowed. "Couldn't find any head trauma. A very slight blood alcohol level on the screening. I'm guessing you'd come from a bar?"

Luke blinked hard. "After work drinks at Mercy's Pub. I only had one."

"Hm. Could he have drugged you or something? Maybe he used something that's not on the standard screening. The police might be able to look more into that."

Drugged? How would that be possible? Hadn't he run into the guy after he'd left? Luke tried to concentrate, but the headache was too insistent.

She pulled out a small plastic package. "Are you in pain? I have some Ibuprofen for you."

He nodded. If it would even take the edge off the headache, he might feel more functional. This was too much like a hangover.

She filled a paper cup from the sink and handed it and the pain meds to him. "Here you are—" her voice dropped off. "We don't actually have your name, since you had no ID on you. I'm assuming your name is not John Doe."

"No," he agreed. "It's Luke Pearson."

She smiled. "All right, Luke. I'm Anna. Is there someone we can call for you?"

He tossed the meds back and sipped the water. "Um, yeah, my fiancée, Erin Baylor."

She pulled the tray beside his bed over and laid a piece of paper and a pen on it. "Put her number down here, and we'll contact her for you. I'll send up a little snack for you while you wait."

"Thank you."

She smiled again. "No problem."

He leaned his head back against the pillows as she left. The sense of disorientation could have been the effects of whatever drug the homeless guy might have given him. He did feel off, like he was still stumbling through a dream. The pain was real enough to make him toss the possibility away, though.

He replayed the events from the night before—the homeless man accosting him at his car with a knife. Why pull the knife and demand more from him if the guy was just going to drug him and take his stuff anyway? He was much more likely to get caught since the guy's grubby face was pretty well etched into Luke's memory.

Even took his shoes.

Well, they weren't that comfortable to begin with. It's what he got for buying the cheaper ones to get him by. He hated spending money on things that seemed so unimportant, like shoes he wore while sitting all day.

The rhythmic beeping around him was steady enough that, with his eyes closed, his mind started to drift. There was that meeting with the Gillespies today. He would have to reschedule.

. .

2

Doom Calling

The noise beyond her office door was a faint buzz around her, hazy and annoying, but easy enough to ignore when she worked at it. Which she was currently doing.

A framed picture sat on the edge of her desk, but Erin's eyes always skittered away from it. And at the moment, she was gazing determinedly out the window.

Nathan was probably just taking off to New York where he'd catch a flight to London, and she wished she was going with him on his business trip. Even if he would be busy the whole time, she could find ways to occupy herself. Lounge around in a hotel robe, give herself a facial, *sleep*—just being somewhere else would be a welcome break.

If only.

It wasn't like she could clear her schedule to make it possible. The to-do list she had in front of her might as well have been etched in metal. Each item was a link on the chain tethered to her wrists, holding her to the obligations. Her shoulders curved inward from the weight of it, her jaw ached from unconsciously grinding her teeth, and her ulcer was back.

The doctor said it was probably too much coffee, too many acidic foods. But she knew the biggest problem, really, was the stress. A vacation was precisely what she needed and exactly what she couldn't afford.

Even just sitting there, the pain sliced through her as she stared without seeing, knowing she was ignoring an overabundance of work tasks. Or maybe because of that fact.

Her phone rang, pulling her mind back to reality and distracting her from the stab in her abdomen. She snatched the phone from her desk without checking the readout.

"This is Erin." The words came out on a sigh, her tone bordering on exasperation.

"Erin Baylor? This is Anna Woodbury. I'm a nurse over at Memorial."

Her heart dropped down to her shoes, and she sat up straighter.

Oh, God. It finally happened.

"Y-yes?"

"Luke Pearson asked that we call you to let you know he's here. It seems someone mugged him last night, but he is actually doing fine. We'll be releasing him today, and he wanted us to call you to come pick him up."

Confusion knit her brow, and she sat forward. "I'm sorry. Luke Pearson?"

The name, she knew, but it took a bit of effort to make sense of it—like a half-remembered dream upon waking. She hadn't thought of him in so long. The images came in a jumbled haze. A dark-haired, lean boy who grinned often and liked to tease. With the memory came darker, more painful flashbacks, and her throat tightened.

"Yes, ma'am," the nurse said, her name already gone from Erin's mind.

Because she was so busy trying to separate her whirling thoughts, to make the pieces fit together, she heard herself saying, "Um, okay. I'll be right down."

She hung up before the nurse could respond and sat frozen for a second, staring down at the phone in her palm as if it would get up and walk away.

Then, with halting movements, she grabbed her purse, stuffing the phone into a pocket, and turned in her chair. As she stood, putting the purse strap over her shoulder, she pressed cold fingertips to her temple, shaking her head at herself. She'd already agreed to go down there, but the impulsive response was one to be filed under *Bad Idea*.

Luke Pearson.

It had been, what, ten years since she'd seen him? Longer since they'd even had a conversation. Last she'd heard, he was living and working in Chicago. So the question was, why was he here? And even more importantly, why the heck would he have the hospital call her?

She paused at the door. *Bad Idea* was starting to feel more like *Terrible Idea*.

And yet she marched through that door like someone was yanking her leash.

"I'm heading out," she told Lotta, the administrative assistant. "I have my phone if you need me."

Lotta shot out of her chair. "When will you be back? Your father wanted to set up a meeting." Her voice rose in volume as Erin continued toward the elevator. There may have been a hint of panic, too.

"Not sure. We can reschedule."

Erin didn't look back, but she didn't have to in order to know what kind of expression Lotta would have on her face. People rarely said "no" to Hank Baylor—least of all Erin. She was about to find out if this was something worth defying her father for. Those elevator doors slid shut, and she was officially committed despite the tantrum he would likely throw later.

She tapped her foot, hand pressed against her stomach, and her father faded from her mind.

Because *Luke Pearson*.

She remembered the laughter that always glinted in his eyes. It was probably why her brother had become friends with him. As serious as Jordan had always been, he'd needed someone to help him let loose. Luke could make him laugh so effortlessly that it had endeared him to the whole family.

She steered her thoughts away as she walked through the parking garage, heels clamorous in the concrete cave. Her hands were slick with sweat, and she fumbled in her purse for her keys. There was more than just confusion about him calling *her*, of all people. Because every muscle in her body clenched just thinking about the possibility of it having to do with their last interaction.

She didn't want to remember that conversation from a decade before. Or what had led up to it.

The anxiety made her drive a little too fast, take corners a little too tightly, as she twisted her hands back and forth on the steering wheel.

No, she wouldn't dwell on the last time they'd talked. But she allowed herself to fall into the memory of that summer before her brother's senior year of high school. Hadn't that been the defining time?

Her family spent eighty percent of that record scorcher at

the lake house, and Luke had been a constant fixture, sleeping there almost every night.

She'd spent most of her time with her friend Jessica since she was a year younger and didn't figure the boys would want her tagging along, though she wouldn't have minded hanging with her brother or, particularly, his best friend.

What had started as an innocent childhood crush, mostly because of how nice Luke always was to her and his nearly constant presence, had blossomed as she'd gotten older. It didn't hurt that he'd become a bit of a teenage heartthrob.

But that was the summer Luke had noticed *her* as more than Jordan's little sister.

Her second year of high school had been good to her. She'd stopped growing taller so she could fill out with more womanly curves, and being on the varsity soccer team had given her the confidence she'd struggled to find during her freshman year. Up to that point, Luke had treated her with fraternal affection. But as the simmering sun languished day after day, his eyes, always crinkled at the corners from his constant grins, started to linger on her in a way that was suddenly and decidedly unbrotherly.

She recalled that afternoon she'd actually spent at her parents' place, painstakingly choosing an outfit and putting on just enough makeup to enhance without overdoing it—a fine line she was still figuring out at that age. When she'd walked down the wooden porch steps to wait for Jessica to pick her up, the boys had been playing catch with a football.

"Hey, Goldilocks! Wanna toss me that ball?" Luke had hollered, jogging toward her.

The nickname, which had always irritated her, grated less when she saw that his steps faltered as he took in her appearance. She'd worn a sundress for the outdoor concert she was going to, and she knew it accentuated her long, tan legs.

He'd reacted belatedly when she'd thrown the football back, exactly as her brother had taught her, and grunted when it pummeled him in the gut.

She remembered giving him a slow smile, the satisfaction in making him stumble spreading through her with delightful warmth. Especially since he was usually surrounded by girls who fawned all over him. That magnetic personality, always free-spirited and light, was hard for anyone to ignore. Even though he'd dated quite a few of them, none of the relationships lasted long. She'd been counting on his new attention on her to change that streak.

Even with the changes between them over the summer, a back and forth of flirting and ignoring had frustrated her so much she'd cried more than once over that next year. But, still, it seemed to set them on a trajectory she'd thought she could track, everything lining up for their lives to intersect in a new way. The waiting was torturous, but the anticipation was going to make it that much sweeter. Even if it would take a few more years for them to get everything in place.

Then it had been ruined.

After that life-altering event knocked them loose of their bearings, there was no clawing their way back to the paths they'd been on before because the trails had been obliterated.

3

Askew

At some point, Luke had drifted off. Just a light doze, the cacophony of the hospital around him forming a background soundtrack that kept him on this side of consciousness. It was light enough that the tentative knock on his partially open door roused him with ease. He lifted his head carefully, forgetting the painkillers he'd taken had kicked in.

Even though the light in the hallway was artificial, it still glowed around her like a halo, silhouetting her lithe frame. She wore a button-up shirt, tucked at her waist into a bright, floral skirt that belled around her hips, the hem stopping mid-thigh. Her shoes were a bright pink that matched the blooms in her skirt. Had he ever seen that outfit before?

"You're all dressed up," he said, automatically smiling.

She stepped further into the room. "I was at work." Her tone was hesitant, uncertain. She sounded so unlike herself.

His brows knit. "Bad day?"

She didn't respond, hovering at the foot of his bed.

He didn't like the way the air felt—heavy, buzzing with

something he couldn't name. "Can you open the shades? Let some light in?"

She moved across the room without a word and did as he asked. Her blonde hair was tucked into a smooth bun at the nape of her neck. She turned toward him, her face tight with anxiety.

"Seriously, is something wrong? I mean, aside from the panic getting a call from the hospital probably caused." He smiled to reassure her. "They said I'm fine. But man, I feel off."

"They said you were mugged."

"Yeah. Dude even took my shoes. Can you believe that? I mean, I hated those shoes. And yeah, I know, you told me so. But still. I'm not sure I have much dignity left after that."

Her eyes narrowed slightly. "Luke, I have to ask. Why did you have them call me?"

He stilled. Was she *mad* at him?

"Hell, Erin. What, you think I did this on purpose? Like this was my fault? A guy held a knife to my gut. Cut me, in fact. I would've thought you'd want to know. Maybe care to see if I was all right." That hurt, and it was worse because it sent him reeling, so unprepared for that kind of reaction.

She crossed her arms over her chest.

Not so much in anger as defense, it seemed to him, and he was reeling again.

"Don't get so upset," she said in a subdued tone. "I mean, I'm glad to know you're okay, but, Luke, I haven't seen you in a decade. I just don't understand why you'd call me instead of your parents or your sister."

He released a breath. Oh. She was messing with him. Terrible timing, but she did owe him. Lord knew he'd played enough pranks on her to warrant even a malicious get-back. The chuckle he gave was short-lived as she tilted her head, genuinely confused.

He flipped back through her words, his gut clenching. "What do you mean you haven't seen me in a decade?"

Her brows quirked up. "I mean, I literally have not seen you in ten years."

He pushed himself up straighter, taking only brief satisfaction that he felt largely normal. "Stop messing around. I get it; I shouldn't have gone out for drinks. I know you don't like those guys, but it was one beer. Wait, did Jordan put you up to this?"

She blanched, taking a step backward as if he'd struck her. "Excuse me?"

He knew her well enough to recognize the danger in her tone. He had misstepped somewhere, but unlike in most other situations, he had no idea where he'd gone wrong, even as he replayed every part of this weird conversation. It had to be a joke, and she was doing a bang-up job of acting it out. Best performance he'd ever seen out of her.

His sigh scraped out of him, proof he was weary of the game. "Babe, come on. I know I'm the biggest jokester you know, and you definitely owe me some retaliation. But I honestly just want to go home and rest."

"Babe?" she repeated, wrinkling her nose. She held up a hand as if to stop him from speaking. "Listen, Luke. I don't know if you were hit over the head with a brick or if you're high or *what*. But this seriously has to stop. It's confusing and, frankly, upsetting. I can take you home—well, Chicago is quite the drive. So to your sister's house or whatever. But please. I don't want to talk about Jordan or play along with your little charade. It's not funny."

Damn right it wasn't funny.

"Chicago?" he echoed. "What the hell does Chicago have to do with this?"

He watched her face morph. She was definitely mad. "Stop it!"

He clenched his fists and his jaw simultaneously. As he knew from experience, that kind of anger brought on her tears. She turned away to hide them.

"Please."

"Erin," he said, his voice now soft.

God, he hated it when she cried. Made him feel helpless when all he wanted to do was fix it. He was feeling more useless than usual.

"What's really going on?"

She half-turned, her eyes glistening. "That's why I came when they called. To find out what's going on. Because I haven't seen you since Jordan's funeral. Last I heard, you were in Chicago."

Ice rushed through his veins. "Jordan's funeral? I saw him two days ago, alive and well, at your parents' house."

Tears spilled onto her cheeks. "Please stop it."

"Stop what? I'm serious, Erin. Your parents had us all over for a family barbecue. Jordan and Kelly were talking about going to Europe in a few weeks for their baby moon."

A sob broke from her lips, a whip across his heart.

"I can't take this anymore," she choked out, turning and bolting from the room.

Luke dropped his head back, squeezing his eyes shut. This must have been some bizarre sort of dream. It was obvious now that she was not joking with him. No, it had to be a nightmare because a world where they were not together was not a world he'd want to be in. And worse, his best friend was dead.

No, there was no way this could be real.

But maybe it wasn't a nightmare. Maybe it was a hallucination.

Had the nurse really only given him ibuprofen? Was it possible she'd given him the wrong medication, intentional or not? Or was it some reaction to whatever the homeless guy might have given him?

Aside from the most confusing conversation he'd ever had with Erin a few moments before, he didn't *feel* like he was under the influence of anything. Despite the hangover sensation earlier, everything was too sharp, too clear to think he could be on anything.

But nothing was making sense!

On top of that crapfest, he realized he would have to find another way home. His car was still at the office. If the homeless guy hadn't stolen it too. Guess that was his first stop.

He went through the check out process as if in a daze, his mind lashing him with the look on Erin's face when he'd mentioned Jordan. Nausea churned in his stomach, stirred by his attempts to reconcile the last image he'd had of her the day before—the way she'd smiled and laid warm lips across his before work that morning, stamping him with her easy affection.

Dressed in his now-dirty suit with no shoes on, he waved off concerned inquiries from the staff. They insisted on waiting for someone else to pick him up, to stop in at the police station to file a report. But the mugging was less of a concern now after what he'd experienced with Erin. He signed the paperwork and was released.

He patted his pockets and felt the keys, grateful to find something tangible that tethered him. Maybe that meant the car was waiting for him in the parking lot.

Lucky for him, the walk was fairly short to the Henderson building, even only wearing socks. Now, other than a slight headache, he felt pretty normal. The weather was so pleasant, he could almost imagine it was just an ordinary day. But he replayed the conversation with Erin, and his gut twisted.

Man, those tears. . . He clenched his jaw.

None of it made sense. Jordan was not dead. The two of them had gone on a camping trip just a couple of weeks prior. And the nonsense about him living in Chicago was laughable. He'd never been to Chicago in his life. So what was going on?

He rounded the corner to the parking lot, a heaviness now in his step. It was filled with vehicles at this time of day, and the weight grew. He weaved through sedans and SUVs and vans, urgency singing in his blood. His eyes shot to the row in which he'd parked his car, scanning the vehicles now lined up there. He started running, gaze moving across the row once, twice, again.

His car wasn't particularly unique, but it was obvious that it was not in its usual spot. He stopped at the row, marched to his spot, designated by his last name on a plaque.

He froze.

Except it was not his name on the plaque above his parking space. Each foreign letter dropped a stone into his stomach. He moved around the car that was not his, heedless of his hands as he pressed them against the glossy paint job.

"Kellerman?" he read aloud. "Who is Kellerman?"

"Hey, man. Get your paws off my machine!"

Luke spun to look at the man walking toward him. The guy was a few years younger, clearly a hotshot new to the game, his haircut a little too sharp, shoes too shiny, eyes too eager.

Luke squinted at him. "That's a pretty fancy car for someone who just started."

The guy pulled up short. "What do you know about it? Move on, buddy. You look like you robbed a homeless guy."

"Close," Luke muttered.

Ignoring the younger guy as he moved down the line of cars, he checked every name on the plaques. Some he recognized; others were not familiar.

Everything he knew of his world was tumbling in succession, each piece like a domino toppling into the next.

He hesitated, afraid of what else would fall if he kept looking. He decided against going inside to ask around the office. His boss was very keen on appearances, and there was no way the man would even entertain a conversation with Luke if he came in bedraggled as he was.

For ten whole minutes, he sat on the curb, trying to weed out his options with his hands in his hair.

His parents lived forty-five minutes away, and despite being a grown man, he didn't want to bring down the judgment that would come with it. They might not make a comment. But everything they refused to say would be displayed on their faces unhindered. They would come get him, of course. They were always willing to help, disapproval or not. But he needed a hot shower and answers much sooner than they could get there.

He could call his sister, but he needed a phone for that. Because, dammit, he didn't know her number by heart. That's what his cellphone was for. He only knew Erin's because she'd insisted they memorize each other's for emergencies.

The only option he could come up with was Baylor Industries, which was only a few blocks over. He risked another emotional encounter with Erin, but maybe she was calmer by this point.

And maybe everything will be back to normal.

That small voice jolted him, even as his logical side tossed every shred of evidence that nothing would be normal ever again. He would never know until he gave it a shot.

So he walked.

By now his feet were protesting the hard concrete, and it was starting to get warm. But it was just a few blocks, and honestly, his shoes wouldn't have been much better.

He made it after about fifteen minutes, his whole body drinking in the air conditioning, his feet singing the praises of the cool, tiled lobby floor. He rode the elevator alone, resting his head against the metal wall behind him, trying to avoid looking at his warped reflection in front of him.

The doors opened to Baylor Industries, and he slipped out, registering changes that threw his mind into a spiral. It had been a while since he'd visited, but the configuration of the space was very different from the last time he'd been there. The next domino knocked into its successor, rattling in Luke's mind, scattering his thoughts.

It wasn't until a cluster of people walked past him that he remembered why he was even here. The man leading them tugged at Luke's memory, and it jolted him back to reality.

Hank Baylor was a lean tower of a man with a full head of gray hair and piercing blue eyes. He had a leisurely slouch to his stance that belied his tendency to command a room and bulldoze anyone who stood in his way.

"Hank!" Luke called.

Hank's head swiveled in Luke's direction, a displeased pinch to his mouth, his eyes narrowed in irritation. The group of people he'd been walking with pooled around him, uncertain about what to do.

The annoyed look shifted, transforming as his mind went through the process of placing Luke's face.

"Lucas Pearson?" Hank said slowly, lifting his chin a little. He flapped his hand at the gaggle of followers to shoo them on.

"Sir," Luke said in response to the formal tone. He strode forward, taking Hank's proffered hand and shaking it vigorously. "I wonder if I might have a word with you?"

Hank took in a deep breath, weighing his answer as if Luke had asked for a thousand dollars. Then he tipped his head for Luke to follow him.

They took a weaving path through a labyrinth of cubicles toward the biggest office in the back. It was odd, given that Hank had retired a year prior, handing the reins of the business off to his children. The office he led Luke to had been transformed into Jordan's workspace months before.

But the suite they entered was a different world. Spartan with abstract art pieces on the walls, modern furniture with cold, hard lines. He couldn't remember having spent much time in Hank's office before it became Jordan's, but this sent waves of heat through him. If Hank had come back, where was Jordan's office now?

Two more dominoes toppled.

"Lucas, I'm going to be straight with you, I don't have much time to offer you." Hank's tone was business-like. His icy eyes shot over Luke in a quick appraisal like a bar code scanner. That quick skim told him everything he needed to know. "You look. . . ”

Luke looked down at himself, unable to think of anything else to do. “I was mugged, sir. And I think someone may have stolen my car.”

And something crazy is going on, he added silently. Hank's distant demeanor confirmed that something was askew.

Hank gestured to a tall, black cabinet in the corner. “You'll find some clean clothes in there. Your shirt is fine, I think. You're more broad in the shoulders than I am anyway. But there are some slacks that may fit, and at least a pair of shoes that'll suit.” His eyes fell on Luke's socked feet because, of course, he'd noticed that detail.

Luke made his way over to the cabinet with trepidation heavy in his bones as Hank flipped through a file he held in his hand. Odd that Hank would keep extra clothes at the office. As Luke reached inside the cabinet, his gaze zeroed in on the shelf with a toothbrush and toothpaste, razor and shaving cream.

He eyed Hank while he used the wardrobe door as a makeshift privacy screen. He could think of few reasons someone would need to keep extra clothes and toiletries at the office, and none of them were good.

“Tell me, son. What brought you back to town and why did you come here?”

Hank's eyes were still on whatever was in the file, absorbing information as his eyes jumped line after line. Erin once said he was a speed reader.

Luke yanked on a pair of chinos, trying to keep a hold of the rapidly building pressure in his chest. The facts. What were the concrete details?

“Um, well, my phone was stolen,” he started, sliding his belt through the loops, taking comfort in the rote action. “I don't know anyone else's number off the top of my head. I figured this was a safe bet for getting that info and access to a phone."

The next part was, admittedly, Luke grasping for confirmation or denial, knowing it would set off another chain reaction of dominoes.

"I thought Erin might be here as well. We got into a bit of a fight. . . " He held his breath as he watched the older man.

Hank lifted his gaze, bushy gray brows pulled tight over his eyes. "You saw Erin?"

The tone clamped Luke's stomach in a vise.

"I had them call her to pick me up, but we seem to be having some trouble communicating." Luke pulled some loafers over his heels then folded his dirtied clothes into a small pile. It was the one thing that he could control in this moment, making that pile as small and neat as possible.

"I'm not sure I'm understanding what you're saying." Hank squinted at him. "Who called Erin? And what on Earth would you be fighting about?" He put a fisted hand on the top of his immaculate desk, his wedding ring scraping the wood.

The sound scratched at Luke's eardrums, too much stimulation against his nerves.

"The hospital called her," he said, uncertain. "They picked me up at some point last night after the mugging. I guess it wasn't so much a fight as a misunderstanding. She went on and on about not having seen me in ten years and—" The rest caught in his throat, held hostage by his urge to deny it—that Jordan was dead. It would certainly set this man off as well if it were true.

But Erin's face, the pain carving an expression that Luke couldn't erase, haunted him.

Hank regarded him for a long moment, his thoughts a closely

guarded secret. But Luke sensed it in the air.

"Is ten years not accurate?" Hank asked, his formal tone a wall that shot up between them. "Perhaps you've seen her at some point in all this time and either she didn't know it or forgot?"

Luke swallowed, the weight of his confusion and despair sending him into the hard leather sofa near the door as his legs gave out. Hank's response suggested that at least part of what Erin had said was true.

"Oh, God," he said, mostly to himself.

Hank raised one eyebrow, unamused and barely sympathetic. "What exactly is going on?"

Luke shook his head, wishing it would knock the pieces in his head loose

He rubbed a hand over his chin. "Last night, I left Mercy's Pub after a drink with coworkers. I worked for Ipsen Investments, called your daughter the love of my life, and saw a future for myself as your son-in-law. Today, I have none of it. And everyone acts like I never did." He shook his head again. "And someone stole my freaking shoes."

Hank's lips pursed. "Sounds like maybe you had more than just a drink last night." He picked up his desk phone and held the receiver out to him. "Give your sister a call. She'll come pick you up, and you can sleep off whatever high you're on."

Luke clenched his jaw and clamped down on his need to argue. There didn't seem to be any ground to stand on. Everything thus far had pointed to him being the crazy one in this scenario.

He slowly stood and took the phone. "I don't know her number."

Hank turned to his computer and logged in, pulling up a search page. "I've got a meeting," he said, a stiff retreat in his words. "You can show yourself out?"

Luke nodded, dazed by the abruptness, feeling dismissed and dejected.

He turned at the door. "It was good to see you, son."

There was a glimmer of the Hank Baylor Luke knew in those words, and a flash of recognition blossomed into a staggering hope. Then Hank's next words came.

"I know we all blame ourselves one way or another for Jordan. But that was never on you." The older man disappeared out the door before Luke could respond.

Luke couldn't help thinking it was so he wouldn't have to see the aftermath.

Who was this man? Distracted and distant, cool and calculating. That was not the man who'd become a second father to Luke.

His stomach twisted. Hank mentioning feeling blame about Jordan's death sent a sharp fear through him. If Luke blamed himself at all, was he responsible in some way?

Had he lost his mind? He'd just texted with Jordan the day before during his lunch break, hadn't he? It wasn't possible he was dead.

Luke shut his eyes as he took a deep breath, the oxygen feeling like a traitor to his lungs as he wondered just what the hell was going on.

He wasn't going to find the answer just sitting there, so he shoved his eyes open and set his jaw, typing Tara's name into the search bar. It didn't take much to find her number.

4

Drowning Sorrows

ERIN

The sun glinted off the choppy surface of the water, the wet peaks stabbing the air with blinding brilliance as Erin stared out the windshield. The air conditioner was on full blast, tossing the tendrils of blonde hair that had fallen from her bun, tickling her neck. She registered nothing that she saw.

Not that she needed to. Though no one in the family had been there for several years, the old lake house was ever the same. Her father still paid a maid and a groundskeeper to maintain the property. Even if it was unused and abandoned, at least it appeared untouched by neglect.

She wasn't sure why she'd driven here, of all places. Maybe because it was the most secluded, quiet place she could think of. Even the thought of returning to the office made her recoil. There was no way she could have gone back, not yet.

She would not have been able to handle her father after the hospital. And her house was too empty to offer any sort of salve for the reopened fissures in her heart.

It didn't make sense that she'd choose here, though, and

she couldn't explain to herself why. Not when it was one more bullet fired from the weapon of her memory.

This had been Jordan's favorite place.

Hank Baylor was able to offer his family the sights in Europe, Mexico, Belize, Australia, and Japan. And out of everything they'd ever experienced, Jordan had most cherished their family vacations at the lake house. Which was why they hadn't come back since those days right after he'd died.

They'd stayed the weekend after the funeral as an homage to Erin's brother, as if it would do anything for them. Her mother had spent the whole time drenched in tears and alcohol. Her father had holed up in the bedroom, making phone calls to clients, checking in constantly at the office, micromanaging every employee down to the janitor.

It had set the precedent for the next decade.

Erin's mind danced away from the stinging memories of her mother passed-out drunk while her father's voice rumbled in clipped tones in the next room. Her gaze settled on the lake. The sound of the water lapping at the pebbly beach through her open windows played the soundtrack to a summer she hadn't thought of in years, one that didn't cause her quite so much pain.

It was the week before her sophomore year. Luke had come for the weekend, driving up in the car he'd just bought, an old Toyota pickup. He and Jordan had taken turns driving it around the lake, relishing the freedom even the junkiest of cars afforded them.

She'd watched from the beach, the water kissing her feet as she sunbathed. They'd skid to a halt in the truck then sprint toward the water, shedding their shirts as they went. Both boys were slender from youth and constant physical activity.

Together, they'd run track and played soccer. Jordan had dabbled in basketball that year.

The echo of the boys' laughter reverberated in her mind, an aural magnet that tugged at her. She got out of her car, walking down toward the water, pulled by the familiarity and a need to apologize like she'd neglected an old friend. She shed her pumps halfway down, her bare feet sensitive to the heat and rough edges of the rocks on the beach. Stopping just at the edge of the water meant the soft waves could lick at her toes. The cold was a shock at first, but she acclimated to a point that it felt good as a contrast to the hot rocks.

Seeing Luke in the hospital that morning was much the same. Stinging heat that seemed like it would burn her, then icy cold. Only now was she leveling out with distance.

So many memories plagued her. Most would have been pleasant if they hadn't been tainted by the grief that never seemed to fade.

But grief didn't blind her to the fact that Luke looked so much the same, only more filled out—his jaw was more square, his hair longer than he used to keep it. It seemed darker than it had been when he was a teenager, the ochre locks curling with the length and falling onto his forehead. He had given her that same ready grin, the teasing look in his eye that she remembered from their youth. He had spoken to her as if they were together, had called her *babe*. Which made absolutely no sense.

When her mind shifted back ten years, exhuming memories of those days leading up to Jordan's death, she remembered Luke's increasing interest in her, her fingers aching to trace the path their lives had once been on. But that had all been buried with her brother, the path split and rerouted in the aftermath.

How could Luke not remember? As if the past ten years had happened in an entirely different way? He must have been drunk. Or had a traumatic brain injury.

But if that had been the case, the hospital certainly wouldn't have been releasing him.

Her cell phone trilled from inside her car, alerting her to an incoming call. The grip of memory and familiarity threatened to keep her at the edge of the water, but she convinced herself it would only drown her in heartache if she stayed, and she trudged back up the beach, snagging her shoes on the way.

She needed to get back, whether she was ready to or not.

After tossing her shoes into the passenger seat, she yanked her purse from the floor, sliding her phone out of its pocket. The readout told her that Nathan had called. Then a text from him came through, alerting her that his flight out of New York had been delayed. She had no intention of calling him back for the moment, even as the guilt washed through her with tidal force.

It was always hard for them to connect when he was on his extended business trips in Europe. Between the time difference and their loaded work schedules, they were lucky to talk for ten minutes every few days.

But that was not really the basis for her guilt.

Her engagement ring still sat in a zipped-up pocket in her purse, a silent beacon of questions locked behind the fabric. On a weird whim, she had twisted it off before going into the hospital, like some part of her didn't want Luke to know she was engaged. As if it was some sort of betrayal of what it was they'd almost had a decade ago.

Such a stupid impulse. Nonsensical, even.

Under the notification for Nathan's text, several other messages let her know her father was not planning to let her blow him off.

She paused while reading one, slowing her dismissive roll. Heat rose in her cheeks.

Ran into Luke Pearson. Said you talked? Seems a little confused.
Call me when you get back to the office.

Always succinct, her father.

How in the world had he run into Luke? As if they'd been out doing errands and bumped into each other at the grocery store.

She tossed her phone back into the purse and started her car, pulling out onto the private drive faster than she probably should have.

God, she was unbalanced.

She made it back to work in less time than was legally deemed safe. Instead of letting her father know when she arrived, she made her way to her office quickly, ducking her head and trying to go unnoticed.

She shut the door and slid in behind her desk, bringing her computer to life. She did a quick search for Lucas Pearson. It was a common name, but she found him easily enough.

He owned a small advertising agency in Chicago. He smiled from a professional headshot on the homepage, the same laughing look in his eyes she'd always known, but there was a shadow there too. A deeper set to his eyes.

That had not been present in his face this morning at the hospital. And a full pause demanded she catalog the fact.

His social media profiles were not set to private, and it looked like he traveled a lot but was somewhat of a loner. Lots of selfies. A few here and there with his parents.

She remembered that a couple of years after he'd settled in Chicago after college, his parents had moved out to be near him. From what she understood, there had been some concern about his life choices. He had floundered a lot in college and for a while afterward, struggling with drugs and alcohol.

According to one of his pages, he'd recently checked in at a restaurant in downtown Chicago. As in twenty minutes ago.

That didn't make sense.

She trapped her bottom lip between her teeth.

Then a picture of his strategically placed latte and lunch plate popped up on his page, again labeling his location as Chicago's downtown.

She leaned forward, squinting, questions bumping into each other in her mind.

A knock on her door startled her, but she knew it was her father before he opened the door, which he did without being invited, as usual. It irritated her, but it was a fight she had yet to win.

Hank Baylor shut the door behind him. Surprisingly, his frustration wasn't visible on his face.

"You didn't call that you'd gotten back," he said, moving across the room to stand by the window.

He never sat in her office. She figured it was a power play. Hank Baylor was never to be on equal or lesser footing than anyone he met with. He was lucky to be blessed with enough height to keep that largely the case even when standing.

"I had a pressing matter to attend to first," she answered. Her tone was not as smooth as she'd been trying to make it.

"Yes, checking your social media is quite critical." It was spoken mildly, but she knew him well enough to detect the disapproval there.

"Believe me," she said, her own voice adopting the edge, "it was not for leisure's sake."

He inhaled loudly through his nose, a measured attempt at calming himself. "What is it you're looking at then?"

She turned her computer monitor toward him.

He moved forward, squinting at the screen. "Luke Pearson," he said, tilting his head ever so slightly. "This post lists him in Illinois. And he was definitely in my office little more than an hour ago."

"With, I suppose, a bizarre story as to what he believes about his life and connection to us?" She leaned back in her chair, crossing one leg over the other. She imagined it was a casual movement, but she was anything but relaxed.

"Something like that," her father replied. "I told him to go sleep it off. But what do you make of this?"

She sat forward, one thread of possibility twisting around several others, and she worked to sift through her jumbled thoughts.

She decided to pull the string that seemed most likely to unravel the whole mess. "Was it really Luke Pearson?"

Surprise flitted across her father's face. "You think this guy is pretending to be him?" His bushy brows contracted over his eyes. "What would he gain from that?"

She lifted her hands, utterly at a loss. "Nothing I can think of. But either that or, as you said, he's on a bender and something's got his mind messed up. Which is not out of the realm of possibility."

He cocked his head, a concession of the point. "Could be. But how would that explain what we're looking at here?" He gestured to the computer.

She chewed on her lip for a moment then lifted a shoulder. "We know he's struggled with drugs in the past. Is it to keep someone, a sponsor maybe, from checking up on him?"

He shifted, drawing her eyes. Hank Baylor wasn't one to fidget. "I don't know. Other than his crazy story, he seemed rather with it. The look in his eyes was focused and serious. Not the eyes of any drunk I've ever seen. I can't say I have much experience with drug users, but I don't imagine any of them being as aware as he seemed to be."

His words sang to a truth inside of her. There had been no evidence of intoxication in his demeanor when she'd seen him either. As she'd surmised earlier, a head injury seemed unlikely given that the hospital released him. And the nurse she'd spoken to that morning gave no indication otherwise. She'd even said that Luke was fine.

Still, the desire to understand what his game was prickled under her skin, like an itch she couldn't find, let alone scratch.

"I just don't understand," she finally said. "Why would he have some story about being at your house for a barbecue, talking about Jordan being married to Kelly, acting as if he and I were together?"

Her father nodded. "He said your relationship was quite serious."

Her brows rose. He had not intimated as much to her. "He acted as though Jordan were still alive and well. What does that mean?"

"He's crazy?" Her father rarely lacked confidence, but there was true uncertainty in his voice.

She tapped one finger on her desk. Then: "Where did he go after you saw him?"

"He called his sister to pick him up."

5

Revelation

Tara's silence as she drove pressed against his skin like an uncomfortable suit. Her gaze was very studiously trained on the road, her hands fisted around the steering wheel, twisting in a way that gave away too much and not enough. She had asked very little when Luke called her, readily agreeing to come get him.

Her hair was cropped much shorter than the last time he'd seen her, the dark locks curling just under her chin. More evidence that something about his world had changed.

"I appreciate you coming so quickly," he said, wanting to peel at least one layer of silence. "I figured it was easier than calling Mom and Dad."

Tara's brows furrowed, and she glanced sideways at him. "Luke, what's going on? Are you using again?"

He blinked, off-kilter. "Excuse me?"

She spoke quickly, her discomfort stiffening up her whole body. "There's no shame in a relapse, but we have to contact someone and get you support as soon as possible."

A flash of heat snapped up his spine. "Tara, what the hell are you talking about?"

"Luke, please. I can't lose you to that life again." Her voice trembled.

Which leeched the defensiveness right out of him. All of the toppled dominoes were now starting to form a picture he was struggling to accept. Everything in his life was gone—his job, his love, his best friend. And now, it would seem as though he had turned down a dark road he never would have thought himself capable.

"I'm not using," he said quietly.

She pressed her lips together, doubt written all over her face, but she said nothing more as they made their way across town.

The world flew by his window, but his mind was incapable of processing anything more than snatches of color and form as he tried to unravel just what the hell was going on.

This was no hallucination, as much as he wished it was. And if it was a nightmare, it felt more real than anything he'd ever experienced in his life. Usually when he had a stressful dream, he could make himself wake up. But he had been telling himself to wake up since his conversation with Hank, to no avail.

Too crazy to be real, too real to be a dream.

If ever there was a time he needed a hand in picking the whole situation apart, it was now. He needed help analyzing, needed someone to offer a different perspective or some kind of explanation that could make it all make sense.

Because his only answer right now was that he had lost his mind.

Erin would have been his first stop for unpacking anything. She was always his best sounding board, the most grounded and simplistic in analysis. But that wasn't an option. Jordan would have been his next stop.

Jordan's dead.

His wish to deny it wrapped itself around his chest and squeezed. It wasn't right, could not be true. How? Why?

"Tara, tell me what happened to Jordan," he said, his desperation to understand overruling his logic.

She glanced at him, a question in her eyes.

He scrambled for an explanation that would satisfy her. "It. . . will help me process. . . things. I just need you to walk me through the whole thing."

That seemed logical, right?

She turned back to the road and swallowed against the emotions that flickered across her face, all of them different iterations of grief. The pain seemed to steal her ability to speak for a moment.

"Um." She took a steadying breath. "Well, it was your sophomore year of college. You guys were at a party. He was ready to leave before you were."

That was pretty standard Jordan.

"You always had a hard time leaving a good party." Her smirk was dark and disappeared quickly. "He opted to walk home instead of wait for you. It was pretty late, on a weekend, and someone was out driving when they shouldn't have been. He was hit in the crosswalk a block over from your apartment, killed instantly. They still haven't found the driver."

Luke's hand became a fist on his thigh as he processed her words.

"You've always blamed yourself," she added softly. "But it wasn't your fault."

This must have been the blame Hank had alluded to. Luke was willing to bet it was a party Jordan had been reluctant to go to. How many times had Luke coaxed him out when he'd spent too much time studying?

But he didn't remember any such party. Not that any particular one would stand out among the rest. College was one long party for a while there. Until he'd finally gotten serious about winning Erin.

This seemed like a defining split in the life he remembered and the one he now found himself in—Jordan dying. Maybe he wasn't crazy at all. Perhaps he had shifted somehow into an alternate version of his life. But how? And what changed to lead to Jordan's death? A choice Luke had made? Or one Jordan had? Or was it outside either of them?

They were silent as Tara pulled into her driveway, and he followed her into the house. It was dark inside, and that darkness called to the black path his mind had turned down as he sifted through memory after memory of days that had melted into each other like candle wax.

Thankfully, his attention was drawn to the interior of the house, noting differences that were small but obvious to him because he'd been the reason why. It didn't have the upgrades he and his father had worked on for her. No fresh paint on the walls from last summer, the holes in the drywall he'd patched the first month after she'd bought the place still there.

A woman stood from the couch, and Tara walked forward to brush a hand on her arm.

"Thanks for watching her, Kim."

"No problem," the woman said. "She was just playing in her room, and since you said she'd had a cough, I figured I'd let her be."

Tara smiled and walked the woman to the door, then turned back to Luke when she was gone. "Our neighbor is always so helpful when I'm in a bind."

"Hannah's home from school today?"

She waved a hand then let it settle on the arm she crossed over her chest. "Yeah, she has a cough. She acts mostly normal, so hopefully it's just a little cold."

From a back room emerged a little dark-haired girl as if she'd known they spoke of her, her large eyes cautious.

"Hey Squirt," Luke said, his face automatically breaking into a grin.

His niece seemed to shrink, her hands grabbing onto the door frame as if it would protect her.

The sight sent a sharp pain through his heart. "What's wrong?"

Tara shot him a look as she brushed past, going to her daughter to reassure her. "She doesn't know you, Luke, and you're scaring her."

That was not the Hannah he knew. The sweet, rambunctious social butterfly would talk to anyone who would listen, ready with the stream of consciousness litany that marched in her head. He'd forged a bond with her from a young age because her father was a deadbeat, and Luke had fallen in love the second she'd been earthside.

"Hannah," Tara said. "This is your Uncle Luke. Remember the pictures Gigi showed you?"

Hannah glanced up at him at an angle, the sharpness of her distrust slicing into him. To alleviate that wariness, he knew he needed to take this process seriously.

He crouched down and held out a hand to her. "Nice to meet you."

Reluctantly, the girl lifted her arm and offered her tiny hand. It was limp in his palm.

"Strong shake. Have you been working out?" He shook out his hand as if her grip had hurt.

Hannah fought a giggle, to his relief. That was more like his girl.

He glanced at his sister, but he didn't see amusement in her expression. She almost seemed suspicious.

"Baby, why don't you go out in the backyard?" Tara tipped her head. "Get you some sunshine."

Hannah nodded, disappearing into her room briefly for a few toys, and they all made their way into the kitchen. Tara opened the sliding glass door for her daughter, her gaze following the girl as she went out.

He stopped by the door, watching Hannah in the small backyard. She moved slowly, cautiously, the dolls in her hands twitching every once in a while like she was too afraid to act out her imaginary scene out loud. None of the frenzied energy he was used to. Her lips moved softly as she carried on quiet pretend conversations.

"You seem different," Tara said.

He turned to fully face her as she set a cup in the sink and leaned a hip against the counter. Her eyes were narrowed as she took him in again.

"I am different."

She crossed her arms over her chest and tilted her head. "What does that mean?"

He took a deep breath, the weight of his inability to explain threatening to knock him flat out. But the opportunity had presented itself, and he needed someone to walk through this with.

"This will sound crazy. . . " He trailed off for a moment, trying to gather his thoughts the best way he could. Then the words just tumbled out. "I feel like I've been sucked into some alternate dimension or something. I seriously don't know what's going on, because yesterday I was walking down State Street to my car, parked in the parking lot of the Henderson Building where I worked for Ipsen Investments. I had just bought a ring so Erin Baylor and I could get married like we've been talking. Jordan was alive and well, and he and Erin ran Baylor Industries since Hank's retirement a year ago."

Through his explanation, her eyebrows had risen higher and higher, practically melding with her hairline. "What the hell kind of story is that?"

The serrated words bit into his skin, but he forged ahead anyway.

"I know it sounds whacked out. And given what kind of life it appears I've led from your perspective, I can see how you would think I've fallen off some sort of wagon. But Tara, you've got to believe me. Something seriously bizarre has happened. I am not the same brother you know."

Wariness narrowed her eyes. "Well, any time I've seen you on a bender, it definitely didn't look like this. But that is the stupidest story I've ever heard. You on something new?"

He bared his teeth in frustration. "Tara, I've never even been to Chicago. I know that's supposedly where I live now. What do I do out there? Investments?"

She tapped a finger against the counter, barely humoring him. "Marketing."

He wrinkled his nose, temporarily distracted. "Marketing?"

She rolled her eyes. "Come on. Quit messing around. Give me your sponsor's number. I should probably give him a call."

Her words ignited an idea. He didn't have a phone—couldn't give her *anyone's* number. But if there was a way to prove that he was a different Luke entirely, maybe this was it.

"Not my sponsor," he shook his head. "Call *me*."

"What?"

"Call me up right now. See if I answer."

She threw her hands up in exasperation, but after he stared at her in earnest, she finally pulled her phone out, grudgingly searching for his name and hitting *call*. She rolled her eyes again as she pressed the phone to her ear, her gaze falling to his pocket where she assumed his phone would start ringing. But as the line at her ear trilled, the room remained silent.

She pursed her lips in dubious irritation until he heard his own voice come on the line, causing her to jump.

"What's up, sis?" Luke's voice said.

The sound of it made a chill run down his spine. He didn't know it would actually work, and now a sick feeling settled into the pit of his stomach.

"Uhh, Luke?" she stammered, brows knitting together.

His voice chuckled. "Yeah, who else? Did you call me by accident?"

Her eyes grew larger as they settled on the Luke in the room with her. "No. Um, I just wanted to see how you were."

Luke felt the tension in his body winding tighter as he watched her, heard his own voice.

A pause. "Now? I'm kind of in the middle of something. And I'm meeting with a client in ten minutes."

She turned away. "Where are you?"

"What does that matter?" the other him asked. "I'm at a restaurant down by the marina."

"Okay. Well, give me a call when you're free later." Her voice was too tense for anyone to think she was just calling to chat. She slowly lowered her phone as the call disconnected, staring at it as if it might come alive at any moment.

After hearing another version of himself on the phone, he thought he would feel the typical brother smugness of being right. But the yawning pit in his stomach grew as more evidence fell into place that something was wrong.

"Do you believe me now?" he asked, his voice a little unsteady.

She wheeled to face him so suddenly he took an instinctive step back. Which was a good thing, it turned out. The blade of a steak knife glinted, winking at him as she pointing it toward his chest. It trembled only slightly.

"Who are you?" she demanded. Her voice was not loud, and he understood why as her eyes unconsciously slid to the girl still playing outside.

Luke lifted his hands to show they were empty, panic clutching his gut. "Tara, please. I'm Luke. I swear. I'm your brother."

"Like hell, you are," she said through her teeth.

He edged around the island between them, inching toward the front door, just in case he couldn't convince her. She shifted in sync with him but toward the back door, ready to bolt for her daughter.

His eyes remained on her hand, the knuckles turning white as she gripped the knife.

"All right." He spoke softly like she was a cornered wild animal. Which was probably what she felt like. He lifted his hands higher, as if in surrender. "Uhh, proof, right? Um. . . I set your hair on fire when I was eight while you were watching TV because I was mad at you for not letting me watch what I wanted. Singed it, really. Mom had to cut four inches off."

Her expression tightened and she tilted the knife a few

degrees as if in question.

Ideas flashed through his brain without clarity as he tried to find something that might convince her. "Um. . . . You realized you were afraid of heights that time at camp on the ropes course." He raised his hands higher when her chin jutted out, like she was daring him to test her. "You had to jump from a platform fifteen feet off the ground, and it took you a half an hour to work up to it."

"Stop it!" She jabbed at him with the knife, and even though there was still a few feet between them, he leaped backward.

He glanced behind him to see how far he was from the front door. "Uh, uh, jeez. Um." A memory jumped to the forefront of his mind, and his index finger punctured the air between them. "You told everyone you lost your virginity to Jeff Coolidge in high school, but it was actually Aaron Kowalski." The words tumbled out so fast, he wasn't sure she'd understood him.

But she suddenly lowered her arm, staring at him like she was seeing him for the first time. "I never told *anyone* that!"

The heat rose in his face, and he was surprised that, through his fear, he could still feel sheepish. "I read your diary."

"Lucas!" she cried, scandalized.

He winced. "I'm sorry, but I was only thirteen."

The glare she gave him was edging toward lighthearted, the actual threat of the brandished knife entirely gone.

As his heartbeat slowed, he realized just how much adrenaline had pumped through his body. He slumped into the chair at the kitchen table as it seeped out of him, leaving little energy to feel appropriately chagrined.

Tara leaned back against the counter, her own energy seeming to wane, the knife held loosely at her side. She pressed a hand to her temple. "How is this possible?"

He only managed to shrug. "I have no idea. I mean, I woke up this morning in this alternate reality. I've just been trying to get my bearings. I feel like all I get is yelled at. The knife was a first though."

She looked at the blade before setting it down on the counter. "Sorry, but I was scared out of my mind."

"I don't blame you."

She glanced out at her daughter who was now crouched in the grass investigating something, perhaps a bug. The Hannah he knew was fascinated by insects of all kinds, so it was as good a guess as any.

"So, you're my brother. But not," she mused. "You said an alternate reality." She looked at him, eyebrow raised in question.

He grimaced, lifting a shoulder. "That's what this feels like. As if I'm somehow locked into this alternate version of my life. And the existence of another 'me' seems to jive with that."

She shook her head. "In your version, Jordan Baylor is alive and you're with his sister?" A small smirk played about her lips as she said the last part, like it was unfathomable.

He gave her a steady look, trying to convey the depth of his heart for Erin Baylor. "Tara, she's the love of my life."

Her mouth dropped open a little. "That certainly proves you're not *my* brother."

He sighed, offering her a grim smile. "There are apparently a lot of things about your brother and me that are different."

Her expression darkened, and she seemed to fold in on herself a little. "You—he—struggled for a while after Jordan passed. The guilt just ate at him."

Luke chewed the inside of his lip, a part of him understanding that in an abstract, hypothetical way. Jordan was his best friend, and to know that he was connected to his death would be hard to move past. Especially so young. He would have hoped he'd be a stronger man than to fall victim to the mindset that numbing the pain was a better option than dealing with it. But he could make judgments all he wanted from the untouched side.

"That's why he moved to Chicago," she continued, her eyes intent on his face. "To be somewhere completely different, away from the memories. And Mom and Dad followed him because, well, you know how they are." She smirked, but it was tainted by bitterness.

"Gotta keep their wild kids in line," he agreed.

He meant it to be a joke, but they both knew it was partially true. Tara had been the rebellious one. She drank heavily in high school, slept around, and ended up with a guy who got her pregnant then left her. Luke was the work hard, play hard type. Which had never sat well with their parents. So neither of them had lived up to expectations that sometimes felt impossible to meet.

"Not any more," she countered, her eyes going to Hannah once more. The love there, the wistfulness, was like a warm, protective blanket.

It was true that the birth of her daughter had changed her, even in his world. But he and his parents stepped in a lot to help. It appeared that, in this reality, she was left to figure things out on her own more. And he could see the effect in her demeanor. There was a tightness about her, as if the constant worry pulled a string taut inside her and didn't release. But there was a hardiness to her too. Like she'd learned to stand more solidly on her own two feet.

"I'm sorry," he said. The apology encompassed more than

just that truth. He wanted to erase this other Luke's poor life choices so that she wouldn't have been abandoned by more than just Hannah's father.

She shrugged, biting the corner of her bottom lip, a move he knew was an attempt to battle back tears. Which she did successfully.

Finally, she sighed. "So what's your next step? What do we do?"

He ran a hand over his face and blew out a breath. "I have no clue. It's not like there's a protocol for this. I might need to crash on your couch for a while."

She hesitated, and he wondered if it was just that she was used to a junkie brother she had to maintain boundaries with.

A twang in his heart made him wince, but he spoke quickly to cover it. "It's all right if you're not comfortable with that."

She shook her head. "No. I'm sorry. You're welcome to stay here. This is just. . . " She blew out a breath.

"Yeah," he agreed.

6

Absurdity

ERIN

The house was small. But there was a vague familiarity to it, like she'd driven by and made a mental note of it for some reason. Or like déjà vu—something from a dream or another life.

Erin shut her car off, not understanding her own reluctance as she got out, the feeling like weights strapped to her body. Her eyes never left the facade of the little brick house, even though her hands fluttered over her clothes and then gripped her purse tightly as if that would bolster her.

Walking up the steps to the door felt foreboding, like she was walking into the gaping maw of the unknown.

It was stupid. She was just coming to test Luke out, to maybe see if it really was him or an imposter. She hadn't ruled out that the one who'd checked in from Chicago was the imposter. And she knew that people could, in fact, check in somewhere belatedly. But it still didn't clarify his story. It was such an elaborate ruse for no obvious reason.

She realized she'd been standing outside on the stoop for a

long time, so she reached out to knock. The door opened before her knuckles connected. It took her a moment to recognize the startled face that stared back at her.

Tara Pearson was as much the same as she was different. Her face was longer, leaner, her eyes harder, but she was still beautiful, still had that devil-may-care glint to her eyes. She raised a brow and a slow smile spread across her face.

"Well, Erin Baylor," Tara said, setting the trash bag she held on the ground.

"Hi, Tara." Why did she sound breathless? She reached to twist her engagement ring around before realizing it still wasn't there. "Is Luke here?"

"Sure. Come on in." Tara stepped back to allow Erin to enter, all the while wearing a small, knowing smirk on her face.

The house was dark, curtains drawn, but light splashed in from a back door through the kitchen. Tara led her that way. But before she opened the door, she paused to smile warmly at the scene out back.

Erin stopped to stand just behind her but gazed over Tara's shoulder to follow her line of sight. Luke was crouched down in the grass, a fat caterpillar on his index finger. A small child, her dark hair and large eyes identifying her as Tara's, studied the bug with intense delight.

Luke smiled, talking to the girl.

Tara opened the door gingerly, probably an attempt to keep from disturbing them.

" . . . into a butterfly. It breaks out of its little cocoon and spreads its wings."

"What color?" The girl was almost cross-eyed as she gazed at the caterpillar, her face inching closer and closer.

"Ah, that depends on what kind of caterpillar this is. We'll have to look it up."

"Can't we keep it?" The child stood straight up, a pout already puckering her mouth, as if she expected she'd need to wheedle a bit to get her way.

"You know, we could." He tilted his head. "But his home is out here, and he needs lots of leaves to eat before he changes."

"Like the very hungry caterpillar?"

"Yes, exactly! He's happiest out here where it's wide open. How would you like being locked up all the time? You couldn't go anywhere or do anything but sit in your room."

She tipped her chin down. "I wouldn't like that at all."

Luke nodded gravely. "Maybe we can see if there's a video online that shows us how he changes into a butterfly."

Her face brightened. "Yeah!"

Tara cleared her throat and Luke glanced up. "Someone's here to see you."

He squinted, and Erin took that as her cue, thinking it was overly theatrical when she stepped out from behind Tara.

It was the strangest thing, though, watching his expression morph. Like she was the sun he hadn't seen in weeks, like her presence alone melted away his tension. But then he schooled his features and shot up to a standing position.

And she had to curl her fingers to keep from reaching for that feeling, to ask him to put that look back on his face so she could bask in it. It was heady to feel like she actually mattered that much to someone. That thought and her impulse made her nervous.

He looked down at the caterpillar he still held and set his mouth. Walking toward a tree nearby, he released the captive bug and wiped his hands on his pants.

He was very guarded as he made his way back to where she

and his sister stood.

"Erin," he said, cautious, controlled.

"Hi," she said tentatively. This was more awkward than she had anticipated.

He looked at his sister, who winked at him and walked out into the backyard, holding out her hand to her daughter and leading her toward the tree to visit their caterpillar.

Erin stepped back to allow Luke to come inside the house, her eyes drawn to the stiff, careful way he moved. As if he knew she was feeling skittish.

"What are you doing here?" He stuffed his hands into his pockets, rocking back on his heels. "Not that I'm unhappy to see you. I just mean—" He shrugged, glancing away.

That look had come into his eyes again, and she felt herself tighten.

"My father said you came to see him," she began. Her pause deepened, and she wasn't sure what to say next. That she wondered if he was an imposter, or that he'd paid someone to pretend to be him in Chicago? That she was worried he was crazy or high or. . . something—given their interaction that morning?

His stillness was like its own entity, heavy like he thought she wanted to say something else. But when she didn't, he tilted his head. "I guess you're wondering why I was acting weird."

She let out a breathy laugh. "Among other things."

He grimaced, turning his face to the floor. "It's hard to explain."

When he didn't elaborate, she glanced outside to his sister. She would know if he was an imposter, right? No way would she have left him alone with her daughter if that were the case.

And standing there, staring at his profile as he looked out the back door as well, she couldn't imagine an imposter looking as much like Luke as this man did. One thing would help her be sure.

She thought back to that day, the summer before he left for college. She'd been reading on the front porch, and he'd shown up to go with her brother to laser tag or paintball—some detail that didn't matter.

He'd tweaked her ponytail and sat with her while Jordan changed after his morning shift at the grocery store. She remembered staring at his profile back then too. But it was when he'd looked at her, the teasing look almost entirely gone from his expression.

He was thinking about kissing her, she could tell. The way his body strained toward her with a buzzing energy called to the live wire nerves inside of her. He must have known her rebuffs up to that point had been half-hearted. She met his gaze, catching her breath when she noted his left eye had this small imperfection, brown like an ink spill in the gray-blue iris.

"Something happened to me, and I'm not sure what." He looked at her now, drawing her mind back to the present. As if the unexpressed explanation had a mass and weight that pulled him down, he sat at the table with a heavy sigh.

She waited a beat then moved to sit in the chair next to him. Her hand fell on his arm, and his eyes swung to hers. It made her breath catch again to see his expression was just like that day. All serious, full of earnest anticipation. And it was with the light streaming in through the back door, that same blossom of brown in his left eye was visible, and her stomach clenched.

"Why are you pretending to be in Chicago?" she asked

abruptly.

His dark brows furrowed. "I'm not. I mean—well." He grimaced again.

"I don't understand why you would set this whole scenario up, unless you were trying to trick someone into thinking you were there, continuing life as usual. But what and who are you hiding from?" The discomfort of not understanding sharpened her tone.

He shook his head, frustration twisting his handsome face. "It's not like that. Erin, I think I'm in an alternate reality or something."

His answer knocked her sideways for a moment because it was the most ridiculous and unexpected explanation, if she would even call it that. It was mockery.

She pulled her hand back as if his skin burned her, disgusted. "Fine. You don't have to tell me anything. I just thought since you reached out, that maybe you needed some help." She stood up, checking her impulse to mirror her father's imperious stare to drive her point home, and turned for the door.

"Please," he said softly.

The desperation made her pause, something about it squeezing her chest.

"Please believe me. Tara does. I convinced her, anyway. We called him—me. In Chicago."

Erin shook her head, the dark mirthless laugh bubbling out of her, burning her throat as it went. How ridiculous. How utterly *absurd*.

"Get yourself together, Luke. And don't contact me again."

She grabbed her purse, heading for the door. Tears stung her eyes, and she wasn't sure where the urge to cry was coming from.

Luke stood from his chair so quickly, it crashed to the floor as he chased after her. "Erin, please."

She sensed his presence behind her, an undeniable warmth that tugged at her, but she willed herself to ignore him as she reached for the doorknob.

"Erin, you need to listen to him." Tara's voice was quiet, but it held a fervent intensity.

Which made her stop. Erin turned, her chest heaving with the pressure of ensnaring emotions she wanted to pretend weren't there.

Tara stood just behind Luke, her daughter in her arms. The child's head rested on her shoulder, dark, curious eyes trained on Erin.

Erin raised a brow, waiting for some heavenly revelation that probably wouldn't come. There was very little they could say that would make any of this okay.

A muscle in Luke's jaw twitched. "Last night, I was mugged while walking to my car. I woke up today to a world and a life that's completely altered. As if some event shifted the trajectory of my life. But there's another me, who's lived that entirely different life, and he still exists in Chicago, unaware I am here."

"I called him," Tara added. "I called my brother. The other version. He's there, in Chicago as usual."

Though there was no sane reason for Tara to corroborate Luke's outrageous story, there was absolutely no reason Erin should believe them. *Could* believe them. And the rage simmered in her chest, begging for release.

"Maybe we can prove it," Luke said, the earnestness in his face absolutely mind-boggling. "Like when Tara called him—me." He lifted his hands like he was reaching out to

Erin. "You said I was pretending to be in Chicago. What did you mean?"

Her nostrils flared with her anger, but she decided, against her better judgment, to humor them. "Your social media accounts."

He looked to Tara, who moved across the room to a laptop on the coffee table. She set her daughter down, who eyed Erin shyly when she caught her gaze. The child's presence softened her just a little. But she still folded her arms across her chest, as if she could ward off whatever nonsense they were going to feed her.

Tara pulled up all of Luke's social media accounts. "There." She tapped a finger against the screen at the check-in location above the image he had posted four minutes prior. "That's where you—*he* said he was when I talked to him on the phone."

Luke was bent over, hands on knees, blue eyes narrowed as he looked with her. The picture showed Luke—or, rather, the lookalike he must have paid—with another man. They were smiling with their hands clasped in posed mid-shake as if they'd made some sort of deal.

He let out a breath through his teeth. "That's creepy as shi—"

"Lucas." His sister's tone was a warning.

His eyes flickered down to Tara's daughter and back to the screen.

"This proves nothing," Erin said, underwhelmed, somehow even angrier at their attempts to persuade her. "You clearly have someone posting these previously taken photos, checking in somewhere in Chicago. But what's your endgame? Why are you doing this?"

Tara's mouth twisted, her anxious gaze going to her daughter as she shrank back at Erin's caustic tone. She pulled the girl into her side, tucking her under an arm.

"I wish I could explain, that I could prove to you that I'm not making this up." His hands raked through his dark hair, pausing to grip at the wavy locks in frustration.

An electronic melody trilled from the computer, pulling everyone's attention back to the screen. Tara was getting a video call.

From Luke.

7

Convinced

ERIN

Imposter Luke, Erin amended, unimpressed.

Tara flapped her hand at the real Luke, and he must have interpreted the communication correctly, stepping out of view as she clicked to answer. Erin shifted back as well, even though she wasn't even in the shot.

"Heyyy little brother," Tara said on a breathy laugh, so far from casual, Erin was sure this was all for her own sake.

The Luke impersonator, eyes hidden by dark sunglasses even though he was sitting in a slice of shade on an outdoor patio, didn't smile back. "Is everything okay?"

Tara gave a tight shrug. "Why wouldn't it be?" Her daughter's brows knit together as she took in the image of the man on the screen, and Tara gave her a couple of reassuring squeezes.

The man on the screen pulled off the dark sunglasses, concern etched into the lines on his forehead. "You sounded upset when you called earlier. I just wanted to make sure you were okay."

"Oh." Tara waved a dismissive hand, her eyes going heavenward. Erin could tell it was a stall. "I had something else on my mind. I suddenly remembered something about work."

"Are you sure?" Even the man's voice was an uncanny match to Luke's. "I know I haven't been reliable in the past, but I am here if you need anything."

Tara's expression softened, along with her voice. "I know that."

The mannerisms, the voice called to Erin, drawing her closer. She'd caught the unique cadence of his speech that was quintessentially Luke. Something so subtle, but so remarkably *him*, that it would take an extremely talented actor to imitate. The man on the screen didn't appear to know she was there, so what was the purpose of keeping up the charade? It seemed unlikely that someone could look identical to another person *and* sound exactly like them.

And so she moved forward like some invisible tether tugged her closer.

Luke reached to stop her, but she yanked her arm away before he could touch her.

"The video," he whispered to his sister.

Tara's eyes flashed to his face as he used his finger to make a slicing motion across his throat.

Her hand shot out to hit the button as Erin came into view of the computer's camera, determined to find that ink spill in this man's eyes.

"Tara?"

"Uh, sorry, connection is bad. My video cut out," Tara said, her voice rising with the lie.

"Oh, that's Okay. You know, I have another meeting back at the office anyway. Let's set up a time to chat later."

"Sure." Her voice sounded choked as Erin pressed in front

of her, hands grasping the screen as he leaned forward to end the video call. His face was suddenly bathed in sunlight and the video froze for a half second when he disconnected before disappearing.

It was enough time. Erin slammed the laptop shut and stumbled backward a few steps.

Luke moved toward her, but she held up her hands to ward him off, and he froze. Her heart stuttered a frantic rhythm in her chest. Why were her fingers tingling?

Tara stared at them for a moment before standing and ushering herself and her daughter out of the room so quickly, it would have been comical under normal circumstances.

"Impossible," Erin managed to say. Her voice was weak, thready.

Luke's lips were pressed into a line and he lifted one shoulder. Almost an "oh well" gesture that seemed idiotic, given the situation.

Two Lukes.

As if this one, with his crazy story, wasn't enough. She looked at him, took in his tall frame, the way the darkened room carved deeper shadows under his sharp cheekbones. The defeated expression on his face fit the other Luke better. That one was thinner, more serious.

Tortured.

"You believe me?" Luke asked, so desperate that hope twisted around the words.

She took a few slow, deep breaths, trying to normalize her heartbeat. "Maybe. I don't know." Her voice was soft. "Or this is one elaborate trick."

"Why would we trick you?" He sounded hurt. As if she'd accused him of a heinous crime.

"That's what I've been asking myself since I left the hospital this morning. Why would you make up some stupid story, hurt me like that? Why pretend we're something we're not?" She heard the tremor in her own voice and moved to the couch. She couldn't say the last part.

Why say that Jordan was alive?

"I'm so sorry," he said. She could tell he meant it.

"Alternate universe." Saying it out loud made it sound even more ridiculous. But she had to admit she couldn't think of a better explanation at the moment. A twin separated at birth? But that didn't make sense. Why would they believe or act like they were the same person?

Her eyes wheeled to him as he hovered, uncertain.

It seemed like he wanted to sit too but was giving her some respectful distance. Abruptly, he walked to the window, likely for want of something to do, and pulled back the curtain.

The sunlight bit at her eyes, and she squinted against it. The silence threatened to steel the oxygen from the room.

Then, finally: "I thought it was a bad dream," he murmured. "Or you were mad at me for something. Once I figured out you weren't playing a practical joke on me."

She recalled their conversation at the hospital with an ache flowering in her chest. His reaction to her had seemed defensive. Like a response to a lover's quarrel.

The ache made her voice small. "We're together? In your world?"

He turned to look at her, and that expression was there again. Intimate. A special kind of ownership in those eyes.

He cleared his throat and looked at his feet and back. "Yes."

"And Jordan's. . . alive?" That was hard to say, hard to imagine, hard to admit to herself how badly she wanted that to be her reality.

Luke's eyes softened. "Expecting his first baby."

She gritted her teeth as if that would keep the stab of grief from bleeding her dry. It was unfair to know that he existed somewhere. To know he'd had a future without her. How would that have changed her life to have him here?

She looked at Luke, knowing at least one major thing would be different. She saw it in the way he clenched his muscles into submission, to keep himself from touching her the way he might have in some other time and place. To comfort her the way he clearly wanted to.

"He's married?" The words came out strangled, and she tried to clear her throat.

"Four years ago." Luke stuffed his hands into his pockets, his eyes on the floor. "That little church outside of town." His smile was faint, quietly wistful.

And she could picture it, and she wanted it—for them and herself. Jordan's college girlfriend, Kelly, was a quirky, down-home kind of girl. And he had loved her whimsy, and she could see him going with the country wedding, in that old stone church with the worn-down pews, darkly wooded against the white walls just because Kelly wanted it.

"How bad was it?" Luke asked, breaking into her reverie.

She met his gaze, forcing herself to hold it. How could she truly make him understand that it wasn't just bad then? It was still bad. That her mother was drinking herself to death to numb the pain of Jordan's loss? That her father was never home, working constantly as his own form of self-medication? That Hank Baylor pushed double the expectation on her without her older brother to shoulder some of the burden?

"The worst."

He looked like he would cry with her, like he felt the pain as deeply as she did, even though he still had Jordan. Except, now he didn't. Whatever had brought him here may not happen again. Which meant that his reality might have shifted to encompass a life without his best friend.

"Luke, what happened?"

His brows pulled low over his gray-blue eyes in confusion. "With what?"

"How did you get here?" She gestured around the room. "Does it even count as a 'here'?"

Understanding smoothed his expression. "I'm not quite sure, honestly." He finally did sit down, resting his hands on his knees. "As you may remember me mentioning, I was mugged last night." He paused and tilted his head. His eyes were not on her but unfocused in front of him, as if he were replaying a scene from a movie in his head. "There was this. . . noise."

She raised a brow, waiting for him to continue, but he was still working to remember.

"The guy had a knife to my ribs." His hand went to the spot automatically, resting there at his abdomen. "It was a buzzing sound. No. Ringing. So damn loud, I thought my ear drums would burst. That's it."

She blinked. "What's it?"

His gaze sharpened, and he looked at her. "That's all I remember before waking up in the hospital with everything messed up."

Again, she sensed his desire to touch her, a pulling presence between them, but he remained immobile. She couldn't imagine what that must be like, for life to be completely upended, for the person you cared for not to be available to you as always. But he had admirable self-control.

"So who is he?" Luke asked flatly, and she was off-kilter again.

This whole day felt like an unending spiral.

"Who?"

He took her left hand to examine the naked ring finger. "You keep feeling along your finger with your thumb like something is missing." His expression was closed off, and she knew it must be the sense of betrayal he would be feeling, even if it wasn't fair. Because, in his world, she belonged with him, *to* him.

She pulled her hand from his grasp and folded it under the other one in her lap. "You wouldn't know him."

"I might." Tightness, even an edge in the tone there. Unintentional, no doubt. But still, she stiffened in defense, fingernails digging into skin.

"You don't," she insisted, checking her urge to slide away from him like a petulant child.

"Fine. I take it it's serious." Not a question. Almost accusatory. Or maybe she was reading into it because she felt so defensive. "So where's your ring?"

She fisted her left hand under her right as if that would stop this line of questioning.

Because she hesitated with her answer, he turned his face away, rubbing a hand over the stubble at his jaw. The sound was like sandpaper against his skin. "I'm sorry. It's none of my business."

Saved from having to lie about the fact she'd intentionally hidden it from him. For good reason, apparently. "It's okay. I'm sure you're just as thrown off as I am about this. It's good to know that if we were together, you care enough to be jealous of another guy."

He gave a snort of derision. "Yeah, I'm jealous, alright."

"So it's serious with us—er, you and her, then, too?"

He looked at her, pulling his bottom lip between his teeth, and his eyes told her what she had been guessing at. Serious was an understatement. It made her uncomfortable, and she shifted a little under his gaze.

He finally looked away, but she didn't feel that release of tension. The discomfort remained, a tightness in her chest, her shoulders pulled inward.

Because Nathan had never looked at her like that. Not even when he'd gotten down on his knee in front of the fountain downtown, man-made geysers shooting skyward behind him, lightly spraying them with moisture.

She caught herself feeling her bare ring finger. Just as Luke had noticed. But he wasn't looking at her, and she knew he was no longer just thinking about her, or the her that belonged to him.

They were quiet for a long time.

After a while, he sighed. "I don't know what I'm going to do."

She resisted the urge to touch his shoulder, to offer comfort of some kind. He sounded like a lost kid.

"I have no money, no job, no way to get either of those things, and I can't mooch off my sister. I just—there's no way to prepare for this kind of thing." He threw his hands up, then stood, pacing. "As if this is something anyone could even remotely plan for! As if anyone should! Like what the actual hell?"

She stilled as he let himself fully unravel, his pacing intensifying.

His words started tumbling out, barely leaving room for a breath. "I can't just ask myself for the money. He shouldn't even know I exist, right? Is there some sort of space-time continuum I have to maintain? Like, will I disappear if I meet myself face-to-face?"

Before she could respond, he plowed on.

"Or is it like a highlander situation? There can only be one, and we have to duke it out to be the last one standing? I mean, I thought that kind of thing would be cool when I was, like, thirteen, but I'm definitely not interested in something like that in real life. I mean, I have bad knees. All that running. And I've never been in a fight before. I work out, but that doesn't exactly translate to hand-to-hand combat."

She fought a smile at that last one and stood up. "Luke."

He froze and looked at her, eyes wide with anxiety. He almost acted like her interruption of his increasingly improbable babble wasn't helpful. But his deteriorating logic wasn't helpful either. She had to put a stopper in it before he really started to freak out.

"I don't think the space-time continuum thing is a problem. Pretty sure that's related to time travel," she pointed out. "And I don't think reaching out to. . . yourself is necessary. I can get you something to at least earn you some money at Baylor. And we can go get you some new clothes now."

He opened his mouth, looking like he was going to protest.

"You can pay me back. You need to do something to keep you afloat while you're—" she waved a hand to incorporate the room—"here. The rest of our time can be spent investigating how this happened and how to get you back."

His breathing was still a little ragged, but his shoulders

slumped. "You're going to help me?"

She shrugged, offering a half-grimace, half-smile. "You didn't actually expect that I'd find out you're from an alternate reality and then say, 'Good luck figuring that one out. See ya!' do you?"

He attempted a smile, failed, and sat down. "I don't know what I expected. Nothing beyond the fact that I couldn't stand the thought of you so angry with me, so hurt. Since that's taken care of, I obviously hadn't thought of what happens next."

She frowned as he placed his face in his hands. He grew very still, and she wasn't sure what to do. She wanted to comfort him but didn't know what was appropriate, given their unequal feelings toward each other.

His dejection was a pale shadow of the pure grief and guilt in his posture after her brother died. She remembered walking into the front room at her parents' house after the funeral. Luke was thinner then, still heavily into cross-country running. She hadn't known how to comfort him then either. She'd never found the words, never reached out. Would it have changed his fate? If she hadn't abandoned him to his grief?

That question spurred her into saying something now, something she wished she'd said to him back then. "Well, I'm here to help. So, how about we just take this one step at a time?"

He groaned, rubbed his hands over his face a couple of times, then lifted his head. As if that had refreshed him enough to power through. "All right. What's step one?"

She pressed her lips together. "Clothes."

He curled a lip, which was the reaction she expected for some reason.

"You need clean clothes. I doubt you'd want to sleep in what you've got. What are you wearing, anyway? Looks like something my dad would wear."

His sheepish smile seemed to chase away the dregs of his despair, and he looked down at himself. "That's because half of this *is* your dad's."

She wrinkled her nose. "Yeah, let's fix that."

8

Shopping Trip

"What am I looking for here?" Luke asked, flipping through the clothes on the rack. "Business-casual? Very business? Very casual?" He snuck a glance at her. "Business in the front, party in the back? Or party all around?"

Erin rolled her eyes, though she didn't look at him. Her face was only visible in profile across the small aisle, but he still saw the corner of her mouth twitch up for a second, which was all he needed. That helped soothe his raw nerves, even if for a moment.

"Business-casual for the office." She flipped through some shirts, paused to look at one, then continued flipping. "Casual for your every day. Pajamas—or whatever you sleep in." She flapped a hand in his direction, working very hard to not look at him.

She blushed, and he grinned, suspecting that she was imagining what he might *not* sleep in. Obviously, it didn't matter if pajamas weren't his usual M.O., he definitely had to wear something while he crashed at his sister's.

"Pajama pants," he said, pursing his lips when she glanced over, trying to hide his amusement. "T-shirts, definitely."

She pulled a short-sleeve button-down off the rack and pressed it against his chest. It was a peach or salmon color. "This would look great on you for the office. Maybe with some olive-colored fitted slacks."

He wrinkled his nose. "Uh, how about some khakis and a white shirt?" He pulled a crisp button-down from the rack behind him.

She raised a brow, inhaling deeply. "Boring."

"My clothing doesn't have to be exciting for me to get my job done. Jeez, even in an alternate reality, we have to have this argument." He took the salmon shirt from her and slammed it back on the rack.

She held up her hands. "Compromise. Khakis, olive pants, black polo, gray button-down."

He accepted every piece of clothing she listed as she piled it into his arms. It was like every conversation he'd ever had shopping with her. She always wanted him to go bolder. Patterns, weird colors, tighter pants. He'd capitulated on some by just letting her go without him. If he didn't go, he was less grumpy, and he lucked out that half the stuff ended up getting returned because he hadn't been there to try it on to gauge fit or how it looked.

She stood on her toes and craned her neck to look around the store. "Dressing rooms," she murmured, her hands pressed against his back so that she could direct him.

The touch from her was like a balm on a wound he didn't know he had. It made him realize how much this messed up situation had taken from him. To ever be with her and not touch her—*be* touched by her—for any length of time, was insanity. How many years had that comfortable, casual physical contact been so much a part of how they interacted?

He wanted to turn, pull her into him, smell her hair, feel her warmth. And his mood darkened just knowing he shouldn't, *couldn't,* because another man had a claim over her.

As she pushed him toward the fitting rooms, he tensed, thinking about the fact that she was engaged to this guy. Which meant another man was that close to her, thought about her like Luke did, touched her in a way that made his head spin with rage from thinking about it. He worked to calm himself, to not picture punching the guy out. It helped that he didn't know what he looked like.

She shoved him into a dressing stall. "Stop pouting. It will go faster if you just cooperate."

He took a deep breath and did as she bid, acknowledging that it would at least be something to distract him. And it was so much like something they usually did that he could pretend it was just another annoying shopping trip. Which meant he could at least spend focused time with her.

He undressed, slipping the first of the outfits on, not bothering to check his reflection in the mirror. Her approval was the only important part. He just cared if it was comfortable.

He opened the door and stood in his socks, holding his arms out.

She tilted her head, pursing red-lipsticked lips as she considered him. It was such an Erin expression, and it was weird to miss someone that was standing right in front of him.

"A good basic ensemble." She twirled her finger in a circle, and he turned slowly as bidden, trying to ignore how quickly he swung from jealous fury to agonizing heartache.

"It's comfortable," he admitted, hoping she didn't hear any

of the emotions in his voice.

"Then it's a winner." She shooed him back in with a flapping hand. Her phone was in the other, twittering out a rhythmic alert, and her focus went to the screen.

He looked at himself in the mirror then, noted his clenched jaw, his tight expression. But she wasn't paying attention to his face. He shut the door so he could pull off the black polo and the khakis.

He leaned back against the wall between changing, looking up at the fluorescent lights in the ceiling as he took a steadying breath. He closed his eyes, set his mind to pretending that it was *his* Erin he was shopping with to lighten the mood, to make it easier, to keep himself from the debilitating thoughts that circled in his mind. He would be crushed under the weight of it all if he let it.

He changed into the olive pants, admitting that they were pretty comfortable but feeling stupid calling them "olive." They were just *green*. He donned the gray shirt, opening the door to model again.

Her bottom lip was pulled between her teeth, her delicate brows drawn together over her eyes. She was concentrating too hard on what she was typing on her phone to notice he'd come out.

"I'm warming to the green pants," he said, stuffing his hands into the pockets.

She glanced up like he'd startled her, and her eyes skipped his face and focused on what he wore. "Turn."

He did as asked, catching her lingering stare at his butt. "Green working in my favor?" he asked as he flexed his glute muscles.

She widened her eyes, pink brightening her cheeks. "Luke!"

Her tone sounded scandalized, but she laughed, looking around as if someone would hear. "It's not green. It's *olive*."

"Army green," he retorted. "More manly."

She rolled her eyes. "Whatever. The point is that they look nice."

He grinned. "I can tell you think so."

The pink blossomed on her cheeks again. "I'm allowed to appreciate. . . things. . . "

He pursed his lips and held up his hands. "You won't hear me complain. It's a nice ego boost." He popped the collar of his shirt with an arrogant flair.

She pressed a high-heeled foot against his thigh and shoved him into the dressing stall, laughing. He could still hear the sheepish note in the sound, but he liked it and winked at her.

"Stop it!"

Her laugh bolstered him and kept his mood relatively elevated the rest of the night. He didn't even mind that she made him try on three more full outfits. It meant she gave him her undivided attention. Her phone was forgotten in her purse, though he suspected what she had been doing. Or rather who she might have been talking to. He only caught her feeling along the naked ring finger once. But he set his mind to making her laugh instead of brooding over it. The sting of jealousy didn't abate, but he could bury it for the moment.

9

Stress Test

ERIN

Erin kicked off her heels as soon as she walked in her front door, tossing the half-eaten burger in its takeout bag onto the kitchen island on her way toward her bedroom. She had already shimmied out of the skirt by the time she reached her walk-in closet.

It was only 8pm, but she was spent. She released her short hair from the low bun, shaking it out. The blonde locks lapped at her face, caught in her lip balm, but she didn't care. She yanked her favorite pair of sweats on and donned an old t-shirt that fell down to the middle of her thighs.

She'd meant to go finish off her dinner, but she threw herself back onto her bed instead. Her eyes followed the circular movement of the ceiling fan, fingers picking at the gathered tufts on her cream-colored comforter.

For the umpteenth time, she replayed the day in her head. How normal it had started—her father leaving her a list of to-dos outside of her daily tasks at work—the paperwork, emails, meetings, all before 10am.

Then that damned phone call from the hospital. Tilted her world sideways, and she was still struggling to find her equilibrium.

She rubbed her hands down her face, voicing her frustration in a groan that morphed into a growl.

Alternate universe.

If she thought it or said it aloud enough times, would it somehow feel real? Or even make sense? She still couldn't rule out the possibility of a weird twins-separated-at-birth theory. Because even though there was no logical reason a twin would try to pretend to be his long-lost brother, that seemed way more likely than a plot twist out of a science fiction novel.

Was one of these men just a psycho obsessed with his twin's life? With Erin, herself? It wasn't as if he couldn't have done research to have a passing knowledge of her or her family. But what had he said to convince his sister? And why not just pretend to be the Luke in Chicago? Why make up an alternate history of his life that included her? And claim her brother was alive when he so painfully wasn't?

More and more questions built on top of each other to the point that her exhausted brain threatened to stab at the back of her eyeballs with a headache.

A knock on her door saved her from further exploring the unending spiral of questions. She rolled to her feet, padding out to the living room and into the foyer. She glanced at her phone, its screen glowing from inside her open purse, and she knew there was a new message from Nathan.

The visitor at the door was more pressing, though she had a guess as to who it would be.

"Hey, Dad," she sighed.

Hank stood with his hands in his pockets, still impeccably

dressed, obviously having only just left the office. No surprise there. His attempt at a casual expression was unsuccessful. Maybe because she knew him well enough to know he would never be casual or relaxed. The gears in his mind turned incessantly.

"Hey, Princess," he said, stepping inside uninvited.

It still irked her that he took those liberties as if she had no space of her own or was allowed to have boundaries. Not that she wouldn't have invited him. But even in her late twenties, the man seemed to view her as nothing more than his little girl. Even the nickname, usually a sweet endearment, grated against her raw nerves.

She clenched her teeth against the old rebuke that never made a lasting impact on him anyway. "What are you doing here at this hour?"

He looked at her, took in her ensemble, checked his watch as if it never occurred to him that it was after eight o'clock. Or that it might be considered late. Which, granted, wasn't actually that late. But he never stopped by her house. She was surprised he'd remembered how to get there. It was always her job to go to him, at his convenience.

"I won't keep you. I have to get home to pack anyway." He moved from the foyer into the living room that opened into the kitchen.

"Pack?" She couldn't help the dismay in her tone.

"I have a business trip to Miami. I leave in the morning." He was appraising the open-concept layout of her small house as if he were deciding if he liked it. Not that his approval mattered. It was her house.

"How long will you be gone?" How was it possible that her stomach was already starting to knot up?

"Not more than a few days." He brought his gaze to hers. They were the eyes she'd inherited. Cold, glacial blue.

She walked into the kitchen to pour herself a drink to calm her steadily increasing anxiety. "Is that what you came to tell me?"

He tipped his head to the side, narrowing his eyes on her as she poured the scotch. He declined when she held up the decanter as a wordless offer.

"I actually came to check on you. After the strange encounter with Luke, and seeing that you left early, I wanted to make sure you were all right."

She swallowed her sip of whiskey, lowering the glass to the counter. It seemed like all their conversations revolved around work and her mother, and she had forgotten what it was even like to have a father who cared how she, herself, was doing. Or that he would think to ask.

What she wanted to say was that she wasn't all right. That she was stumbling along on numb legs, confused, sad, lonely, anxious. But she forced the smile, forced herself to give him a steady look.

"I'm fine."

Because he was hard to read, had been so distant from her for so long, she couldn't tell if he believed her or simply wanted to. But he nodded and glanced away.

"I should be back by Thursday."

"I'll check in on Mom," she replied, answering the unvoiced request, the age-old expectation.

He nodded again, his eyes falling on her hand wrapped loosely around the glass resting on the counter. Maybe he wondered how many she'd had, if her mother's alcoholism had been transferred to his daughter. Or maybe he was just thinking what a mess the stuff had gotten their family into. He never said anything about any of it, so neither did Erin.

"Have a good night, Dad."

He inhaled suddenly, giving her a grim sort of smile. "You too, sweetheart."

She walked him to the door, drink in hand. When he was gone, she leaned her back against the door, chewing the inside of her cheek. She looked down at the finger of amber liquid in her glass and grimaced. She no longer had a taste for it and went to the kitchen to pour it down the sink, setting the empty glass on the counter.

The anxious knot in her stomach didn't loosen, and she pressed a fist to her gut. She always felt this way when her father traveled. Her mother was a high-functioning drunk, and none of her society friends likely knew the extent of her problem. Even when she seemed to fall into a darker abyss every time her husband traveled. She didn't do well alone.

Erin shut her eyes and took a deep breath, saying a silent prayer to ask for this time to be different. Maybe her mother had gotten a better grip over her demons. Or maybe this time Erin's presence was enough to keep her from leaping over that precipice. Because she was tired, oh so tired, of having to drag her back. Last time, she almost hadn't. That was the scariest car ride she'd ever experienced, trailing an ambulance that carried her unconscious mother to the E.R.

When her father returned home from his trip, early of course, and took her mother home, they carried on as if it had never happened.

Erin's phone vibrated inside her purse, and she jerked, knocking her empty glass into the sink. The crystal crashed loudly against the stainless steel, shattering into glittering shards.

She whispered a curse under her breath, glaring at the broken glass in the basin. Instead of cleaning it up immediately, she went to her purse to check her phone.

During her shopping trip with Luke, she'd had a brief conversation with Nathan via text. But she'd quickly become distracted and hadn't responded in hours. It wasn't the only thing she felt guilty for.

The way she'd laughed while Luke teased her, allowed him to flirt with her, and even responded.

Nathan's last message:

Maybe we can connect tomorrow. Love ya.

She swallowed against the lump in her throat and set her phone aside. She unzipped the inner pocket where she'd stashed her ring. Instead of putting it on right away, she stared at it, the facets in the diamond catching the light, glittering benignly as she moved it back and forth.

Her phone vibrated again, snapping her out of the trance. With shaking hands, she slid the ring onto her finger before she checked the readout on her phone.

This is Luke. Got a temp phone. . . Call me if you need anything.

She all but heard the hesitation in that last line. Like he wasn't sure if he was overstepping. But it was as if he knew she'd be struggling.

Her thumb hovered over the screen as she fiddled with the engagement ring she'd put back on.

Luke hadn't even been there for twenty-four hours, and she

was already feeling torn. The past yanking her back, her future luring her forward.

And, still, all the questions. She stood, paced, looking at the phone every few seconds as if it would get up and walk away.

She still wondered if this was a weird ploy. Some deception she couldn't figure out. But she couldn't reconcile any theory with his weird story of another life because there was no discernible endgame. What would he stand to gain if she went along with the alternate reality story?

And his panic earlier in the day, the way he'd grappled with how to move forward after his realization either meant he was telling the truth or he deserved a freaking Oscar for the performance.

Everything boiled down to the biggest question in the smallest package: *why?*

She wrestled with herself for several more minutes, her pacing getting more frenzied. Finally, she lunged for her phone, hesitated for only a minute more before calling the number Luke had texted from.

It was stupid that her heart was pounding, that she became overly aware of her lungs pulling air in and out. Like a teenager making her first phone call to a crush.

"Erin?" His voice was soft, quiet. He was trying not to wake anyone else. Because, of course, he was staying at Tara's.

"Hi," she managed, breathless from nerves. "How are you?"

He sighed, and she could picture him running a hand over his face. "Not great."

She nodded in understanding even though he couldn't see her. "I wouldn't imagine so."

"And you?"

The silence stretched. How much could she really trust him

with? Everything about him told her he was Luke, even ten years of dust didn't remove all of the memories of before. Because he had always been more than just her brother's best friend.

She finally settled on an answer that was true but also kept her from feeling too vulnerable. "Struggling."

He waited a beat too. His hesitation had a weight to it, almost something she could grasp with her hands.

"It was the green pants, wasn't it?"

Her startled laugh surprised her, and she heard his soft chuckle on the other end, pictured him smiling in the dark. It was so characteristic of the Luke she remembered. Always ready with a joke, always teasing her, always trying to make her feel better when she was down.

"Do you remember that time you stole my coke?" she asked, the memory playing back in her mind, images and colors dull with age.

"Hey, you left it unattended. You can't expect a guy to ignore a freshly poured fountain drink when it's all alone and lonely."

The playful defensiveness came easily. "I only went to the bathroom to wash my hands."

"I'd just run five miles for cross country! I was thirsty."

"I had a water, too."

He tsked. "You expect a seventeen-year-old boy to pick water over a refreshing coke when calories and eating healthy wouldn't need to be on his radar for at least another ten years?"

She grinned, tracing the patterns in her marble counter top. Admittedly, that was an easy test. But it still wasn't something he could've just faked his way through with so little effort. And no amount of research would've led him to such an innocuous, insignificant memory.

Still.

"Do you remember our first kiss?" This question was asked in a more subdued tone. It seemed ridiculous that she would feel like she was betraying Nathan just by asking it, when it was something in the past, and nothing to be ashamed of. How many girls had Nathan kissed? But she couldn't help the fact that thinking about it still made her stomach flip.

Luke was silent, this time the hesitation was heavy with something different. Hurt, maybe?

"Are you testing me?" He didn't exactly sound hurt. But his tone suggested he was bothered.

"I just. . . " What? She was, wasn't she? "I don't know. Maybe?"

She heard movement, and she pictured him sitting up in the darkness, like he could defend himself better in that position.

He didn't defend himself though. "It was at that party. Who was it again? Alison Weber?"

"Ashley Weber," Erin supplied.

"Right. You were a junior. Jordan wasn't there. I forget why. But he told me to keep an eye on you."

"He was studying for his SATs."

He grunted. "Right. Because he was sick the first time."

"Strep."

She remembered that party. She'd felt so out of her element, always having been more of the bookish type. But there were some seniors who'd taken a marginal interest in her. Girls from the soccer team after she'd made varsity. The music was loud, people pressed in all around her, and she'd worn a dress that was a little too tight. Someone had poured beer on her.

"Right," Luke said slowly, remembering. "I was upstairs, holding the hair of that girl I'd been hanging around while she upchucked.”

“Mallory Tuttman,” Erin supplied again. She’d come up the stairs to find the bathroom to try to get the beer smell out of her dress because she knew her parents would ream her if they thought she’d been drinking.

“Mallory Tuttman,” he repeated. “Jeez, what ever happened to her?”

“College out of state.”

He made a mildly irritated sound in the back of his throat. “How do you remember all of that?”

“Because I had a crush on you. Half the reason I went to that party was because I knew you’d be there. I wanted to seem mature so you’d notice me as more than just your best friend’s little sister.”

He gave a breathless laugh. “Oh, trust me, I’d noticed you. That little dress you wore that night.” A soft whistle through his teeth.

She couldn’t help her grin. That had been the point.

“You barged right into the bathroom while Mallory gave me a visual that likely put me off that little hibachi grill for life.”

“I didn’t barge in. The door was half open.”

“Well, it’s not like she was peeing or something.” He was only mildly defensive.

“I wouldn’t personally want someone walking in while I threw up.”

“She was plastered. I’m not sure she cared. Or even remembered the next day.”

Erin waved her hand through the air as if to disperse the words. They had to stay on track, though the longer they dwelled even on those insignificant details, the more she believed this was the real Luke.

"Anyway," he said. "You looked kind of upset and Mallory's friend—"

"Kendra."

A tsk— "offered to take over once Mallory was more or less done introducing the contents of her stomach to the porcelain bowl."

"Stunning visual," Erin said dryly. "I'm glad you didn't just abandon her."

"Never. I helped Kendra get her downstairs and into her car. Kendra had clearly been more responsible with her time."

Erin smiled a little, glad to know that he'd been a gentleman even if he couldn't remember their names.

"I went back upstairs to find you. In one of the bedrooms. It wasn't occupied, thank God. I think it was Alison's parents' room—"

"Ashley."

"Whatever. She had made a very vehement announcement earlier not to even touch the door handle or she wouldn't be sharing any of the booze."

"How do you remember *that* detail?"

"I'm just not great with names." She pictured his one-shouldered shrug.

"You broke the sacred oath," Erin prompted.

"I only had one beer." Another shrug.

"Only one?"

"I had a meet the next day. And I had a lot of goals I didn't want to jeopardize at the time." He paused, weighing an addition. "Getting you being one of them."

She suppressed another smile, though it didn't matter if she grinned like an idiot. No one could see her.

"So I followed you into the parents' room, where you went

straight to the bathroom, slamming the door in my face. I heard you crying."

"I was embarrassed. I felt stupid, and totally out of my element. I was freaked out, to be honest."

"Because you thought your parents were going to kill you."

"And this random guy had come on to me, and I was not prepared for or skilled at handling that kind of thing."

"That was the guy who poured his drink into your lap for rebuffing him." Luke's tone tightened with anger.

"It was fifteen years ago, Luke."

"Yeah, but that guy was always a douche."

She had no doubt. He hadn't even been drunk when he'd hit on her and then continued to follow her around, persisting despite her resistance and outright refusals. He'd tossed his cup of beer straight into her lap and said "oops" flatly, so she knew it had definitely *not* been an accident.

"I wanted to wring that guy's neck after you came out and told me what happened," Luke continued. "You were crying, saying how you didn't know what you were going to do about the stain and the smell."

She smiled, able to look back with some fondness now that the crisis was weathered by age and upstaged by much deeper and worthwhile concerns. "And you just sat with me on the bed and let me put my head on your shoulder."

She heard his exhale. "And then you looked at me with those admiring baby blues, and I just couldn't resist. I'd been thinking about it all year."

She remembered the way he'd stared at her, tucked his finger under her chin, and tipped her face up just slightly. She'd been thinking about it for a long time too. But she also wasn't as confident and broke the kiss pretty quickly.

"Then you ran off, called Mandy to pick you up. And when I came over the next day, you acted like nothing happened." Even all these years later, he sounded hurt.

Softly, she said, "So did you."

"It ate at me. Because I couldn't tell Jord. I knew he wasn't going to like it. Not yet anyway. So I had no one to unpack it with. The rest of that semester was hell."

"And then you graduated."

"And you dated that football player." The playful disgust in his voice was obvious. She remembered the ongoing, mostly friendly, rivalry between the different sports teams.

"He was a nice guy," she insisted.

"Water under the bridge," he said, dismissively. "It all worked out in the end." A pause, agonizing. "Well. It had."

She touched a chunk of broken glass that had bounced back out of the sink, feeling the weight of his words, shouldering some guilt she shouldn't.

"Did I pass your test?"

The sadness in his voice didn't abate; her guilt became heavier. "Yes."

"Were you starting to question my story?"

"Wouldn't you?"

"Believe me, I still am." His breathing was ragged, and she wondered if he was close to tears.

"I'm sorry, Luke. It's difficult for me to swallow, but I can't imagine what it must be like to be going through it."

He cleared his throat. "I think I just need a good night of sleep to reset. Everything's easier after rest. Who knows? Maybe I'll wake up tomorrow and everything will be back to normal."

"I sure hope so."

10

Don't Quit Your Day Job

LUKE

Erin walked toward him with big sunglasses hiding her eyes and a pinched look to her mouth. She carried a tray with a couple of to-go coffees, her keys dangling from her fingers. One charm caught the morning sunlight, winking at him.

Another dress, this one svelte and form-fitting, taunted him. Red. It had always been her color.

He fought the compulsion to lick his lips, reminded himself that this Erin was off-limits. It was like that last semester of his senior year all over again. The one girl he wanted and couldn't have.

He stood from the bench in front of Baylor Industries, trying his best to look unruffled by her presence.

"I'm not going to ask how your night went," she said. "I figure it went about as well as mine."

He could hear it in her voice and knew she probably had a triple shot in that venti cup.

She didn't stop walking, so he followed her to the door, leaping forward just before she reached for the handle to open it for her. A smile flickered briefly across her face in thanks.

He followed her silently to the elevator, up to their floor, into the main office area, then to her personal office. He glanced around the space, noting the different choices in art—abstract and pretentious—and how few personal pictures there were.

She set the coffee tray on the corner of her desk as she walked around it to put her purse away and wake up her computer. The glasses came off, and she released a heavy sigh as she ran her hands through her loose blonde locks.

"Your hair's shorter," he said in surprise. His first words of the morning.

Blue eyes, framed by what looked like false lashes, flickered to his face. She had fire-engine red lips again, and she pursed them.

"I don't hate it," he added.

She straightened, her gaze aloof. "I'm so glad you approve."

He clenched his muscles to keep it from hitting like the sucker-punch it was and turned to look out the window. Of course, his approval would mean nothing. Or would come off as overly familiar where he had no right. He wasn't even sure why he'd made the comment.

She sighed. "I'm sorry."

He turned so that he could see her. She placed a hand on her hip. A bandage was wrapped around one finger, but he decided it was better not to ask about it just yet.

"The lack of sleep, the implications of what's happened, have made me. . . thorny." She tucked her chin length hair behind an ear. "That cup is for you."

He made no move to get it. "No apology necessary. I was the one out of line. What is my job going to be?"

She raised a brow, and a hint of humor twinkled in her eyes.

"Basically my errand boy."

"At your beck and call." His grin was slow. "Just like at home."

Finally, the tightness he'd seen in her the moment she walked up loosened just a fraction as she laughed. "I'll have you start with some data entry. I'll show you a cubicle where you can work. I have. . . " She exhaled in irritation suddenly, picking up a tablet of paper from her desk he hadn't noticed. "A list of tasks my father left me."

"Hank isn't here?" Luke asked.

He caught the fleeting sour look, there and gone.

"He has a business trip. He'll be gone for a few days."

He tilted his head, watching her roll her shoulders back almost unconsciously. It bothered her, stressed her that her father was gone, and he wondered why it was such a burden to her. He had already seen that something about Hank and his dynamic with Erin was off. And of course, things would be altered after Jordan's death. But there was something else there. Some other tension.

Would she tell him about it? Or would he have to work for that kind of trust? At the very least, he could get started

"Well, show me to my desk, and I'll get started."

* * *

The morning passed in a blur of mindless busywork. It was the sort of job a recent college graduate might have. But he couldn't complain too much. It was his only option at the moment.

A few people introduced themselves, and a woman named Lindsey had lingered for quite a while, flirting mercilessly.

Erin hadn't said anything, but he caught the shrewd look in her narrowed eyes when she'd spotted the buxom brunette hanging around his cubicle.

As it neared lunchtime, Luke stood to stretch and check how many people were still around. Not many opted to work through their lunch, and though his stomach gurgled out its own opinion about what he should do, he sat back down and pulled up the web browser to do a search.

He typed in *parallel universes* and drummed his fingers on the desk for the five seconds it took the results to load. Wikipedia and YouTube were the top links, which he clicked on respectively to at least get a baseline idea of what he might be dealing with.

Then he found an article that delved a little deeper but explained in easy-enough terms. As he read, he lost all sense of the time that passed and what went on around him.

Even in layman's speak, broken down in cutesy stories to explain the concept, he struggled to grasp it entirely, and he was reminded why he had not gone on a science route in school.

"I think if you sit closer, you'll be able to see better."

Luke flinched, startled by Erin's voice so close.

"I came to see if you wanted to go get lunch," she said. "And then you were squinting at that screen so hard, I had to wonder if you need glasses."

He took a deep breath and rubbed both hands over his face. He felt a little like he was walking through a dream, slow and sluggish. Everything was so surreal.

"I don't need glasses," he said finally. "I'm doing some, uh—" he paused to glance around. "Research on parallel universes, and I'm just working hard to understand any of what I'm reading."

She leaned down, her hand dropping onto his shoulder as she read from behind him. "Quantum mechanics?" She gave a low whistle. "Zombie cat?"

He laughed darkly. "It was an example this guy used to illustrate the idea that for any given choice, the timeline splits for each possible outcome. So in one case, a gun goes off and kills a cat or it doesn't go off and the cat lives. But because there are now two timelines occurring simultaneously, the cat is technically both dead and alive at the same time. Hence, zombie cat."

She grimaced. "Okay."

He waved that away. "Just ignore the zombie cat part. But focus in on this: every decision you make—and there is apparently some debate about this—causes a split into as many timelines as it needs to accommodate every option and its outcome. The debate is if it truly is every decision, or simply every *impactful* decision. Take your dress, for example."

She looked down at the red number then squinted back at him, dubious.

"You chose to wear this red dress instead of, say, a blue one. If there is a split for every decision, there's a timeline that split when you chose the blue dress, and your day unfolded how it would if you'd made that choice. But say that your day played out exactly the same whether you chose the blue dress or the red one. Maybe it had no impact whatsoever. Therefore, that split might not have even happened. So, one part of the theory postulates that anything that interacts in a way that isn't reversible is where the split happens."

If possible, her eyes narrowed even more as she sighed. "So you think you have a grasp on this?"

He winced. "The general theory, sure. But none of this

explains how I ended up in this alternate timeline. Not to mention where the split happened to make this one and my own diverge."

She chewed the inside of her cheek. "So how do we figure that out?"

He turned back to the computer screen and backed up to the previous page. "Find an expert on the subject."

This was where he felt the need to tread lightly. His knowledge of Jordan's death was so cursory that he wasn't sure how this would affect her. But it was one of his only options, and one convenient enough to be worth pursuing.

"Did you find one?" she asked, apparently sensing his hesitation. Her eyes had become guarded.

"Keep in mind that you wouldn't need to come with me." He clicked on the page he'd been on before—the faculty page that listed one of its professors of quantum mechanics and physics.

Her expression darkened when she read the name of the college at the top of the page.

"I only did a random search, and this happened to come up. But it's the easiest trip for me to make to at least start the investigation into what happened to me the other day. Even if he doesn't have answers, maybe he can shed some light on it and point us in the right direction. Maybe help us figure out how to send me back."

His words had continued to tumble out as her silence grew heavier. She hadn't moved, but he almost felt her shrink.

Her eyes were still focused on the name of his alma mater, knowing abstractly that she must hate the very place, what it represented as the location of her brother's tragic death.

"Like I said, you wouldn't have to come with me." Her stillness made it feel necessary to lower his voice, to speak gently. She seemed so fragile in that moment, like a sudden move, a loud noise, would shatter her.

She blinked, and the moment passed. She was no longer breakable, pulling some inner strength around her. It was obvious in the flinty look of her eyes. "I'll go. I'm going to need some answers too."

"All right. When is the earliest we could leave?"

Her lip went between her teeth again, a habit he was noticing. It was not one he had noticed his Erin doing. "I have some things I have to take care of this evening." Her voice shaped the word *things* oddly, like it wasn't the word she actually meant. "If I buckle down and get some stuff done today, maybe work a bit later tonight, we could play hooky and go tomorrow."

He clicked his teeth thoughtfully. He would really rather go sooner, but he had no vehicle, and she'd already lent him money for his clothes. He really needed to do his duty by her and work hard now. "Tomorrow will do."

She nodded once, decisive, her mind already appearing to shift into high-gear work-mode. She turned to head back toward her office.

"If you have anything I can help you with to get your work done faster, I'm more than willing," he offered.

A sly grin was on her face when she looked at him, walking backward. "Data entry a little too mundane for a genius like you?"

He shrugged, his smile mirroring hers in attitude. "I mean, I don't mind busy work. But I certainly have more to offer than completing mindless tasks."

She placed a hand on the doorjamb to her office and winked. "I'll see what I can dig up."

11

Mom Probs

ERIN

True to his word, Luke had been helpful with some of the additional tasks her father gave her so she was able to complete every priority project before the day was over. It made her seriously consider getting herself an assistant that worked solely for and with her. They had a number of administrative assistants in the office, but none were directly dedicated to any one executive.

Her father claimed that he didn't want anyone to feel like there was a distinct hierarchy, or at least to make that gap seem less wide between the employees. Which was odd considering the man liked to emphasize the disparity in rank in business meetings and among some of the upper-level execs.

Hell, even with his own family, he liked the obvious authority he held as the head of the Baylor clan.

Erin walked to the big window that spanned almost the entire south-facing wall of her office trying to shed her frustration, but it was only replaced by tension.

She dialed her mother's cell. When she didn't answer, Erin

tried the house number. Still, no answer, and her stomach twisted as if someone was wringing it like a washcloth.

"I swear you're going to chew a hole in your cheek if you keep doing that."

She spun to look at Luke in the doorway, leaning against the jamb with one ankle crossed over the other.

God, he was a lovely sight to behold. He'd been a good-looking kid, but he'd become a *very* attractive man.

He raised a brow, and she realized she was staring and hadn't acknowledged his words. It took her a second to remember what he'd even said to her.

She rubbed a hand absently down her arm. "What do you mean?"

"You're always chewing on your lip or your cheek. Nervous habit?"

She clicked her tongue and smiled to hide the heat rising to her cheeks. "Yeah, probably." She looked at the phone in her hand. "My mom isn't answering my calls. I, uh, I'm supposed to check in on her while my dad's gone."

Because she might have drunk herself to death or fallen into the pool in a drunken stupor, she added mentally. She knew her expression had darkened.

He tilted his head, probably noting the change in her face. "We can go now. That way you can run by your parents' before you drop me off."

Her body threatened to shrink at the very thought, but she fought the urge. Two fears battled within her: one that something was wrong with her mother, and she needed to get there as soon as possible to check on her; the other was that Luke would find out her family's dirty little secret.

"Let me just get my stuff," she said in a subdued tone, trying to work past steadily rising panic to think of an excuse not to bring him along.

But the only things her mind conjured were her worst fears about her mother and nothing productive.

She moved across the room to pack everything back into her purse and shut down her computer, all while running scenarios in her mind. Her mother, face-down in the swimming pool or in a puddle of her own vomit. Luke coming in behind her to see her worst fear and greatest shame.

She looked up at him as if he could see every scene rolling in her mind. He no longer lounged in the doorway but stood straight with muscles snapped tight. He was poised like he sensed something was off and was waiting for it to break open.

It made her eyes dance away from his face, and a cord of tension snapped up her spine, gripping her own muscles in a choke hold that had a headache brewing.

She turned off the light as they left and pulled the door closed, all the while feeling too aware of Luke as they walked. She could tell he was overly tuned in to her too.

It must have been the tether forged long ago in youth. She never would have guessed that connection could remain across distance, time, and even universes. But there it was, just the same. And there was a time that this secret, this family skeleton would have been something she *would* share with him. Or at least something Jordan would have. Back then. When Luke was more or less an extended member of their family. But her mother hadn't had a problem then. And she probably wouldn't have it now if it weren't for. . .

Jordan.

Erin shut her eyes, leaning her head back against the wall as they rode the elevator down in silence.

"Are you all right?"

She lifted her head to gaze at him. His expression was as soft as his voice had been. She could almost feel his want, his desire to touch her, to comfort her. It vibrated off of him, made her whole body tingle in awareness.

Her heart seemed to respond to that unspoken communication, beating with a force that called out, and she swore he'd hear it. How she longed for comfort like that. Nathan had been gone for only a few days, but it felt like forever since someone had simply held her.

She sighed. "I'm fine. I have a lot on my mind. It's given me a headache." Which was true enough. But it still felt like she was lying to him.

He stared at her for a long moment, those intense eyes gauging her, trying to read her mind, maybe. Then he looked away, and she couldn't explain the odd sense of abandonment she felt in that moment.

She clenched her fists and set her mind to bolstering herself. There was no reason she should need comfort or help. She was capable of so much, and this was just another hard thing in a life full of difficulties.

"I appreciate your help today," she said, noting with satisfaction that she sounded firm and in control again. She led the way out of the elevator and through the lobby.

He shrugged. "I'm just glad I can do something to pay you back in some way for everything you've done and are doing for me. The clothes, the job, driving me to, ah. . . Well, helping me figure some things out."

As if dancing around the subject would keep her mind from jumping exactly where neither of them wanted it to. She should let it slide. Just like she let it slide every time it had come up in conversation with people who knew what happened to Jordan. How many times had someone stumbled over their words, backed up, apologized profusely for saying what they thought would hurt her or remind her of something tragic that she never could forget anyway? She never said anything, but it drove her crazy.

She especially hated it coming from him.

"Don't do that," she said, pressing her key fob to disarm her car's alarm system with unnecessary violence.

He paused in the act of reaching for the passenger side door handle. "Do what?"

"Tip-toe around it. Jordan is dead. You can say it." She couldn't help how the words sliced out of her. She got in the car, knowing she was a coward for not wanting to see the effect they would have on him. Not that she could avoid it for long.

He got in the car as well, though he didn't look upset. More like he'd been chastised. Which, she supposed, was kind of what had happened.

She turned to him, working to soften her voice. "It's going to come up. A lot, I'm sure. Yes, it's painful to be reminded that he's gone." She paused to get control of her voice, which had cracked a little on the last word. "But his death is a part of me and my life, this timeline. So just say it if you have to. Because when you start and stop, it doesn't make it less hard. It just makes it annoying as hell."

He remained silent as he absorbed her words, and they both reached for their seat belts.

As she started the car, she felt his intention to speak before he opened his mouth, and she braced for whatever it was.

"I didn't mean to seem insensitive. Or maybe overly sensitive to the subject, as if you're too fragile to hear me mention it." He stopped, but his tone had lilted up, meaning he wasn't finished. The moment stretched. Then: "Some of my stumbling has to do with the fact that. . . it's hard for me, too. In a different way. Because I'm here, maybe permanently, I have to deal with the fact that my best friend is gone. And that means I have to grieve too. But as if it just happened."

She slid a glance in his direction. He was looking straight ahead, his jaw clenched. He'd spoken steadily, but there was something just under the surface—maybe the threat of a quaver.

It called up emotion in herself, and she swallowed against it. Because he was absolutely right. This would be a fresh wound for him, and he'd likely go through all of the phases she'd had to ten years ago.

They drove for a few minutes in silence. Abruptly, she reached over and took his hand. He gave hers a grateful squeeze. But he didn't look at her, nor did he keep her hand because he must have remembered it didn't belong to him.

And that, too, she thought, was a kind of grief he'd have to grapple with. If this were, indeed, a permanent thing, he would have to process the loss of her as well. It seemed like an odd thing until she thought of the past relationships she'd invested in that had ended. They always involved a grieving process, to some extent or another. Always a death of what had been or what never would be.

When she looked at Luke again, he seemed lost in thought, his lips puckered absently.

So she turned her attention back to the road, using the silence to mentally build up some protection for whatever she was about to encounter at her parents' house.

There had only been a couple of really scary experiences

in the years that her mother had spiraled into the mire of alcoholism. Maybe there was more than she was aware of. Her father didn't talk about what went on behind closed doors, even to her. She had no idea what it was like in the day-to-day with her mother's problem.

Still, when it was all on her, she couldn't help but think back to that one scary experience. So every time her father traveled, the anxiety balled up in her stomach, wreaked havoc on her appetite, her sleep, even her ability to concentrate.

They pulled into the driveway of her parents' sprawling one-story home. It appeared that every light had been turned on, curtains open to let the brightness blaze against the dusky sky.

She squinted out the windshield at the front window, hoping to catch movement so the fist around her heart would loosen.

"Do you mind waiting here?" She looked at Luke, hoping he didn't sense her inner turmoil.

His gaze remained trained out the front window. "Nope. Go ahead."

She pressed the buttons to roll the windows down then shut the engine off. "I don't know how long this will take, so there's some fresh summer air for you."

"Gee, thanks." The first hint of a smirk appeared. "I'm pretty sure it's illegal to leave your dog in a hot car, but why not leave the human to bake?"

His tone was light-hearted, and she tried to match it despite her stress level. "You're not broken. You can open the door and get out if you need to."

He gave her a half-smile, which almost made her anxiety ease. Almost.

Despite the fact that there was no porch light on, she could see the walkway to the front door easily enough with all the light spilling out the windows. On impulse, she tried the knob without using her key and found it unlocked.

That was enough to set her closer to the edge, and when she saw the living room and the kitchen were empty, she continued through the rest of the house at a near run, whispered fears turning to shouts in her mind.

"Mom!" She searched through the first two rooms, a guest room and office space respectively. Empty, though she hadn't really expected to find her there. It still kicked her heart into a more panicked rhythm.

The last place she had to check was her parents' bedroom. She skidded to a stop just inside. Even the bathroom light blazed. The blankets were mussed as if her mother had just gotten up. But what stopped her heart for a split second were the french doors that were thrown open to the back patio, the swimming pool, and the guest house just beyond.

Her breath came in huffs as she moved across the room. The urgency twitched at her muscles, but she felt like she was moving through water and everything around her was distorted. Sound, light, even her own thoughts.

She had to steady herself with a hand against the frame of the door leading into the backyard. Her eyes scanned the water first, but there was nothing and no one in it. It was still light enough outside for her to see the area was entirely empty, the guesthouse dark.

Erin's hand clutched at her throat as she cut through the patio to the side gate that would let her go around the west side of the house and to the front again.

She froze when she rounded the corner. All of her anxiety seemed to condense and morph, or maybe just mask itself with irritation. It took everything in her not to stomp over to the car where her mother was leaning into the passenger side window. The martini she held was half-full, and it sloshed around as she talked, gesturing enthusiastically.

Luke's baritone laugh mingled with her mother's own as Erin walked up.

"Hey, Mom."

Her mother was probably far enough gone that she wouldn't notice it came out through clenched teeth.

Gloria Baylor straightened and spun around, the amusement not fading at all. Her cheeks were flushed, her eyes glassy from drink, and her grin widened on seeing her daughter.

"Erin, this young gentleman is a delight. I'm sad you weren't going to bring him in!" She touched Luke's arm resting on the door.

His expression changed from polite amusement to shrewd understanding when he met Erin's gaze.

Okay, so he knew her mother was *currently* drunk. But that didn't mean he had guessed that this was her general state of being more often than not.

She tried to shake off her frustration. "Sorry, Mom. We were just stopping by to check on you. I was dropping him at home after work. But while I'm here, I thought I'd see if you wanted to have dinner? I could bring something over after I drop him off."

"Is it dinner time already?" Her mother looked at her bare wrist as if she expected a watch to be there.

"How's Chinese sound?" Erin took her mother's arm and gently tugged her toward the house.

"Hmmm, orange chicken?"

"Sure."

"With chow mein? And some spring rolls!"

Erin opened the front door. "Of course."

Her mother brought her hands together, and realized one held the martini glass. She rewarded her surprised delight with a hefty gulp of the drink.

As soon as Erin had her mother settled on the couch with some home renovation show on TV, she assured her she'd be back within the hour and snuck out the front door, taking her first unrestricted breath.

She caught herself chewing her lower lip and stopped before she climbed into her car. The flush in her cheeks was no doubt visible, but she didn't look at Luke to see if he noticed.

He said nothing until after they had backed out of the driveway and were halfway down the street.

"Your mom didn't recognize me."

She glanced at him, not expecting that to be the first thing he said. She realized that despite there being no way for him to guess, she still nursed the fear that he'd somehow figured it out.

"That's probably for the best," she said carefully.

"I'm sure it helped that she was a little worse for wine. Or, rather, vodka, if I had to guess."

"Yeah, there's that," she said, trying to gloss over that casually, so she quickly plowed on: "But it's been a long time since she's seen you, and you don't exactly look like the college boy you once were."

"Is that a good thing or a bad thing?" His tone was teasing.

She paused a moment to gather her thoughts instead of saying whatever came to mind immediately. What she wanted to say was *a very good thing.*

Instead, she said, "Not bad."

He grinned in a way that made her feel like he knew what

she'd been thinking anyway. She couldn't fight the heat that rose to her cheeks.

"Stop doing that."

He laughed. "What?"

"That flirting thing."

"Sorry."

He looked decidedly *not* sorry. And she couldn't help smiling, which made it clear to her that things were definitely getting more complicated than they already were. She fidgeted with her engagement ring almost unconsciously, but it drew her eyes to it as the guilt swept through her.

"Now I really am sorry."

His voice had changed, and it drew her gaze to his face. His lips were pressed into a tight line, and he was eyeing her ring with abject disdain.

"Nice little skating rink you've got there. Makes the one I got you look pathetic."

Somehow, his words made her feel like she was the inadequate one instead of the other way around. Not that the ring size had any bearing on the happiness of the couple, or the success of their marriage.

"I didn't choose the ring." Damn it, she sounded defensive. "It was his grandmother's."

He pursed his lips, no doubt noting her tone. "Old money, then."

She couldn't help the irritation that spiked through her. "You disapprove."

He folded his arms across his chest as if to deflect the disapprobation in her own voice. "Did I say that?"

"No, but your tone implied it."

"Read into it all you want."

It wasn't a denial, and she was sure it was his way of confirming exactly what she accused him of. But she chalked it up to pure jealousy, trying to dismiss his words as nothing beyond that, and worked to convince herself his opinion didn't matter anyway.

She pulled to the curb in front of Tara's house, unable to bring herself to look at him. Instead she stared at the white-knuckle grip she had on the steering wheel, focusing on her breathing.

"I can't help feeling like something's off. Like, is this really the guy you want?"

She turned an incredulous gaze on him. "What are you basing that on? A diamond that puts your puny ring to shame? You don't even know him! You don't know *me*, for that matter."

He drew back slightly as if she'd slapped him.

She turned away, not wanting to let him see that she was shaken. Because even though she'd spoken true—that he knew nothing of Nathan, herself, or their relationship—he'd found that little nagging suspicion that had been in the back of her mind all along. Why else would she take the ring off before going to the hospital?

"I'll pick you up at seven tomorrow morning," she said in a tone that sounded alien, even to herself.

He said nothing. But she heard him shift, open the door, shut it.

She didn't watch him walk up to the front door or disappear inside. And she was grateful for darkness and drive-throughs, for the solitude to give in to a short crying jag.

<h1 style="text-align:center">12</h1>

Answers and Apologies

The mug of coffee his sister had left for him felt more like a prop than anything as he stared out the front window. It was too early for Erin to be there yet, but he had this sick fear that their disagreement the day before was enough to make her flake on him. She wasn't the type to do that, of course, but he wouldn't blame her if she did.

He'd spent half the night awake, agonizing over his stupid, impulsive words. The other half of the night was spent dreaming that he was chasing her, trying to apologize, and she was always disappearing around a corner or vanishing right in front of him.

He curled his lip every time he took a sip of the tepid, low-quality coffee, but he was going to need the caffeine for the day ahead. He needed to be alert, to operate at his mental maximum to understand anything the professor might have to offer him. And to keep himself from saying more idiotic things to push Erin away.

He tried to keep from replaying the conversation again, but it was on repeat in his brain against his will. He could admit that a lot of what he'd said came from the malicious jealousy that stole through him whenever he thought of her with another man. There had been no evidence that she was unhappy with her fiancé, though he could tell after he'd said it that he was at least somewhat close to the truth from the way she blanched.

But it gave him no sense of satisfaction. Because, even here, where he couldn't have her, his sincerest wish would always be for her happiness. And whether he was right or not, he'd hurt her. It was worse knowing that some part of him had wanted to. It was like that reeling, tortured part of himself wanted someone to be miserable with him.

He downed the last of the coffee as if the acrid taste would wash away that pain, wishing that it wasn't seven a.m. so it would be socially acceptable for it to be something alcoholic.

Erin's car pulled to the curb as soon as he came back from putting the mug in the sink, so he went straight to the door.

She was chewing her lip again when he reached for the door handle. He wouldn't comment on it. He'd decided the first words out of his mouth definitely needed to be an apology.

She was already looking at him when he turned to her. "Erin, I'm so sorry."

She raised an eyebrow.

"I had no right to say what I did."

She pursed her lips skeptically as silence stretched. "There's no 'but?'"

That threw him. "Why would there be?"

"There usually is." She spoke softly, so it almost seemed like she was saying it to herself. She furrowed her brow quizzically, but she said nothing more, opting to put the car in drive and head out instead.

He couldn't help noticing the way she fiddled with the engagement ring, and he wasn't sure if it was because she was purposely trying to draw his attention to it or if it was because she was thinking about what he'd said the night before. He hated himself for hoping she was second-guessing any decisions to marry the guy.

"So what's the game plan?" she asked.

Down to business, tone crisp and distant. Like her father that first day. Hank Baylor had always had an aloofness about him, but the coldness he'd maintained when Luke had talked to him was disconcerting. Even more so when Erin did it too. This was not the Baylor family he knew and loved.

It was hard to reconcile, even with the knowledge of the painful and irreversible damage Jordan's death had caused. He'd always known abstractly that the loss of a loved one was deeply impactful, especially when it was unexpected. He'd just never witnessed it firsthand. Both his mom and dad had lost one of their own parents respectively, but it was somehow less life-altering, if only marginally, because they had expected it, and it was the natural order of things to eventually lose your older relatives. But Jordan's death had done something more.

He was starting to see that for himself as he fought to understand it as his own reality, even if temporarily. Because there was no guarantee it wasn't permanent.

"Luke?"

He looked over, realizing he never answered her. He gave his head a quick shake. "Sorry. What was the question?"

"Is there a plan for when we get to the college?"

Shutting his eyes, he tried to center his thoughts. "Uh, there was no option to set up an appointment with the professor, but he has office hours I figured we could shoot for."

She nodded.

The air in the car vibrated with the words he could tell were coming. It took a long time for her to say what was on her mind.

"Thank you for the apology. I realize that some of this is difficult for you too."

"That's not an excuse."

"No, but I want you to know I understand."

He shrugged it off, though her words made something in his chest tighten.

Silence lengthened again, but it held that tension once more. There was so much reluctance in her to speak, like she was afraid something she didn't want him to know would come out. And he was very sure there were some things she wanted to keep from him.

Erin's reaction to his accusation about her fiancé made him fairly certain that was one.

The other seemed related to her mother. And if he had to guess, it had to do with the drinking. Gloria Baylor, in his own world, was a capable, independent woman. She wouldn't need her grown daughter checking on her while Hank was away on business.

Erin's whole demeanor had spooled when she'd mentioned checking on her mother. Especially when he said they could do it on the way to his sister's. Like she hadn't wanted him to come. After seeing Gloria well into her cups, he figured Erin had known she'd be in such a state. So either it was a frequent occurrence whenever her father was out of town, or it was worse than that. Given Erin's increasing tension on the drive over, he guessed it was the latter, and her father's absence likely exacerbated the problem.

"You're awfully quiet this morning," Erin murmured.

"Takes one to know one."

She rolled her shoulders. "You're right. We need to loosen up. And I need to prepare myself for. . . " She wrinkled her nose. "Now I'm doing the thing."

"The avoiding-talking-about-it thing?" He smirked.

She pointed at him. "That."

"Just because you don't want to tip-toe around it, doesn't mean we *have* to talk about it."

She blew out a breath. "Then what do we talk about?"

He considered, tilting his head. "How disappointed I am you're not wearing that red dress?"

She laughed.

"Actually that gets me thinking," he started, pieces falling together in his mind in a way that formed a pattern.

"Oh, no," she groaned.

"No, just listen." Excitement tingled along his skin. "When we were talking about the parallel timelines, and I used the example of the blue dress versus the red dress, right?"

"Sure," she said slowly, obviously not sure where it was leading.

"I mean, does the color of your dress matter? Would it send your life on even a slightly different trajectory?"

She was only half taking him seriously, squinting bemusedly at him. "I doubt it."

He turned slightly in his seat. He had meant the original comment in jest, but then he remembered what had run through his mind after their brief discussion before. "So, think of it this way: the red dress is. . . noticeable." He paused to give her his devilish grin as punctuation, and she rolled her eyes. "Say you walked down a busy street. The red dress definitely draws the eye. And let's just say you don't look like a bum in it. Even a nice guy like myself notices that kind of thing."

A wry smile. "Ha."

He held up a hand as if to stay her. "Say some poor schmuck is driving down the street, sees you in the red dress. He's distracted enough to be a second too late in putting on his brakes, rear-ends the car in front of him. Would your life stay exactly the same if you'd worn the blue dress, hadn't been noticed by the guy, and no accident had occurred at all?"

Her brows furrowed , and she did the lip chewing thing. "So it could have been something just as innocuous as a red or blue dress that sent your life in your timeline on a different trajectory than your life in this timeline?"

He took a deep breath. That hadn't occurred to him. He was assuming it was Jordan's death that had caused the divergence. But maybe it was something small before that which led to those events. "Could be. At this point, there's not much to go on. I'm just trying to get a better baseline of understanding before we meet with the professor."

She nodded. "Well, obviously he won't know what could have caused the split. He doesn't know your life."

"True."

"I guess we'd have to go back and trace your steps to know ourselves. And there's only so much we can do in that arena. Your other self would really be the one we'd need in order to know what might be different."

He shook his head. "That would only tell us what makes the timelines different. It likely wouldn't tell us what brought me to this one and why. And therefore, how to get back. Which is why we need the professor." He studied her profile, an unexpected wave of yearning washing through him. He had to clench his hands before they betrayed him.

"There's no real way to know if it was my life, or *only* my life, that shifted the direction of this timeline, either."

She winced. "Man, this gets complicated fast."

"Hence the need for an expert."

She rested an elbow on the window and rubbed her temple. That was a universal Erin move for when she was trying to get a handle on multiple emotions. Usually frustration, exhaustion, stress.

He turned to his window, running his hands through his hair to fight the unholy rush of homesickness that nearly crushed him.

It didn't take long for him to register that they were close to the school. How many times had he made that drive? When he'd gone home for a weekend so his mom would do his laundry for free, for her unrivaled home cooking, or just to watch a football game with his dad? He'd relished his freedom, the sense of growing up that going off to college had given him. But he had never been one to need hundreds of miles between him and home.

He remembered making the trip in his beat up pick up, usually with Jordan in the passenger seat. They'd crank their dumb punk rock, chug some cokes, or commiserate about papers, finals, and girls. Until Jordan met Kelly. And Luke had finally buckled down to earn Erin's affection.

Jordan hadn't gone home nearly as often after Kelly got a hold of him. He'd never seen his best friend so enamored with any girl. He'd sure gotten stupid for a couple, but not the way he did with Kelly. Luke wondered what happened to her in this universe. Had she become a teacher like she'd wanted? Gotten her master's so she could eventually become a principal, per her plan?

He tried to remember what Erin and Tara had said about Jordan's death, when it had happened. How long had he been with Kelly by that point? Deep enough to alter her life path too?

He definitely needed to fill in some of those blanks, at least for his own peace of mind, and he hadn't had time to do much research on his own. Too much time spent just trying to get his bearings and to figure out if he could get back.

In the distance, several of the brick dormitories loomed, orange and ugly against the blue of the end of summer sky. As they got closer, several of the shorter buildings became visible, the signs posted out front announcing their focuses on mathematics or humanities or sciences. Those were tucked into the huge, mature trees that seemed to encroach, hugging the edifices in habitual possessiveness.

The school year had barely begun, and there was a constant flux of students cutting in and around the buildings on foot. It reminded Luke of an anthill. They always followed the same trails, flowing in lines back and forth.

"Which building?" Erin asked.

"Uh, the sciences building. You'll want to park in the Buxton lot." He pointed. "That way."

She nodded and pulled in. They drove around for a while before a car pulled out, and they were able to take its spot.

As soon as they got out, Luke was nearly bowled over by memories. Almost all of them were good. He certainly remembered the nights he'd partied too hard or had stayed up too late studying. But his years here with Jordan were some of his best.

"You're looking wistful all of a sudden."

Luke looked at her. By contrast, her shoulders were hunched as if she were being buffeted by a heavy wind.

"I know this probably seems foreign to you, but I have a lot of good memories here. I did a lot more than book learning."

"Let me guess. You got some life lessons about being an adult, taking chances, how to earn your lady love."

He knew her caustic tone was due to all of the negative things this place represented, so he was able to keep her words from really getting under his skin. He couldn't blame her. Even if this was a permanent situation for him, accepting that his best friend was gone would never give him the negative association with where he'd died. This place wouldn't exacerbate his grief.

"Sorry," she said. "I didn't mean to be harsh."

"That's okay," he replied in a subdued tone. "Let's just get this over with."

She nodded, and he couldn't help noticing how pale she looked, how she wrapped her arms around herself like she was cold, despite the heat of the late summer morning. He would have put an arm around her shoulders, comforted her, if that damn ring wasn't winking at him in the sunlight.

So they walked in silence, Luke feeling useless and irked, Erin looking alone and small. He hated everything about this timeline, couldn't wait to get home. But it would always sit with him, this experience, this knowledge that in some world, he didn't have Jordan, *couldn't* have Erin, and everyone was broken and hurting.

13

Professor Oddity

ERIN

The professor's office was easy enough to find. This early in the semester, it wasn't likely anyone was utilizing much of his open office times. Indeed, crowds of students thronged through the halls, but none came or went through the door.

Erin didn't feel quite so sick, so twisted inside. Maybe because she'd never been inside the college, this didn't feel so connected to her memories of the weeks after her brother's death.

Still, when she failed to knock on the professor's door, Luke stepped up to do it for her.

A shuffling sound from inside alerted them that he was inside. There was a thud and then a low oath before a man's voice called, "Come in."

She trailed in after Luke as he opened the door.

The man behind the desk had his eyes narrowed as he looked up at them. He seemed less settled than he should have appeared, given that he was seated, and she wondered at his heavier breathing. He was in shape, almost fanatically fit for an older man, though she gauged his age to be mid- to late-forties. His dark hair was only lightly grayed at the temples.

"Can I help you?" he asked, his voice gruff.

Erin didn't feel the inclination or the confidence to answer, so she left it to Luke. This was his endeavor, and he had more of a grasp on it all than she did, anyway. But he seemed to shrink before the obvious irritation that hung about this man like a cloud.

"Yes, we had a few questions for you," Luke began, rocking back on his heels a little.

The professor's gaze shifted to the door and back to them. "You don't look like students."

"Ah, no." Luke clasped his hands in front of him, clearly letting his nerves get the best of him. Or maybe it was the professor's closed-off demeanor. "But we had some questions about a particular topic you seem to be somewhat of an expert on."

A blatant wariness entered the man's eyes now.

"I apologize. My name is Luke Pearson. This is Erin Baylor." Luke turned to indicate Erin before offering his hand.

The professor hesitated before he shook it. "Doctor Eli Thibald." The wariness lingered, and he didn't sit down. "What topic are you needing my expertise in?"

Luke's unease seemed heightened when the professor failed to sit or invite them to do so. She was starting to suspect this man wasn't going to be as helpful as they'd hoped.

Still, she felt emboldened by Luke's long pause. "We had questions about parallel universes."

Thibald pulled his head back slightly, his eyes becoming steely. "What about them?"

She jabbed her elbow into Luke's back when he didn't answer

right away, and he almost leaped forward. "Uh, we wanted to know if they were possible?"

Thibald crossed his arms over his chest. "Mathematically speaking, yes."

Like pulling teeth, she thought.

"Okay. . . Well, is it possible to be transported between two timelines?" Luke's voice seemed to reflect her own frustration.

"Why on earth would you need or want to know an answer to that question?" Actual antagonism now.

Luke lifted his hands as if in defense. "We just want to understand the theories a little better."

Thibald was poised on the balls of his feet, fingertips brushing his desk as he leaned forward. His expression was not friendly. "There's no reason for you to need to understand them beyond what you may find on the internet, honestly. If you were studying quantum physics, I would be more willing. But by your own admission, you're not students, so I'd rather not waste my time."

"Aren't you a teacher?" Erin demanded. "Why not educate someone seeking knowledge?"

"I'm *paid* to educate. I don't answer idle questions curious people happen to have." He turned to gather some papers and a briefcase.

"This is more than just idle curiosity." Luke's voice was a sharp slice through the air as he took a step forward.

The professor's body went rigid. Skepticism was written in every line of his body as he regarded Luke.

"It might seem like an odd topic for the average person to be interested in, but it doesn't make my need for answers any less valid."

Was Luke aware of the edge in his own voice? It made Erin

tense up, unconsciously anticipating a fight.

The professor drummed his finger along his briefcase, perhaps debating something. "Shut that door." He continued to gather his things, but as Erin did his bidding, he seemed willing to at least humor them. "How much do you know about parallel universes?"

"Not much," Luke admitted. "Just what I've found online."

"All right. If you've done any research, you may know about the Many Worlds Interpretation," Thibald began. He looked for some kind of confirmation in Luke's face. There was an extra sharpness to his scrutiny too. Like he was looking for something deeper.

Luke shifted as if he sensed it too. "On a basic level. Every choice we have splits to accommodate the outcome of any decision we make."

"Yes. And some theories posit that all the possible outcomes still exist all in one place, but we experience only one at any given time. But we can't observe every possible state because, when we observe, the multiple possible states collapse into only one observable state."

Erin squinted at the professor, trying to untangle all of his words. The more she tried to parse the language down, the more it confused her.

Luke appeared a little more secure in his ability to follow than Erin did. "So, how would someone cross into another 'state?'"

The question seemed to stop Thibald in his tracks, and that incisive look came into his gaze again. "Is there a reason you'd want to know about crossing?"

Erin felt it—something beneath the surface. It was as if this answer was more important than it appeared, but she couldn't fathom why that would matter to him. And they couldn't very well get into the reason without him kicking them out for being crazy.

Luke seemed to realize it too, his hesitation a weight on the air. "I guess I just wondered if it was possible."

Erin rubbed the hem of her top between her thumb and forefinger, an inexplicable tension building inside of her as Thibald stared at Luke, weighing his answer.

Something caught his attention at the door, and his expression morphed, like he'd seen a ghost. Then he shook his head. "I'm afraid I got more into this than I intended. I have somewhere I need to be."

Luke waved his hands as if to clear the air of what the professor had said. "Wait, that's it?"

Thibald focused on him, but a frenetic energy rolled off of him. He was already moving around the desk. "I don't have time right now to get into this with you." His eyes went to the door again.

Luke stepped forward, and Erin moved with him as if they were tethered. His sense of urgency was plain in his demeanor, and it was rubbing off on her.

"Professor, please. This is important." He placed his hands on the desk. "Can we schedule another time to meet?"

Whatever Thibald saw in Luke's expression must have given him pause because a debate waged in his eyes. Then he shook his head. "I'm sorry. I can't."

The professor rounded the edge of the desk ushering them toward the door.

Luke's rigid posture made Erin think he wasn't going to be rushed out, but he gave a curt nod. "Thank you for your time. Let's go, Erin."

She blinked, thrown off. "Uh. . . "

Luke didn't wait for her, and she chased after him as he stalked out into the hall.

They pushed through a crowd of people, students who thronged in the halls and paid little attention to the urgency of anyone else around them. She bumped hard into the shoulder of a man who grunted at the contact as he was working his way in the direction they'd just come from.

She glanced back to try to offer an apology, but he wasn't paying any attention to her. In fact, his eyes were trained on the professor's office with an intense sharpness that made her think it was his destination.

But Luke's long strides carried him off to the nearest exit and outside, and she sped up to catch him before he stalked off and lost her. It wasn't where they'd come in, but Luke didn't seem to care.

And all she could think was that they were missing something. Maybe more than one thing.

14

Sleuthing

LUKE

"Luke," Erin said softly, hand cupped over her eyes to shield them from the bright sun. It was a full sentence in one word.

But how could she even think he could calm down? The buzz of frustration was too raucous, too grating against his nerves for him to even consider it.

"The guy clearly knows what he's talking about," Luke said, rising to her attempt. "Did you hear that? Even that little bit he finally gave us was life-changing. And then he stops, refuses to help any further. Talk about dangling the t-bone in front of a starving dog."

"Luke," Erin said again.

He stopped and turned to her, though he was still too incensed. He clenched his hands, trying to steady his breathing. How close they could be to getting him home, away from the torture of this place, and the guy was so dismissive and half-distracted.

"This is my *life*, Erin. Everything I had is gone." That last word scraped up his throat, painful to say, painful to hear.

Her eyes softened, and she took his hand. "I know. I understand."

His heart gave an agonized lurch. Her comfort was a burn on his skin, the wrong hand on his. He pulled out of her grasp. "I don't know that you do."

She pressed her lips together and glanced away. After a moment, she turned back. "It's not over yet. You have his email, don't you? Maybe he'd be more willing to answer questions that way."

He took a deep breath and worked to settle his mind. "I doubt it."

Erin moved to stand beside him and lifted a hand to touch his shoulder before thinking better of it, dropping it back to her side. "It's a place to start. Don't give up yet."

Luke took another deep breath, told himself not to get so dramatic quite yet, but the anguish hadn't receded, wouldn't listen to logic, even if Erin was right. They had a little something still. And maybe the professor would be more helpful in that medium now that he had met Luke, knew his face and name.

"All right," he said, nodding, hoping that saying it would make it true. "All right. Let's get going."

Erin followed him onto a winding path and let him lead the way since he knew exactly where to go.

He wished he could shake off the melancholy, the despair he felt. What he wanted was to enjoy the walk, at least a little bit, to pretend it was just a random visit to his old college. Maybe then he would get the relief from the renewed grief pulsing through him.

It wasn't the first time he and Erin had walked these grounds. That one summer between his junior and senior year, he'd taken a couple of extra classes so he would graduate on time. She'd been home after her sophomore year at a university several hours away.

Before the summer session had started, there had been her parents' Memorial Day barbecue where he'd finally made his move. Erin's hair had been long then, falling past her shoulder blades. She'd already had tan lines from running every day, and her long legs were on display in that miniskirt she'd worn. And he couldn't stop staring at her.

Jordan had noticed.

"Just ask her out already," he'd said, exasperated. He'd been irritated for two reasons. The first being that Luke had been too chicken so far and, second, that he was interested in the first place.

Luke remembered the heat creeping up his neck. "What are you talking about?" Even then, his eyes had ghosted to where Erin stood with friends, laughing freely, a cold drink in her hand.

Jordan had scoffed, giving Luke a dark look. "Come on, man. I know you guys have had this *thing* for a long time." His tone had been mildly caustic, his lip curled a little in brotherly disgust. "And now I'm kind of okay with it. I might change my mind, so seize your opportunity while it's there."

So Luke had found a moment later on, when the sun was down, and the fire pit held a dancing flame that made her glow. He remembered the light reflecting in her eyes when she'd smiled at him, agreeing to go with him to an amusement park for a first date. Which had lasted all day, crept into the night, and she'd tucked herself in next to him on the Ferris wheel.

And from that point on, she'd spent any free moment she'd had with him here, often walking on campus in the dark, when he'd been free from classes and homework.

Luke was pulled from his reverie when he heard Erin's sharp intake of breath, and he had to clear his mind from that time, from what followed, from the expectation that this was his Erin. He resisted the urge to take her hand.

But then he saw her face. All color had drained from it, one slender hand resting against her throat. She slowed, her eyes focused to their left.

"Are you okay?" Luke asked.

She swallowed. "This is where it happened."

He didn't have to ask what she was talking about. Tara had said two blocks from their apartment. He hadn't realized it had been right by campus.

Erin walked forward, toward the huge maple that stood sentinel beside the street. He watched her circle around to the front, dragging her fingers along the rough bark of the trunk.

"They think the driver hit the tree right before he hit Jordan. Like he over-corrected and plowed right—" She clenched her teeth and shook her head.

Luke slowly made his way around the tree to look where she did. An aged scar was gouged into the trunk like someone had ripped a square foot of bark about an inch deep off the tree.

"There was a whole mess of flowers here for months after he died. A little white cross with his name written in sharpie on it." She was seeing some image he could never access. A memory that would never be his.

The pain, on some level, though, would become his. If he could never find a way back, he would take on this hurt without even trying, without wanting to. He would have no choice but to navigate his life as if this was what had happened to him, too.

And even as he touched the bark with his own fingers, the hard, rough texture matched the feel of this grief. It was living, too. Permanently marked, but solid, and growing in spite of it.

He didn't want this to be what he dwelled on, what he tried to understand. Because there had to be something else. He didn't want this permanent mark in him, unhealed, with too many questions still unanswered.

"They never found the guy who did it?"

Erin took a deep breath then shook her head. She never took her eyes from the gash in the tree, like she was memorizing the size, the shape. Maybe fitting that wound in with the one that matched on the inside of her.

"Did they find anything? Paint chipped off? Shards of a broken headlight?"

Erin blinked, her mind shifting. "I don't—I don't remember." She shook her head again.

Too distracted by the grief, no doubt. The shock and the gaping wound her brother's sudden death would leave was a hefty weight, something that would be hard to see around.

But Luke could separate himself from the incident. He squinted across the street to the shops there. The Hill, as it was known, was where all the college kids hung out. With two small venues for concerts, a bookstore, a tattoo and piercing shop, restaurants, it was a great haunt for anyone looking for something to pass the time. The restaurants stayed open late, catering to the all-night studiers, the post-party snackers, the after-concert crowd.

A row of shops faced the side of the street where the accident happened, and Luke remembered the guy who ran the sandwich shop. He'd had his fair share of middle-of-the-night snack attacks, remembered joking with the guy, becoming friendly enough to chat with him on more than one occasion.

"Did they question the shop owners?"

Erin finally looked at him, saw him gazing across the street, her expression tightening.

"I don't know, Luke." Frustration lanced her tone. Like she didn't care, was annoyed he did. "I wasn't really in the loop about every detail of the investigation."

Her tone and unwillingness didn't discourage him.

"Someone has to know something," he muttered.

She crossed her arms over her chest. "If anyone did, they would have gotten as much information as there was available back then."

Her testy tone caught his attention now. Maybe because her resistance grew in direct parallel to his desire to know more.

"You don't want to see if maybe they missed something?"

"Why?" The word snapped on the air, almost hurt his ears. "Why would that help?"

Luke stared at her. The way she'd curled in on herself again, the moisture in her eyes, punched him in the gut. His arms ached to hold her. It took all his strength not to move.

"He's dead," she hissed. "Asking questions won't bring him back."

Her pain seared him, but her words weren't a deterrent. Because he wanted to know. He *needed* to know if there was some way to get justice for Jordan's death. If he couldn't have his life the way it had been, he wanted whoever ruined it to pay.

15

Unwanted Questions

She picked at the edge of the lid on her coffee cup, a barely controlled aggression in her movements. She sat alone at the wiry outdoor table, college students swarming around her. They moved in that frenzied state of excitement and anxiety the beginning of a semester always brought.

She ground her teeth as she tried to see into the window of the sandwich shop. She could make out movement, had seen Luke sit down with whatever he'd ordered to use as his prop for talking to the owner. But it was hard to make out what was happening from where she sat.

She could have gone in with him, even regretted not doing it. Pride kept her rooted in place. Not to mention the anger. God, the anger. She was livid that he was persisting.

But why? Didn't he have a right to do what he wanted? To run around in circles like this just to get to the same place her family had gotten? He would need to make peace with the fact that they didn't have answers, wouldn't get them, and move on.

Because we've *moved on.*

She ripped the empty sugar packet in front of her into tiny strips, irritated that the voice in her head sounded so sarcastic. And that it was right.

She checked her email on her phone to distract herself. No response yet to the email she'd sent to the professor on Luke's behalf. That made her more anxious and annoyed. Didn't normal people check their email every ten minutes? It couldn't just be her.

She locked her phone and set it down, looking away, but her eyes froze on the tree across the street.

Tilting her head, she tried imagining the scene: a car careening around the corner, swinging wide to side-swipe the tree. The driver yanking the wheel too far, sending the vehicle to where her brother was walking. He'd almost made it across the street, just a few feet from the sidewalk. Not that it would have helped. Tire marks on the concrete walkway showed how far up the car had gone. Mere inches from crashing into the building.

She gripped the edge of the table as if she could ground herself as she fell into the memory of the police describing what had happened. The driver had hit and run over Jordan, stopped and backed over him again. She thanked God that the initial impact had been what killed him.

Still, she had to shut her eyes, breathing deeply to calm herself. Her parents had insisted she stay home when they'd gone to identify him, and she would forever be grateful to not have that picture in her mind. What she imagined was traumatic enough.

"Are you all right?" Luke's voice, velvet and cautious, cut through the awful images in her head.

She decided to answer honestly for once. "No."

She looked up at him. The concern knitted his brows over those gray-blue eyes, and a lock of dark, wavy hair had fallen onto his forehead, giving him a very Clark Kent/Superman appearance.

"Let's go then." He held out a hand to her.

She stared at it for half a second before deciding to take it.

He helped her stand, his eyes already scanning up and down the street. His mouth twisted in the way she remembered when he was contemplating something, speculating. She'd already seen it that day.

"What are you thinking?" She heard the wariness plain in her voice as they began walking.

His eyes flickered to her and back. He shook his head. "I was thinking about what Leo said."

"Who?"

"Sandwich Shop Guy." He jerked his head toward the shop. "He said he had a box full of old tapes from the security cameras around his place. Dating back a long time."

She gave him a skeptical look. "What exactly is 'a long time?'"

He glanced at her again. "He wasn't sure how far back. He doesn't really seem like the fastidious type." He did a brief imitation of someone taking a toke from a joint. "But he remembered the accident. Remembered the police checking with him after it happened. Dark-colored car, generic body style, so not much help there."

The irritation spiked again. Why didn't he sound defeated? It didn't seem like he was close to giving up at all. And she felt more nauseated than before.

"So what are you thinking?" She said the words slowly, but

they still came out with an edge.

Finally, he gave her his full attention. "I'm sorry. If you want to go, that's fine. I can stay and find a ride back. Maybe call Tara if she isn't too busy."

She stopped walking, and he halted beside her. "Why do you need to stay? What could you possibly want to know now?"

He lifted one shoulder, this time intentionally avoiding her gaze. "I'm all the way in this now. I want to know as much as possible."

Her earlier words ghosted through her head: *Why? WHY?*

It wasn't going to bring him back, and she knew from experience that it was all a dead end. All the questions would give them was pain. Wasn't he in agony already? It was fresh for him now. Why wasn't it crushing him? It was a decade-old wound for her, and she nearly collapsed from the torture of it.

With their gazes connected, she could see it there in his eyes. He *was* in pain. For more than one reason. Like he'd said before, he was grieving the loss of everything he'd known. And this was the one thing he was trying to grasp at, get a grip on.

"I don't want to hurt you, Erin. I know it's hard for you. But I can't stop until I know everything."

I can't stop.

She shut her eyes, clenching her fists as if it would strengthen her. She had to try moving past her own ache to be sympathetic to his. Because he had very few people in this world to rely on, and he'd lost more than she had.

She opened her eyes and forced her fists to relax. "Where are we going next?"

"The police station. I want to see how far they got." He grimaced like he expected a negative reaction.

She took a deep breath, stuffing her reaction into a tiny box in her mind. "All right. We'll head there, then."

His grateful smile tilted his mouth up on one side.

She couldn't stop the slow returning smile, remembering that small smirk was the one she'd always liked the best. It was harder-won than his full, beaming grin. It reminded her of his joking side, the one she'd gotten a few glimpses of the last couple of days, and she realized how much she'd missed it. Missed him.

His grin widened, like he knew what she was thinking. Or maybe because she was staring at him with a dumb expression on her face.

She looked away, toward the sandwich shop, heat creeping into her cheeks. And that was enough to distract her for a minute because the shop owner was standing outside, staring at them. He definitely fit the look of someone who smoked a lot of pot, as Luke had hinted. But his eyes at that moment were sharp as he surveyed them. Like he was trying to memorize their faces. But when he caught her gazing back, he smiled and waved awkwardly. She returned his smile and dipped her head, and he disappeared back inside.

Luke glanced over to see who she'd acknowledged, but the shop owner was gone.

"Sandwich Shop Guy," she said by way of explanation. "Ready to head out?"

"Before we do that, have you gotten an answer yet on the email?"

She sighed, struggling to switch gears. The whole day, the attack from grief made her feel sluggish. Hell, the last couple of days. Luke's presence alone.

"Uh." She pulled out her phone. A cursory glance at her emails showed nothing new, aside from an "urgent" one from her father with another list of tasks he wanted her to complete while he was gone. "Nothing."

Luke tried to keep the disappointment off his face, but she still caught it in the way his mouth turned down. "All right."

16

Detective Stonewall

LUKE

The sun blazed hot through the windshield as they drove due-west. Luke squinted against it, holding a hand up to shield his eyes. Erin was unreadable behind big sunglasses, her lips bright red again, pursed in thought.

"Do you need to call it a day and check on your mom?" he asked.

Her head jerked in his direction as if she'd forgotten he was there. He suspected it was deeper than that, though.

"Um, no."

There was a false note there, obvious to him because he knew her so well. There were some subtle differences, but she and his own Erin were essentially the same.

"Erin."

She looked at him again, that bottom lip caught between her teeth, brilliant white against the red. "I. . . " She turned back to the road.

He waited to see if she would continue, but she didn't, at war with herself.

So he said it: "She has a problem, doesn't she?"

Her chin lifted slightly, like she was trying to hold onto her dignity. As if it was any reflection on her, or it was her shame to bear.

"Because of Jordan's death." He meant for it to be a question, but as he'd spoken, it felt more like a statement he recognized as true.

She shook her head, but not in denial. "At first, it just seemed like something to calm her nerves. She'd drink before the police came to question us, when they picked out the funeral arrangements, before the funeral itself. But then I noticed it happening more. After she and my dad had an argument, during any get-together with friends, when Dad started working late more and more. She was alone a lot." She took a deep breath. "And then I went back to college. Every break, she seemed too much like her old self. Unnaturally unfazed by the grief that made me almost flunk out that semester. But I smelled the alcohol on her breath, every time she hugged me. She was always a little bit sloshed. Always."

"What did you do?"

"Nothing," she snapped, her hands gripping the steering wheel like she wanted to rip it apart. "I was nineteen. I was still reeling from Jordan's death, and I was away at college. So for the next semester, I took the easy classes and scraped my way through until summer."

He could hear it in her voice, how dark that time had been. There was an edge, not really anger, but something deeper. Dark, heavy, toxic. And yes, there was some anger there too. At the unfairness of it all. It sang to something inside him. The impact of a loss and a grief there had been no way to prepare for, no road map for navigating after.

Because, *hell*, now he had to work through it. And add to it the loss of what he'd had, who he'd been, what he'd *be*. If he really thought about it, it wasn't only the implication that this was possibly his new life—without Jordan, Erin, their family, *his* family—but also that if he went home, he knew he was already irrevocably changed. He'd always feel this loss, know that this world existed. It had been the possible outcome of a decision either he or someone close to him had made. How many times did people talk about how one split-second event could have ended badly but didn't? Late to work, but it pushed them just past the window of time when they would have been involved in a violent car accident.

Except he was living it now.

"It got better for a while."

Luke blinked, turning his attention back to Erin. She had spoken so softly, he'd barely heard her. It took him a moment to even remember what they'd been talking about, and he felt guilty for getting so wrapped up in his own thoughts and emotions. This was the hell she'd been living for years.

"I didn't do anything because getting through that year was about all I could manage. And then she seemed to do better, and I decided to believe she would be fine." She shrugged, but she was uncomfortable, not dismissive.

"You don't have to defend yourself. I wasn't trying to put that on you. You were still a kid, really."

She smiled a little, very sadly. "I know. I just—I always feel like maybe there *was* something I could have done. But she had my dad too. I kept waiting, kept *thinking* he had everything under control. He certainly acted like he did."

He offered a grim smile. "Still does, I'd wager."

She looked at him, that quick jerk of the head again.

He knew it for the question it was. "You forget that I know you all so well. And this thing hasn't changed the essentials of who you are. Your dad is. . . " He grimaced, trying to find the right words.

"Hank Baylor?" she supplied.

They both laughed because it was true that his name was like its own entity, and he embodied that smart, gets-whatever-he-wants, bow-to-me, imperial demeanor that likened him to a warrior-king. And the damned thorn of it all was that he was still so likable, if not a bit frustrating.

"Normally, my mom is. . . manageable? I don't know if that's the right word." She pressed her lips together. "More like you wouldn't know that she'd had anything to drink. She holds herself together, follows conversations, walks a straight line. But there are times. . . "

He could picture it. "So Hank pretends everything is fine since she's presentable."

She nodded. "Yeah." There was a bitter twist to her mouth. "Not that there's much he could do. She's never admitted to having a problem or expressed a desire for help."

"She probably doesn't want to face what she's been hiding from. The grieving process will hurt just as bad, if not more, whenever she does finally deal with it."

He decided it wasn't worth it to add his final morbid thought: Gloria could avoid dealing with it indefinitely. But that meant she would likely drink herself to death.

Based on Erin's grim expression, he could tell she knew it, was thinking the same. She nibbled her bottom lip absently, and he got lost in staring at her. Not just because she was beautiful. There was that too. Always that. But he marveled that the bright red lipstick didn't end up on her teeth. Like what kind of voodoo did these makeup manufacturers use to keep the lipstick from smudging onto everything?

"I guess I don't have to pretend anymore," she said, turning to meet his eyes. It was clear she'd been unaware of his gaze, and her cheeks colored a little.

It took him a moment to gather his wits. "Pretend what?"

"I was planning to go to my parents' after I dropped you off." She shook her head. "I was so afraid you would figure out the family secret if you came with me again. But, honestly, I'm relieved."

He could see that she was. The anxiety about it now hung openly on her, but the tension from keeping it together was gone. Like telling him alleviated some of the pressure. And it made him wonder if anyone else knew. If there had been anyone she'd been able to vent to, get comfort from, share the burden with. It didn't seem like Hank would be the one. No Jordan to take that up with her.

His eyes fell on her ring glinting in the afternoon sun and a stab of jealousy lanced through him. It would make sense that her fiancé would know. If he was around as much as Luke was back home, there would be no way to hide it.

He tried to make himself glad that she wouldn't have to bear it all alone. And he was. A little. But he also couldn't help wanting to punch his fist through a wall.

He took a deep breath, frustrated with himself for thinking this way so constantly. The jealousy was making him miserable. Making him act in ways and say things he shouldn't. It was against his nature, and he had never been one for rage. Had never been violent in his life. But this was a lot to acclimate to. It was probably a natural response when faced with so much loss.

He rubbed his hand against his chin, trying to strong-arm his thoughts into submission. This was *not* his Erin. He had to get it straight in his head before he drove himself bonkers.

Easier said than done, he knew. But at least he could bury himself in something to work his mind away from the unpleasant feelings he was dealing with. That was the promising thought he paused on as they pulled into the parking lot of the police station.

Erin pulled off her sunglasses, revealing her squinted gaze as she stared up at the edifice. Tension carved a line into her forehead.

"You ready for this?" he asked.

She sucked her bottom lip between her teeth again for a second before she must have caught herself. "Nope. But we're doing it."

They opened their doors simultaneously, walking in silence. Both lost in their thoughts, emotions. Hers would, no doubt, be very different than his own. It didn't matter to him that the case had never been solved, he still felt an eager anticipation to know every detail, to immerse himself in searching through whatever clues he could find. Drive himself crazy with that instead of thinking about Erin with another guy.

They went inside and walked to the front desk where a middle-aged, well-exercised police officer sat in a crisp uniform. He held up a finger and gestured to the chairs nearby as he cradled a phone against his ear.

Luke and Erin sat. She crossed one leg over the other, wiggling the elevated foot. She tugged nervously at the hem of the black and white striped shirt-thing she wore, and he tilted his head, considering. Too long to be a shirt, too short to be a dress. She had some thin black pants on underneath.

Leggings, he recalled. He remembered the conversation they'd had before. Not tights, as he'd erroneously labeled them. Obviously not jeans. Too form-fitting to be sweats.

"What do you call this long shirt thing again?"

She gave him a startled glance, tucking her loose blonde hair behind her ear. She looked at her outfit as if noticing it for the first time. "It's a tunic top."

"Tunic. Like they wore in the middle ages?"

She smirked. "Sure."

"This is more of what I'm used to you wearing."

She lifted a brow. "Casual clothes?"

He lifted one shoulder. "Well, on your days off, sure. But I've seen you wear more dresses than I'm used to. I'm not saying I don't like it—not that my opinion matters," he added hastily, and he was proud the bitterness wasn't obvious in his tone. "Just weird is all."

Her eyes narrowed on his face, as if she were trying to figure him out. Or maybe it was whether she wanted to say what she did next. Which was: "My father once said he preferred it."

The conversation had the desired effect. She stilled, the tension lifting just slightly. But it bothered Luke because it was another reminder of something that was off between Erin and her father. She would never bend over backwards to make her dad happy like that. Of course, she cared what he thought. He was her father, after all. But already, it was obvious how she took on the weight of his expectations in this world. The added list of duties while he was away, the burden of babysitting her mother, the fact that she was this underling in the company, like she was still proving herself.

The uniformed officer motioned them forward, snapping Luke out of his thoughts.

"What can I do for you?"

Erin hesitated.

Up to me, then, he thought.

"We're wondering if we could get access to some case files for an incident from ten years ago."

The officer narrowed his eyes as he appraised them both. "For what reason and under what authority?"

"Authority?" Luke repeated. "Like legally? I mean, we're not lawyers or anything." He paused, trying to gather his thoughts, build a convincing, if not entirely true, reason. "It was a hit and run on campus. It was her brother." He slid a hand over her shoulders. "She was too young to be very involved with the investigation, and her therapist suggested finding more information for her to be able to move on. Get closure."

She stiffened under his touch at the last part but didn't deny it. Which was a blessing, given that she hadn't even wanted to come in the first place.

The officer appraised them again. "Police records aren't open to civilians. Any public information can be accessed through a formal process down at the courthouse or online."

Erin placed her hands on the desk, perfect manicure glimmering in the fluorescent lights. "See, it didn't go to court. So technically we can't get it through those channels. It's a cold case. They never found the driver of the car that killed my brother."

Either she had warmed to her role, or she was legitimately feeling the desperation she injected into her voice. The officer's expression softened slightly.

"Were you here ten years ago?" Erin asked. "September 25th?"

The officer placed his hands on the desk, fingers interlaced.

"Out by the big tree across from the Hill. Jordan Baylor?"

Recognition lit in his eyes. "Yeah, I remember the case." His voice was subdued. Kind of sad. He pursed his lips, considering. "I'll be right back."

Erin turned to lean against the counter, giving Luke a sideways glance. "Pretty slick."

He couldn't tell if there was censure in her tone, so he shrugged in response. If they were going to argue about it, he certainly wasn't going to get into it here and now.

The policeman was walking back toward them anyway, a plainclothes officer following in his wake. This man was heavier-set. Not exactly looking like he didn't take care of himself, but more like he was built muscular with natural padding. His gray hair was thinned, his eyes lined from too much squinting, but there was a shrewd look to them. No bullshitting this guy.

Luke shifted uncomfortably after his partial lie. But the man wasn't looking at him. The eyes went straight to Erin, as if he recognized her or even knew her.

Luke looked at her too, curious. There was a reciprocated familiarity in her expression.

"Miss Baylor," he said, reaching out to shake her hand.

She didn't smile, but her expression softened to borderline friendliness as she took it briefly. "Detective Brant."

This, Luke had not expected. Erin made it seem like she hadn't been involved or kept informed about the investigation. So it was surprising that she would be remembered by the cop on her brother's case. But maybe that was Luke's assumption. Had she actually said she wasn't involved?

The detective looked at Luke then, giving him a calculating once-over.

"This is Luke Pearson," Erin said, gesturing stiffly. "You may remember him."

A lift of the chin. "The best friend."

Luke offered his hand, realizing that, of course, his other self would have been involved in at least part of the investigation. He was at the party that night. The reason Jordan had walked home alone.

Brant shook his hand, then turned, nodding his head for them to follow him to a sequestered space in a back room. It looked like a crappy teacher's lounge. Worn couches, small refrigerator, microwave, coffee maker, tiny window covered by dusty, bent blinds.

The detective gestured for them to sit, then took a chair opposite them. He perched on the end, elbows resting on knees. Luke thought it was maybe a power play, to convey that he was doing them a favor but really wasn't going to spend the time they wanted. But as Luke settled into the couch, a feeling like he might fall right through to the floor made him wonder if it had more to do with not wanting to look like an idiot trying to climb out of the sunken chair.

"What can I do for you?" Brant asked.

Erin didn't even glance at Luke, and he wondered again if this had become more real for her, rather than an attempt to placate him.

"Well, Luke and I have recently reconnected, and as you might expect, a lot about Jordan's accident has come up."

They both looked at Luke now, so he cleared his throat. "We, uh, just wanted to get a clearer picture about the case, I guess. Since we were so young and so grief-stricken, I just felt like I couldn't get a grasp on things back then."

She nodded.

Brant tapped his thumb against his other hand. "What are you hoping to gain from going over the accident again?"

Erin and Luke looked at each other. He supposed it was a bad idea to admit the full truth. No doubt, that would come off like they were trying to start their own investigation.

"Closure, maybe?" Erin said, turning back to Brant.

"I don't think you're going to get that from reading the files," Brant said, shifting his weight a little. "The case died without any promising leads. Gives you more questions than answers."

"Is that your only objection? That we might be disappointed?" Luke asked.

Brant leaned back slightly, scrutinizing Luke again. "It's not exactly kosher to let civilians read case files. I know it's a cold case, and you might have some insight that I don't. I just. . ." He took a breath, eyeing them. Finally, he placed his hands on his knees to help propel him to his feet, nodding for them to follow.

Luke and Erin followed suit, trailing just slightly behind as Detective Brant led them farther back into the station, through rows of desks, separated by half-cubicles. Semi-private but with the option to collaborate.

Brant stopped at a desk with a couple stacks of papers and files. A few were fanned across the keyboard in front of the computer. He tapped one with a stubby finger, a grim half-smile on his face.

"Couldn't tell you why, but I was looking at your brother's case recently." He grimaced. "To be honest, I pull it out periodically."

Erin was looking at the file like it was a poisonous snake about to bite—afraid but morbidly mesmerized.

Luke's fingers itched to open it.

Brant did another rhythmic tap on the file, sucking his teeth for a moment. "The rub is I don't really have the freedom to just give you what I have."

Luke clenched his jaw. What the hell was this guy doing dangling it in front of them then? He almost said it out loud, but then Brant looked at him, then Erin. The slightest twitch of his mouth, an infinitesimal tilt of his head, and Luke knew the guy was trying to say something he didn't want anyone else to know about.

Erin gave him a pinched smile but the knowing glint in her eye was unmistakable. "I understand, Detective. Thanks for your time."

The detective placed a hand at her back as they all turned toward the front of the station to leave. No one seemed to pay any attention to them, but they were surrounded by suspicious cops who made a career out of noticing the not very noticeable.

Still, despite the detective's subtle hint that he might be able to offer them something, Luke still couldn't help feeling dejected.

17

An Offer

ERIN

There were two things she sensed simultaneously. First was Luke's palpable disappointment. She wanted to encourage him that this clearly wasn't over yet because the second thing was that Detective Brant wanted to give them information. He just didn't want anyone else knowing he was doing it.

The detective's hand hovered at her back, and he was walking almost at an awkwardly close pace. He ducked his head, speaking low and barely moving his lips. "Someone stonewalled the investigation back then. Has some ability to keep it stuck in the mud, even now. I'll get you the info you want."

She tried not to look at him or indicate that she heard him at all, knowing he was taking a risk telling her that. But it also felt surreal, like something from a conspiracy movie. It almost made her laugh, the secrecy, even thinking something darker and more nefarious could possibly be going on. Obviously, her brother's death was no laughing matter. But to think there was anything beyond a hit and run with no leads seemed laughable.

"You take care," the detective said as he stopped just inside the lobby.

Erin gave him a small smile, while Luke nodded, his brood already darkening his gaze.

She didn't want to let it irk her, but she couldn't help the irritation as it clutched at her muscles. It had seemed like a waste of time in the first place. And she wanted to rub that in.

Except, she had to admit that maybe it hadn't been a waste after all. She glanced back at the station as they walked to her car. She chewed her cheek as she pressed her key fob, the alarm chirping in response.

Brant had something to give her. And to be fair, she hadn't really been privy to the details the way her parents had been. The possibility that there was more than she really knew was somewhat. . . intoxicating? And to know, that on top of that, there might be something even deeper than just a simple idiot who was too much of a coward to take responsibility made her almost eager to pursue more information.

And yet, beside her, Luke brooded as if he were a two year old who'd been denied the ice cream treat he'd begged for. Maybe she was being a little harsh, her nerves raw from too much being brought up all at once, and it put her on edge.

"He wasn't really telling us 'no'."

He raised a brow. "He wasn't exactly helpful. Two strikes."

"He said he'd give me the information another way."

Luke jerked to give her a sharp look. "What? When?"

She couldn't help feeling a bit smug. "Just as we were walking out. He said someone has been keeping the investigation stalled all this time. I'm guessing that whoever it is must be powerful, and Brant could get in a lot of trouble if he helps us out."

Luke's dark brows knit together as he absorbed the information, seeming to mull it and the implications over in his mind. She certainly was.

If there was someone powerful involved, that meant there was not a guarantee of who was trustworthy in the police department. Which was a scary thought. But beyond that, Erin didn't understand how her brother's death could possibly be tied to anyone with that much influence.

He'd been a college student. Her father had a successful business and made a decent amount of money, but it wouldn't make sense that he'd be a target for corporate espionage or some sinister plot to get to his business or assets. Because it hadn't affected his business at all.

As if reading her mind and almost sounding like he hadn't meant to say it out loud, Luke said, "Why would anyone need to go to those lengths to cover up a hit and run of a random college student?"

She shook her head, squinting at the road in front of her. As she considered, it seemed less and less likely it had anything to do with who her brother was at all. He wasn't anyone of note. Smart, cute, kind, promising in his field—yes. But no one worth targeting. But the more she thought about it, the more it seemed like it had to do with who had hit him.

"Because they needed to cover their own butt." She said it softly, mostly to herself, like saying it aloud made the realization solidify.

Luke frowned, his apparent confusion keeping him silent for a few seconds. She waited for the meaning to slide home.

"So, you think the driver was the powerful guy, and he couldn't have a black mark like vehicular manslaughter to his name?" He spoke slowly, as if translating from another language in his head. "That does make a lot more sense. It's not like Jordan could be a threat to anyone as a love-struck engineering major. Dude had hours of homework. He didn't have the time to get involved in something that would put a target on his back."

She twisted her hands on the steering wheel. "So the question would be who is important and influential enough around here to stall out an investigation for ten years?"

He pursed his lips, shaking his head. "I'm trying to remember if there was anyone worth note at school back then. Anyone we know with a big name around here?"

Erin was glad Luke wasn't looking at her. Because the name that came to her mind would certainly qualify even if it made absolutely no sense, and she'd never in a million years think he could have been the culprit. But he counted as a big name, even if it was only his ambitions at that time he'd had going for him. No, she had to think that one through on her own before she shared it with Luke.

She shrugged, deciding that was the safest response. Not an outright lie, but she certainly wasn't being on the up and up.

Luke was too lost in his thoughts to even notice her shrug, and she was grateful the question had been more rhetorical than she'd initially taken it to be.

In her peripheral vision, her ring glinted as she absently played with it. Another unconscious habit she needed to break. Especially since it always seemed to catch Luke's attention and trigger him.

Right now, the ring felt uncomfortably heavy, weighted more by her emotions than actual mass.

A movement from Luke's direction caught her attention. He was rubbing at his back, shifting around, a wince pulling at his handsome face.

"What's wrong?"

"Hmm?" He looked at her, his expression smoothing.

"Does your back hurt?"

"Oh." He didn't seem to have been aware of it. "Yeah. Man, it's weird to be reminded that I'm no longer a spring chicken."

She gave a puzzled laugh. "Meaning?"

"Tara's couch is not the most comfortable thing in the world, and my body no longer tolerates even the mildest abuses. I used to crash out on the floor in my college days with no issues."

She laughed, imagining. Of course, she'd seen him asleep on her brother's bedroom floor on more than one occasion growing up. "I might have a solution for Your Highness."

He gave her a sour look. "If you're accusing me of being the chick from the Princess and the Pea, I take great offense."

She scoffed. "How in the world did you catch that reference?"

"I happen to be the world's greatest uncle to the world's most adorable niece. And Princess and the Pea was a particular favorite at bedtime for a while there."

Oh damn it, she was a puddle. The pride in his voice was like the summer sun in Phoenix to a cheap popsicle, so melted was her heart. It was in that vulnerable state that the idea struck, and she offered before she had time to think it through.

"We have a *very* comfortable guesthouse at my parents' that you could use. King-size bed, jetted tub, full kitchen, even a home gym."

"Not to look a gift horse in the mouth or anything, but are you sure that's a good idea?"

He must have sensed it too, that the offer was somehow crossing some line. Though she wasn't sure exactly what line that would be. It wasn't as if he were an ex or anything.

Not technically. And it's not like he was staying at *her* house. But her feelings, the reluctance they were both experiencing, intimated that it was much more than her letting an old friend stay at her parents'.

"Absolutely." There was no false note in her voice, but she felt the pinch in her chest. "No one's using it, and I'm sure your back will thank you."

"I don't want to overstep, but I'd definitely appreciate it."

She nodded, mentally adding that maybe he'd be an asset when it came to babysitting her mother, and that certainly was convincing enough for her to allow herself to feel less guilty. For the moment.

18

Self-Realization

LUKE

I understand that we kind of dropped in on you the other day, but I was wondering if you'd be able to take the time, even just via email, to answer some of my questions? Please get back to me as soon as possible.

Luke Pearson

He reread the email, wondering if it seemed too vague or too weird. He wasn't sure the professor would remember him or take the time to read the email even if he did. And he knew that Erin had already emailed, but it didn't hurt to try again, right? Maybe their desperation would be obvious enough to garner at least an acknowledgment.

Erin hadn't given him any indication Thibald had gotten back to her in the two days since their initial attempt, so he figured a follow-up was an acceptable next step.

The TV flickered in his periphery, but he'd turned the sound off. He pounded his fist against his thigh, frustrated with the lack of response, his inability to get traction, that he couldn't *do* anything.

He stood and walked to the small kitchenette for a glass of water. He would be eternally grateful for Erin offering up the guesthouse at her parents' so that he could have a bed and privacy. But just then, he felt lonely. The small, two-bedroom house was too quiet and empty.

He pulled out his phone, let his fingers hover over her name in the contacts list. But he decided against bugging her. Surely she'd had enough of his dogged determination to learn everything there was to know about Jordan's death and how that brought up so much of the pain in her life.

Instead he opened the web browser and did a search for an article or mention of the accident. He couldn't even remember the date and had to simply do a search with the name.

September 25th, almost ten years to the day. There wasn't much information to be found. It had been reported in a couple of local newspapers very briefly, and none of the information was helpful, nor more revealing than what he'd already been told.

Local student, Jordan Baylor, was killed in a hit and run Saturday night. Authorities are on the search for a dark-colored sedan with significant front damage. Baylor, an engineering student, had been on his way home from a campus party nearby when he was struck. Any information on the incident is to be reported to police. . .

Luke racked his brain, trying to remember a party so early in the school year, but ten years and a habit of attending any party he'd been invited to made for a difficult time recollecting. Erin had gone off to her own college by that point, and he still hadn't made his move. That was the year she'd dated *that guy*.

Maybe he was just prone to jealousy because the dude had seemed decent, considering. But Luke had hated his guts. Only met him once, over fall break. No—Thanksgiving.

The guy's grandparents had lived the next town over or something, so he'd stopped by to see her for a few hours the Saturday after the holiday. He was the slim, intellectual type. Might have even worn glasses. Biology or Chemistry major. Scientific.

Luke had fought hard not to spend the whole time glaring at the guy when he'd come over to play video games with Jord, who'd been strict about neither bringing their systems to school since he knew what kind of work load the year would bring. And it was just as well, because Luke's grades had slipped enough to make him glad for one less distraction.

She hadn't called that skinny dude her boyfriend, but they'd been affectionate enough to be a step beyond casually dating. Jordan had caught Luke staring at them more than once.

What was that skinny dude's name?

He huffed a breath, knowing Erin would have remembered. She remembered everything. But wait, she wouldn't this time. Because that was the Thanksgiving right after Jordan had died in this version. Skinny Dude had probably never gotten past the first or second date, if at all.

When had Jordan said something about it? Erin wouldn't have told anyone about the relationship until something had progressed to noteworthy status, but she'd told Jordan first.

Luke tried to remember when, though he definitely remembered how. Jordan had mentioned it casually, but he'd had that sly look in his eye. One that Luke had become quite familiar with. Jordan had been aware of Luke's interest in his little sister for quite some time. Probably after Luke's diatribe when she'd started dating the football player her senior year. Maybe before that. He'd never asked.

All he remembered was how his gut had clenched.

"I'm driving home this weekend. You want to ride together?" Jordan had asked.

"You are?" Luke had been surprised because Jordan's homework load had seemed to double, and he'd gotten more serious about Kelly. He hadn't been home since school started, and Luke had stopped asking.

"Well, Kelly's busy and I made sure I got my work done early. Erin's supposed to be there for my parents' party, and I wanted to see her."

Must have been Labor Day weekend, Luke thought now. The only time it had been worth the drive for Erin to come home was a long weekend, and her parents basically had a party for every holiday. So, in this timeline, she might have started seeing Skinny Dude.

"Need to hear more about this new guy she's seeing."

Luke remembered stiffening as he'd stuffed his books into his backpack, and the way Jordan had slowed his movements, watching Luke from the corner of his eye.

"New guy, huh? Big brother grill sesh on the itinerary?" Luke had worked to sound casual, but he felt anything but. *"I think I'm going to stay here. I have a paper due in my econ class."*

It was bull, and Jordan knew it. But Luke was not going to listen to Erin gush about some guy that wasn't him. Not that she'd ever been the gushing type. But it didn't matter. He didn't want to hear about it, and he certainly didn't want his misery to be on display for every mutual acquaintance to see.

So he'd stayed at school, partied instead of studying. Kept that rhythm for a while and was pleasantly distracted if not actually happy. He'd wasted half that year drinking his wallow away, breaking his oath to himself. And Jordan had made no comment, even as Luke's grades floundered.

Burying his pain. So insignificant in comparison to what Erin had endured during that same time frame in this reality. And his other self. Apparently he *was* prone to self-medicating. Or that particular time in his life, he'd been vulnerable to the call of it. Either way, he felt the disappointment at the realization.

Christmas break was the defining moment in his world. The one that snapped him out of it. Erin had ditched Skinny Dude sometime between Thanksgiving and Christmas, and she'd noticed Luke was not living his best life.

He'd been thinner, he knew. He'd stopped working out, and he was the type to almost instantly lose muscle mass when he got lazy. He'd seen it in his own eyes. Dark circles underneath from too little sleep. Even his attitude had been punkish.

You didn't seem the type.

Isn't that what she'd said? A bit of disgust in her tone. A dagger right to his chest.

Even now, the shame twisted at his heart. It reminded him of the fight they'd often had over the years whenever he'd go out drinking with friends. She always seemed angry, and he'd never made the connection until now.

Was there something in that, something about himself he'd never seen but she had? Like he'd always been poised on the edge between self-control and losing himself to addiction?

That was a heavy thought. His alternate self had spiraled out of control, and Luke had been disdainful, even going so far as to consider this other version of himself weak. But they were one and the same, and he realized he'd been too blessed to ever recognize his own weakness and see what his lack of self-control could really cost him.

He set his elbows on his knees and dragged his hands down his face. Who knew an alternate reality could reveal such a dark piece of himself? He'd always thought he was pretty self-aware, but he'd been blind about this. And Erin had not.

A knock on the door pulled him from the grim thoughts. The only person it could really be was Erin. He supposed it could have been her mother, though not likely.

The knock sounded again with some urgency behind it, which left little doubt in his mind, and he thrust himself to his feet.

He was sluggish with self-loathing, and he couldn't muster up his usual smile. He opened the door and said "hey" on a heavy sigh.

Her knock had been insistent, but he saw from her face that she was excited, not anxious. She'd changed out of her work attire—a flowing green deal that had belled at her hips and showed her slim, muscular legs—into some kind of short pants thing and a comfy looking black t-shirt. The dress was appealing, but he liked seeing her so casual, so comfortable-looking. With her hair pulled back, she looked more like his Erin, and that made his heart squeeze painfully.

She didn't seem to pick up on his mood right away and pushed past him. "I got all the notes from Detective Brant on my brother's case."

Luke shut the door and said nothing.

Erin didn't need encouragement. She was frenetic in her movement, pacing the small space between the kitchen and the back of the couch.

"I read through some of it, and honestly, I don't know how he keeps info together. It's pretty jumbled. Or maybe it's just the nature of the case. I'm not sure."

He took a deep breath, determined to shake his melancholy. After all, this was what he'd been after just the other day. So he'd learned something less than ideal about himself. That meant he could do better. This was the thing that he'd felt such a compulsion to understand, and he needed to focus. Moping would do him no good.

He forced the enthusiasm he didn't yet feel. Fake it 'til you make it. "Okay. So did you learn something new? Something helpful?"

"Luke, it's insane. Exactly like the detective said. Someone has been making it incredibly difficult to gain traction in the investigation."

"In what way?"

"Witnesses recanting information they shared or are no longer available or cooperative. Like, even on mundane things." She finally stopped pacing, but she drummed her fingers against her leg.

He pursed his lips. "Okay, so people backed off, but was there anything in initial interviews that we can use?"

Her eyes, so icy blue, seemed to glow with secretive knowledge. "Sandwich Shop Guy."

"Sandwich Shop Guy," Luke repeated.

"He saw someone get out of the car. Said it was a young guy."

Irritation made Luke curl his fingers. He'd talked to Leo. He'd seemed willing to help, and yet he made no mention of this and from the sound of things, he'd changed his story back then, too. "He didn't say anything like that to me the other day."

For the first time, Erin seemed to sense Luke's already black mood and tilted her head. "Of course not. Whatever, or I should say *whoever*, got to him back then probably still has some hold over him now."

Luke grunted, less inclined to hide his frame of mind since she'd picked up on it.

"That's not the important part. Nor is it that he denies what he said previously. He said he thought he maybe recognized the guy. Or at least something he was wearing."

"Did he say what?"

She shook her head. "According to Brant, the guy was flying pretty high during the interview and wasn't always making sense, which was the excuse he gave for changing his story later."

Luke stuffed his hands in his pockets. "Huh."

The buzz she'd been riding as soon as she'd walked in fizzled. "That's all you're going to say about it?"

He felt the fight come to life in him, like it had been waiting just beneath the surface. "What do you want me to say?"

She rose to the tone in his voice, but she was equal parts confused. "You're the one who was pushing for us to investigate what happened, remember?"

He needed a good sparring match. Even as he thought it, he felt like crap for wanting a fight just to fight, just to clear the depression. Because, sure as hell, anger was a whole lot easier than sadness.

"And you didn't want to deal with it, *remember*?" Well, shit, that just sounded petulant.

The flash in her eyes was like a blade catching the light.

"Don't you dare turn this around on me." Her voice was low. Low and dangerous.

His fingers tingled in anticipation. But he took a breath and battled himself back. The burn had scorched out the coldness of his gloom, which had been his goal. But now he just felt like a jerk.

She watched the emotions play across his face. "Just what the hell is the matter with you?"

He pressed his lips together and shook his head. Then he turned away, walking to the window. He stared out at the swimming pool and the french doors beyond, which led into her parents' house.

He folded his arms across his chest. "I have some other things on my mind. I'm sorry. That wasn't fair."

"No, it wasn't," she murmured. "That felt like you were just looking for something to fight about."

Crap. This wasn't his Erin, but she could almost read him as well.

He grimaced. Not just because she'd nailed him, but because they were about to have a third join their party, and it was not likely to be enjoyable.

19

Daddy Issues

ERIN

"Your dad is heading this way."

Erin wasn't sure why that felt just as much like a sucker punch as their argument had. Maybe because she knew that her father was not going to approve of her letting Luke stay at the guesthouse. Add to that the fact that they were looking into Jordan's death, and she knew she would be in for another conflict.

When he knocked and Luke opened the door, she suddenly wished she wasn't dressed so casually. With her dad, it was always a power play, and she didn't want to look like she didn't have every aspect of her life under control.

Stupid that dressing comfortably could give off that impression, but there it was.

She forced herself to stand straighter as the arctic blue eyes settled on her. How conflicting it was that his eyes seemed to brighten with an angry flame.

"Lucas," her father said, turning to offer a polite smile. "What a surprise to see you here."

Luke's sour disposition shifted to discomfort. If what he'd said was true, he knew her father almost as well as she did, and he, no doubt, could sense what was behind Hank's rigid, polite greeting.

"Sir," was all Luke offered.

"Erin, your mother told me you were here with a guest. I came to say hello, but I also realize I have some things to discuss with you. Might I have a minute?"

Overly formal language. She was definitely going to hear it. No matter how old she was, her father still managed to make her feel like a kid caught with her hand in the cookie jar. But, damn it, she would not act like one.

"Sure, Dad." She walked forward, hoping he would follow her lead out of the guesthouse instead of rudely making Luke leave. Whether he wanted him there or not, Luke *was* their guest.

Hank's mouth pinched into a tight line. He disapproved, but he wouldn't say anything in front of Luke.

She shut the door behind them, though she had no doubt Luke would hear at least part of what they said. She watched the built-in lights along the pool wall shimmer and distort under the ripple of the water. They cast an eerie glow around them and illuminated her father's face just enough to make him look gaunt as well as angry.

"What is going on here, Erin?" His tone was mild, but the look in his eyes was not.

"Luke needed a place to stay, and I offered the guesthouse to him. He'd been sleeping on his sister's couch."

Easy, Erin, she told herself. *Don't be defensive.*

"Without asking first?"

She chose to play obtuse. "Mom said it was fine with her."

"That's not what I meant."

"I know what you meant," she snapped.

She took a deep breath. *Power play*, she reminded herself. Losing her temper would give him purchase, and she wanted to win for once.

She fought the urge to cross her arms over her chest. "It's her house too, you know. And she likes having people stay here."

His jaw clenched, and she wondered if he'd actually lose control of his anger this time. Wouldn't that be nice? To get him to let go for once.

"From what I understand of Luke's past, should you really be enabling him?"

She snorted. "That's a good one coming from you."

He snapped to a more rigid posture. "What did you say?" Oh, he was definitely losing control now.

The thought that she'd elicited a reaction was heady. "Luke is not on a bender; he's not hiding from anyone; he's committed no crime. He simply needs a place to stay."

"What about that bullshit story he fed us? Or was that just a misunderstanding on my part?" One of his gray brows arched with the question.

Sarcasm. No, he certainly wouldn't have misunderstood anyone. The man's memory was uncanny. And irritating. Damn Luke for telling her father.

"He'd been mugged. Hit his head. Don't you think you'd have some weird things rattling around in the same situation?"

Her father was unconvinced, but his anger had diffused a little. "I don't think it's wise having him stay here. Your mother. . . " He pinched the bridge of his nose and shut his eyes. Of course he wouldn't say it out loud.

Anger flowered inside her, but she kept herself quiet for a moment. "The secret's not getting out through him, if that's what you're worried about. And he already knew."

"Probably could tell, knowing his struggles." He dared to sound judgmental, but before she could call him out on it, he plowed on. "He's not staying long."

She opened her mouth to argue, but he brushed past her to head back to the house. She tamped down the urge to stomp after him, frustrated that her attempt to actually win an argument with her father failed because he'd still had the last word.

It was just like him.

At least she was "off-duty" with her mother. As if that would actually lessen the tension that pulled at her, the stabbing pain of the ulcer eating at her stomach. She pressed a fist into her abdomen, then took a deep breath, willing herself to exhale the frustration.

Still, she was reluctant to go back in to Luke. She didn't look forward to dealing with more conflict. Or being Luke's therapist since something else had been bothering him, and he'd picked a fight just to release that tension. Whatever. Just what she needed—more burdens.

But she couldn't just walk away from him. This. Not after what she'd found out about Jordan's accident. She was sure that Detective Brant sent her the information not only to help her get the closure Luke had lied about her needing, but to give her a starting point to do her own digging. Because that hole had been festering far too long, the unanswered questions lingering in the background like an infection that prevented healing.

And she couldn't stop now, even if she wanted to.

"You're chewing that lip again."

She started ever so slightly. She hadn't heard him open the door, and her back was to it, so she hadn't seen him either. But she turned to find him leaning against the door jamb, arms crossed, face half in shadow.

"I figured you might be debating about coming back inside." His tone was subdued, apologetic. "I definitely wouldn't want to deal with me."

She smiled, trying to ignore the fact that, in this lighting, leaning so casually, he was actually quite appealing, and her stomach clenched at the sight. "Is that your apology?"

"No. This is: I'm sorry. You caught me in a bad moment, but it's no excuse." He looked down at his feet.

Her heart squeezed. Wasn't this one long bad moment?

"Damn, Pearson. You sure know how to apologize."

He smiled, devilish, and it sent a tingle through her. "It took a lot of fighting with you, but you trained me right."

Fighting with him could be a fun activity despite the aggravation, if he looked at her like this every time afterward. And an apology to boot. She fiddled with her engagement ring behind her back so he wouldn't notice, and anxiety shot through her, even as she felt the pull.

She forced herself to smile as if nothing else were on her mind. "If I ever get the chance, I'd like to thank me."

His own expression turned more serious. "Let's hope you don't get the chance. That would mean someone else is in a universe they don't belong to."

Goosebumps broke across her skin, even on this warm summer night. "Going to yours might not be so bad."

She hoped he would know where she was going with the sentiment. She didn't want to say it out loud that seeing her brother, what his future could have been, would be worth any heartache that came along with it.

He winced, obviously thinking about the other complications, but he caught the look on her face. She heard his small, sharp intake of breath, and her chest tightened.

Just the fact that he knew, that he could imagine what she was feeling made tears spring to her eyes. Why she would feel such an extreme emotion just by knowing he understood, she didn't know. It made her feel ridiculous. And exposed. Weak.

He pushed away from the door. In his face she saw the expression he'd had that first day, when he'd struggled to separate her from his Erin. He'd had commendable self-control up to this point, an almost supernatural ability to keep everything in its appropriate box. Until now.

She lacked any desire to put a stop to it. Because hadn't she been burdened too long with everyone else's grief as well as her own?

He drew her gently against him, and she almost melted into the warmth and comfort that he offered. How long, she wondered, how long had it been since someone had held her in acknowledgment of all the pain she felt and demanded nothing of her?

She felt like she could actually release the tension in her body, like the world wouldn't fall apart around her if she did.

"It doesn't seem like your father is very happy I'm staying here." His voice rumbled against her ear as neither made a move to separate.

"No. But he's rarely happy about anything, let alone any decision I make." She laughed, but it was shaky, and she ached at the admission even though it was meant to be a joke.

Just thinking of her father induced her to pull out of Luke's embrace. For all she knew, he was watching them from the house, and she would get a diatribe of disapproval later.

Luke let her pull away, but it seemed to cause him pain. His grimace was quick, a flash across his face.

She grappled with her own ache at the separation and only moved back a step, unable to fully detach herself. She could still feel the heat of him tugging at her as she met the intensity of his gaze.

His hands hovered over her shoulders but didn't quite touch her, as if he expected her to move further from him.

She should, she thought. Tracing her thumb over the band on her engagement ring, she felt the guilt distantly. Felt something else more sharply, something that demanded much more of her attention.

"Do we have a plan?" he asked, his voice soft enough that she wondered if he'd actually spoken at all.

She tilted her head, a little puzzled as to what he was talking about. A plan for whatever might happen between them if she ignored that guilt, already so faint?

"Should we go talk to Sandwich Shop Guy?" he clarified.

Warmth crept into her cheeks. Could he tell what she'd been thinking? Not that she needed to feel embarrassed. Right? She wasn't a teenage girl with a crush. She was a grown woman, and he was a man who was technically already in love with her.

Still, this felt all too much like those days when they danced around the mutual attraction between them—when she was young and naive. And unattached.

She took another step back, giving a faint, half-hearted smile. "I suppose that would be a place to start. "

It was hard to focus on practicalities when her mind was so muddled in fantasy and possibility. When he was still just a foot away and looking the way he did—looking at *her* the way he was. Because he definitely wasn't entirely focused on practicalities either. But he had more self-control than she did.

He cleared his throat and stepped back himself, stuffing his hands into his pockets. "So, maybe we can take the time and pay him a visit? If it wouldn't be too much trouble?"

She took a deep breath, still needing to steel herself for it, even just in conversation. "That's the only way we could ask the questions we want."

He nodded, but he was obviously too in tune with her. His expression was knit with concern. "I could always go by myself. I want to check in with the professor again anyway."

Her chest was tight with the uninvited anger. Of course he'd want to make the most of the trip. And she had to remind herself that she was the one who'd brought up the sandwich shop owner, had gotten excited at the prospect of new information. But she couldn't help but feel like it was being hijacked for a run-around errand. She didn't anticipate any good coming from a meeting with the professor. He'd seemed pretty set on not helping them the last time they'd seen him.

Her silence provoked him into defending himself. "I know he wasn't very forthcoming with information before. But maybe it was just an off day."

She forced a smile, silently admitting that she understood the desperation there. "Sure. Of course. We can go tomorrow if you'd like."

She expected his usual enthusiasm, but it seemed that whatever had been bothering him earlier still had a grip on his mood. "Sounds good."

20

Dreams Come True

LUKE

She'd left her hair down, but he could tell it was irritating her. The windows were down as the weather had proved to be a little cooler. An odd rainstorm churned overhead, blocking the sun and coaxing a breeze from somewhere north. The wind blasted into the car as they drove, whipping the short, golden locks around her face, and she reached to tuck them behind her ear every minute or so.

He had his elbow resting on the door, his chin nestled lightly in his hand, and her movement caught his eye every time she brushed her hair out of her face. He watched her yank one lock of hair that had stuck to the shiny lip balm she'd applied just before they'd left, wondering how many times he'd seen his own Erin do that and never really paid attention.

He marveled again at the sting of missing someone who was technically right there with him. But he understood it more now, had even convinced himself to view this Erin differently. Last night had proven to him that he was treading on unstable ground. Holding her had felt so right because she fit against him like she always had. His puzzle piece.

And yet, it had felt so off.

He'd lain awake a long time after she left, the ache of homesickness radiating deep into his bones. What had finally given him enough peace to sleep was a promise to himself that he would keep his emotional distance. Treat her like the friend she was without the romantic aspect. Ignore that side of their relationship entirely.

Admittedly easier said than done. He had already partially failed. Noticing anything about her looks fell under that romance category, though it was hard not to do it automatically. He would always find her beautiful.

Maybe, he thought as he forced himself to stare out the window, maybe he could come at it more academically. Comparing the subtle differences in how they dressed and behaved. The way this Erin always seemed to opt for more formal attire—dresses and skirts. The way she worried at her lip with her teeth.

And he'd noticed, too, when he'd held her the night before that she seemed a smidge thinner, more fragile than his Erin. No, not fragile, exactly. More like brittle. She wouldn't shatter, but pieces of her had been chipped away, and more would easily come away in his hands.

He looked at her now, able to keep that speculative bent in his observation. She had always been slim, athletic, but he could see that she looked just this side of gaunt. He had definitely noticed the way she picked at her food more than ate it.

"I can feel you staring at me," she said, not taking her eyes from the road.

He felt no need to scramble for an explanation. "Just taking note of how you're different."

She raised a brow, a slight curve tugging at her mouth. "Different from what? Your Erin?" Her expression narrowed. "In good or bad ways?"

"Neither."

She gave him a shrewd look. "Afraid to say, in case you get in trouble?"

He snorted. "I've spent half my time here in trouble with you. There's no reason to avoid it now."

She was wearing sunglasses, but he knew her well enough to know when she was rolling her eyes at him. Must have been a sixth sense.

"So what conclusions have you come to?"

Getting in trouble wasn't even on his radar despite her mildly antagonistic tone. But he hated to hurt her again in any way. He decided to go for levity. "The lipstick, the chewing your lip thing, the dresses."

She feigned offense. "Your Erin doesn't wear lipstick? But these are *great* lipstick lips." She puckered her mouth as if to prove her point.

And crap, if it didn't.

"No arguments here." He held up his hands. "Believe me, if I get back there, she and I are going to have a very serious conversation about the lipstick."

She gave a short laugh, more loose than he'd heard in a while, and he reminded himself that this was Friend Erin. He repeated it several times until the urge to touch her faded.

"And what's the verdict on the dresses?" she asked.

He grimaced. "Well, that's complicated."

She tossed him a skeptical look. "How is a dress complicated?"

He pressed his lips together. Maybe he *was* a little afraid of getting in trouble.

She smiled wryly. "It can't be any worse than your lipstick comment."

True enough. "Well, I definitely like the dresses," he began. "You have great dress legs."

She dipped her head, as if conceding the point.

"But. . . "

She waited.

He stalled. Grimaced again. Debated. "I like it better when you dress for comfort."

This time her pause felt heavier, crackling like she was preparing to be angry, even though she couldn't fully understand his meaning. "What makes you think I don't find them comfortable?"

He tilted his head, wincing slightly. He had felt she might be upset by his answer, and he wasn't sure if she was subconsciously reacting to his feelings or if she had actually figured out where this was going.

"I'm sure you're used to them by now. But I guess I worry about your motivation."

The anger sparked, but he also sensed the question now in her silence.

"My motivation?" she finally said. "How is that relevant?"

There it was. This anger echoed with the voices of all the women who questioned how anyone had a say about the motivation in their choices of attire, which, of course, was not at all what he was getting at.

"I mean that if you wore those dresses for your own preference, I certainly wouldn't mind. But you said to me the other day that the reason you wear dresses so often is because your father prefers them."

"And why would that bother you?" Definitely mad.

He almost sighed, wearying of the constant conflict. It wasn't an exaggeration that he'd spent half his time here in trouble with her. He supposed it was a hazard of the situation he found himself in.

"Because it's not from a desire to cater to his whims out of love."

She was quiet but breathing hard, like she was fighting her own heated reaction.

He continued because he'd already stepped in it. And this felt like something she needed to hear. "Everything about your relationship with your father is off. It's like you're constantly trying to win his approval or acceptance in some way. Now I know Hank, and the man has the highest standards of anyone I've ever met. But to see what the effort is clearly doing to you. . . You're not yourself, Erin."

Her hands twisted on the steering wheel, a flush reddening her cheeks. "What you really mean is that I'm not your Erin."

"That is *not* what I meant," he started.

Her chin jutted out, and he knew that look, could picture the glint of danger in her eyes. But she took a very deep, very tremulous breath. She didn't say anything for a long time, and he fought the urge to apologize.

He *was* good at apologizing when something was his fault. But this wasn't on him. And he didn't really regret saying it. Because she'd already admitted the strain in her relationship with her father, intimated that she often failed at gaining his approval.

"Let's not talk about it anymore," she said softly.

Her tone suggested tears, but he didn't see them. She pressed a hand to her stomach as if it pained her, which was something he'd noticed her doing on occasion. But he decided to just let things be instead of pushing on another possible hot-button issue.

After a few more minutes of wind-whipped hair, she finally gave in and rolled up the windows. No doubt the emotion she was experiencing made her tolerance drop to nearly nothing.

As the sound died down, the song that was playing on the radio became audible and caught his attention.

He tapped his foot to the rhythm, settling on another experiment to see how this Erin compared to his own. And to just lighten the mood because he felt like he would drown in the tension.

They hadn't been alive long enough in the eighties to guarantee they'd even know the songs, but if she was even remotely the same girl he loved, this would maybe pull her out of the funk.

He sang along softly to *You Make My Dreams* by Hall & Oates, glancing out of the corner of his eye.

She stiffened, though it didn't seem like it was from any sort of strong emotion. She'd tilted her head like she was trying to decide if she'd heard him singing or it was her imagination.

He continued to sing, this time a little louder.

She was fighting the smile now, and he turned to look at her, eyebrow raised. She pursed her lips against her amusement, pretending to be irritated as he started to wiggle his shoulders.

He fumbled through the next line, and she snorted.

"Those aren't the words," she said, still fighting her grin.

He rolled his eyes playfully but continued.

She snorted as he tried to match Daryl Hall's vocalization. "You've got terrible pitch."

He turned the volume dial up, but only so he could sing

louder, leaning toward her.

She gave an embarrassed laugh, leaning away from him as he danced in his seat.

"Stop it! People will see you!"

He shut his eyes and danced more vigorously. Or as well as he could while buckled in. "Come on, I know you know the words."

She laughed again, still not joining in. But he heard the release of tension in her laughter that he was going for, and his own body unwound in response.

He looked at her, grinning, and saw that her cheeks were flushed with embarrassment and humor even as she tried to shield her face from his scrutiny. Her whole body shook with mirth.

And, man, if he never got home to his Erin, he could survive living in this world if they got to have moments like this more often, if he could make her laugh, draw out her smile. Gone was the pain lurking behind her eyes, the stress pulling her shoulders inward, and the serious tilt to her mouth.

His eyes dropped to her lips as she mouthed the words to the song, finally, finally, loosening up. And he reminded himself that he definitely needed to have a serious conversation with his Erin about the lipstick when he got home.

21

Closed Doors

ERIN

Luke outstripped her as they walked, his long legs and impatience to meet the professor again getting the best of him. She didn't have much hope that this would get them anywhere, but their desperation to send him back was getting to them both.

That thought almost stopped her in her tracks.

Send him back.

Was that really what she wanted?

He brought up every wound in her heart, every little thing that was wrong in her world. And he muddled her mind. If he was gone, she wouldn't have to deal with any of it.

The heat of the moment was just a fire in her belly, and she wasn't sure if she did want him gone. But she didn't know if she could handle him being here either. She was engaged to another man, after all.

That thought alone put the fire out with a cold, hard guilt.

Ahead of her, Luke's progress faltered when they heard some commotion down the hall. As he slowed to a stop, she worked hard to keep herself from putting a hand on his arm and simply glanced around him to see what was going on.

A crowd of students milled around, nervously grabbing at backpack and purse straps, shuffling from foot to foot, craning their necks to look beyond the police officers who held them back with stony expressions.

Ice water rushed through her veins as the fear clawed up her throat. She was taken back to darker memories she hated to relive. She let herself grab Luke's arm this time, if only to steady herself.

He glanced at her for only a second, his face ashen. Wordlessly, he moved forward, her hand on his arm drawing her with him.

For some inexplicable reason, students sensed his presence and parted until he was toward the front.

Several more uniformed officers moved in and out of Professor Thibald's office, and a set of men in hazmat-looking suits, making her heart beat pick up. Then she caught sight of a tan blazer that was just a smidge too tight, the man wearing it like a statue compared to the frenzy going on around him. He had always been a barrel of a man, but with age had come the padding he hadn't bought a new wardrobe to accommodate.

"Detective Brant," she murmured, her chest getting tight.

The muscle in Luke's arm twitched in response, but he said nothing.

Brant was a homicide detective, and that thought kept repeating in her head. Bursts of memory blinded her like the flash of a camera. Glimpses of Brant's face, less wrinkled, as he delivered the news. Her mother's agonized cry as she turned into Hank's arms.

Erin forced herself to focus on the commotion before them,

tuning in just as another detective stopped to confer with Detective Brant before the two went into the office together.

The tension snapped tighter, and despite the fact that she told herself to take slow, deep breaths, Erin's heart punched an erratic rhythm into her ribs.

"Hey, maybe retract the claws a bit?" Luke spoke low and calm, so it didn't break through her slowly building panic at first.

When he looked at her hand on his arm, she followed his gaze and realized she was digging her nails into his skin. But it still took a concerted effort for her to release her grip.

Detective Brant appeared in the doorway of the office to squint out at the crowd. The uneasy chatter in the hallway died away with his scrutiny, like everyone sensed his suspicion.

"Clear this hallway," Detective Brant said. His voice was quiet but firm and some of the other officers moved to push the crowds farther back from the professor's office.

"Move along, folks." An officer flapped his arms at them.

"Wait, no." Luke craned his neck to see back toward the office. "What happened?"

The officers ignored his question, continuing to push the crush of bodies back.

The reluctance, morbid curiosity, and frustration that permeated the crowd crashed into Erin as she was forced back, amplifying her own mix of emotions.

Before Brant went back into the office, his eyes lit on Erin and Luke and narrowed with distrust. Of course their presence would seem odd. But how in the world could they be connected to whatever had happened in there?

Erin felt like she'd been caught holding a smoking gun. She dipped her head a little as his focused gaze remained on her, despite the fact that the other detective had come to speak to him in low tones so as not to be overheard.

"Wait," Brant called.

Erin jolted, knowing he was calling to them. She wanted to disappear, melt into the background, forget any of this had ever happened.

Luke stopped more eagerly, rocking very lightly back onto his heels as if Brant's voice physically pulled him.

When the officers stopped and turned, Brant nodded for them to let Luke and Erin through. Increasing apprehension filled Erin's stomach.

"Detective Brant doesn't look happy to see us," Luke murmured.

"And our reason for being here would seem a little more than strange if we tried to tell him." Erin attempted a smile but could tell she barely made it to a grimace as they approached the older man.

"Detective," Luke said, offering his hand to Brant.

"Luke, right?" The detective looked him over as if taking better stock of him for future reference.

"Yes, sir."

Brant's eyes transferred to Erin, making her palms grow slick with sweat, even though she knew they weren't guilty of anything.

"Interesting that I find both of you here today."

"What happened to the professor?" The anxious question shot out of Erin before she could stop it.

Brant's jaw shifted. "He's been reported missing. Do you know him?"

"We met with him once. The same day we came to see you," she said.

The detective became very still except for his eyes as he divided a look between Luke and herself. "Met with him about what?"

Luke took a loud breath, prepared to launch into some explanation Erin was tensed to hear. "I am somewhat of an amateur enthusiast about the topic of quantum mechanics, and we had some questions. Erin and I happened to be in town for some errands today, so we thought we'd see if the professor was free for another session."

At the word "errands," Brant's eyes tightened, but he didn't acknowledge their words beyond that. He pursed his lips for a moment. It was like he was trying to find a reason to be more suspicious. It certainly seemed a little dubious.

"Did he know you were coming today?"

"No," Luke said. "It was just a whim, really."

Brant's expression narrowed further.

Erin's fingers curled into her sweaty palms, and she looked around, searching for an explanation that would throw his skepticism in another direction. Her eyes fell on a redheaded woman who was watching them from some feet away. Her interest was different than the curious gawkers that had lingered. The intensity of her gaze made Erin shift uncomfortably.

"What can you tell me about that first meeting?"

Brant's question drew her focus back, and she tuned in again.

"Not much. He was pretty agitated," Luke said, glancing at Erin as if for corroboration.

"Agitated?" Brant asked. "About what?"

Erin glanced over her shoulder to look at the woman again, but she was gone. Something tingled along Erin's spine, and she wondered if the redhead had something to do with whatever had happened to the professor.

"He was just distracted, rushing to get out the door, dismissive. It was part of the reason we didn't get far in our meeting."

Brant's chin jerked up at that. "Did he say why he was rushing?" His suspicion morphed into determination. He was on the trail he really needed to be on now.

Luke shook his head. "What was it he said?" He turned to Erin.

She squinted, trying to remember. "He didn't have time to discuss anything. He claimed he had somewhere to be."

"He said nothing about where that was?" Brant asked. "Did he mention anyone? Threats?"

Luke shifted his weight. "Threats?"

Brant seemed to debate for a moment before deciding. "He hasn't been seen in days, and there's a suspicious blood stain on his floor. Office was tossed."

Erin swallowed. "Bloodstain?" She shook her head. "He seemed a bit preoccupied by something outside the office. He'd started to answer our questions, then bum-rushed us out before we could get very deep into it."

Brant tipped his head to the side. "Did he see someone?"

Luke held up his hands. "I didn't notice anyone."

Erin shook her head. "We left, and there was a crowd of students. I ran into a guy who seemed like he was heading for the office though. If that helps?"

"Did you recognize the man?" he asked, voice sharp.

"No. He was older. Not a student. But it seemed like maybe he was on his way to talk to the professor. I couldn't say for sure though."

Brant wrote something in his notebook. "Anything else you can tell me about the meeting?"

Luke shrugged. "Not much to tell. Literally just had questions about how parallel universes work."

"Theoretically," Erin added.

Brant squinted at them. "So if he wasn't very helpful, why come back?"

Erin's mouth went dry, a panicked tingle rushing through her.

But Luke seemed prepared for the question. "I know, right? Wishful thinking. I was hoping maybe we'd caught him on a bad day, and he'd have more for us today."

Brant stared at Luke for a moment, his skepticism not diminishing at all. "You attended this school."

Luke stiffened at the accusatory tone. "Yeah, with Erin's brother."

That loosened Brant's expression, but only a little. "Did you take any classes from the professor? He's been teaching for twenty years."

"Nope. Communications major. My interest in quantum mechanics is recent."

The nerves must have been getting to her. She almost snorted but covered it with a cough.

It drew Brant's eye anyway. "Did Jordan take any classes from Thibald?"

That stopped her breath. It hadn't occurred to her that they might be connected, but it wasn't like she would know what classes her brother took back then, let alone the names of his professors.

"There's no connection to Jordan," Erin said softly, but it felt like those words were a hot branding iron for how they seared the air. Like the pain was searching for someone else to burn.

As if it wasn't already a stinging wound for her.

"Alright." Brant sighed. He seemed to deflate with the exhale of air. "Alright," he said again. "Thanks for the insight."

She gave him a grim smile, nodding. "Let us know if you have other questions."

22

Intrusions

ERIN

She knew she was chewing the inside of her cheek. Luke had pointed it out enough that she'd become more aware of it, but the thought didn't induce her to break the habit. Not yet.

She was already on edge after the fiasco at the college, but then she'd gotten a phone call from her father. She listened to her father's instructions with half her brain as she watched Luke sitting on the bench several feet from her.

They'd both needed a minute to regroup after the professor, and the shady spot under a huge oak seemed ideal for a breather. Talk about hitting a wall—one that was officially insurmountable.

God, it made her stomach hurt to think of it. Too much a stirring of memories, that. Everything up to this point had been painful, of course. But to see the same homicide detective, dealing with what she suspected might be a murder—though they hadn't confirmed it yet—on the campus where her own brother was killed. . .

It was excruciating.

But add to that her father's ridiculous demands, his clipped tone, his ready criticism for whatever she did. If he didn't like how she did things, why the hell did he always tell her to do them?

"I'll take care of it," she said instead of telling him off like she wanted to. She hung up without waiting for his acknowledgment or good bye.

Even though her phone call had ended, she wasn't quite ready to walk back and join Luke in his cloud of misery and dejection, only to have it amplify her own.

She knew, on some level, that it wasn't a disappointment to her just because it meant they'd lost their connection to sending Luke back. It meant that they didn't have the option to understand how it worked and how to use it.

And some part of her—though she admitted how stupid it was—had hoped that maybe it meant she could travel too. Like some kind of character in a sci-fi show.

Erin fought it but couldn't help the tears that sprang to her eyes.

She'd seen Luke's jealousy, felt it every time his eyes caught on the engagement ring that had been given to her by another man. But she didn't think it could compare to what she felt.

Her jealousy—that this Luke had had the last ten years with Jordan—was beyond anything someone else could imagine. She would travel to a thousand other universes, lose whatever she had now, if it meant she could have Jordan back.

What did she have now that was worth keeping, anyway?

That thought jolted her, flushed her with shame and guilt, and not a little bit of fear about the state of her life and her mental health. She had plenty to live for, to fight for.

Didn't she?

Her phone buzzed in her hand just as Luke came to join her, but she didn't immediately check it, lost in her introspection and shock at her own morbid thoughts.

"Someone is calling you."

She glanced at him, hearing the blackness of his tone. She checked the caller ID, understanding why. Nathan's name was on the display with the little ring emoji she had assigned him after he'd proposed, giddy with girlish excitement.

It seemed stupid now.

Her cheeks grew warm, and she opted to answer the phone instead of giving any sort of defense or explanation. She didn't actually owe him either. Still, she turned away, so she wouldn't have to see his expression.

"Babe! Glad I caught you," Nathan said, breathless. "I got back early. Just landed."

"You did?" She tried to muster the appropriate enthusiasm. After all, she hadn't seen him for a week. She *was* excited. That's what that little flip in her stomach was, right? She made herself smile to get the feeling going.

"Want to meet me for drinks?" Nathan's excitement didn't abate. "That place downtown we like? I still have to stop at home to unpack and change. My dad has some stuff he wants me to handle, so I can't do dinner and the works."

She glanced at Luke. "Um, sure. When?"

It was quiet a moment, and she pictured him checking his Rolex. "About an hour?"

"Yeah, sounds good."

"Great. Love you!"

She cleared her throat. "You too."

He was more energetic than usual, though he was generally like that when he'd had a successful trip. He'd be in a good mood when they met up, probably order the fanciest drinks.

She gripped her phone and turned to Luke. His expression was unreadable. Not angry, not overly controlled. Just blank.

"I, uh, need to head back toward home," she said, still feeling the need to tread lightly. "I'm going to meet my fiancé for drinks."

His expression didn't change. "Okay."

"Is it alright that we're cutting this short? I know you wanted to talk to Sandwich Shop Guy."

It was weird that she'd hoped for some push-back, an argument. Something.

But he was quiet, rubbing his palm over his chin slowly, pensively. "It's fine." The dull look in his eyes sharpened a little. "You know what? You go ahead. I'll get an Uber or something."

Unease coiled in her belly. She wasn't sure why. "Are you sure?"

He wasn't even looking at her, like he had already forgotten she was there. Deliberate? Or was he really just that one-track?

"Yeah. I need to get some momentum on something, so I'll check in with Sandwich Shop Guy on my own."

"I can drop you," she offered.

He shook his head, his body already shifting north toward the shop. "No, thanks. I'd rather walk."

"Okay." The word was drawn out, almost a question, as she waited for him to turn back, take her up on it.

But he left her standing there alone, staring after him like some sort of pathetic, abandoned puppy.

Stop it.

She looked at her engagement ring as it glinted in the sunlight. Wasn't she the one doing the abandoning?

She shook her head.

No guilt, she told herself as she straightened her shoulders. *Go see the man you're going to marry.*

23

Replay

LUKE

Luke tapped his fingers against the top of the wiry outdoor table, but he ceased the staccato rhythm when it started to wobble. Absurdly, he found himself gripping the edges as he wiggled it and bent down to examine the legs as if to confirm one was shorter than the rest. Sort of like tripping over a raised crack in the sidewalk and turning to glare at it as if it had lurched up just as you were walking by.

He was just nervous. Aggravated. Thrown off balance. Like that table, he was permanently unstable.

He needed to focus on something else.

While he waited for Sandwich Shop Guy—Leo, he reminded himself—to bring his order, he scowled toward the marred tree across the street, imagined the car swinging wildly around the corner. Or had it weaved back and forth?

It wasn't dark now, but Luke could picture it. Had seen the campus lit only by street lamps and moonlight, roads nearly empty save for a car here and there. He could picture Jordan walking too.

Back then, Jord was slouchy. He'd been too swamped with homework and Kelly to get in any workouts. And he'd spent so many hours hunched over his computer, he'd jacked up his back.

So, the slouching lope, hands in pockets. Maybe whistling. Maybe brooding over a math problem.

Definitely the math, Luke thought. Jordan was too serious of a guy to whistle.

He would have been engrossed enough not to notice the sound of the approaching vehicle, even as the headlights washed over him, casting his lanky shadow against the tree that would later bear the scar of the accident.

Luke shuddered, his stomach protesting the images his mind was conjuring, even if the gore he imagined was somewhat cartoonish. He had no first-hand experience with anything close to what his brain was trying to construct.

"Hey, man. Your sandwich."

Luke jerked out of the Stephen King visual he was painting for himself and looked up at Leo. His eyes were unsurprisingly red-rimmed, but they were a little sharper than usual. More like the beady eyes of a crow, though. Not really any particular intellect there; just a brain that was attracted to shiny objects.

"Thanks."

"You were staring pretty hard over there," Leo observed. His tone implied a question.

Luke debated for a second. "Let me ask you something."

"Shoot," Leo said, stuffing his hands into the pockets of his very worn, loose-fitting jeans. They had to be at least a decade or more old. Long enough to get worn out, fall out of fashion, and come back in as seemed to be the prevailing routine of the fashion world. *Not* that he really knew. Erin paid attention and railed when something that went out ten or more years before came back around.

"*Should've kept that!*" she'd inevitably say as she marched off.

"Hey, man, you get lost in la la land more than me!" Leo said, interrupting his thoughts again. He gave Luke his full smile, crooked teeth and all.

"Sorry. Just pretty introspective today, I guess."

"There's a college word for ya. Hear 'em all the time. Big surprise." He gestured generically toward the campus. "But I'm just a simple guy. Not much to introspect. Or whatever." He gave a short, wheezed bark of laughter.

Laying the pothead routine on a little heavy-handed, Luke thought. As if Leo wanted to drive home that he was absent-minded and two-sheets to the wind at all times. Like he knew what Luke would ask about.

"You remember me from the other day?" Luke asked.

"Sure. Corned beef sandwich. Always remember a solid sandwich order." He bobbed his head in approval.

"Do you remember what I was asking about?"

That beady-eyed bird look sharpened his gaze again, but he frowned, now playing the thinking-is-too-hard card.

He looked out across the street where Luke had been focused before. "You that guy who wanted to know about the hit-and-run a few years back?"

"That's me." Luke placed his hand on the wrapped sandwich and considered.

Maybe he was reading too much into it. Maybe he was being too suspicious of the guy, but he wasn't quite the high-flier he seemed to be.

"You were his friend or something, right?"

Luke sighed, startled by the emotional punch that gave him. Innocent question, though it was delivered with less finesse than most people have when talking about the deceased.

"Yeah. Yeah," he said again, raking a hand through his hair. *Need a haircut*, he thought absently. "I just wondered if there was anything you remembered from that night? You'd mentioned some possible security footage on some old VHS tapes?"

"Yeah, man." Leo nodded in agreement. "I sure did say that."

Luke lifted his eyebrows when the guy didn't elaborate. "Do you know where you put them?"

He tried not to let his irritation show, but he could tell that Leo was intentionally making him work for the answers. Because he wanted to be difficult or because someone was putting him up to it, Luke wasn't sure.

"You know, I'm not sure I even remember." He stroked his scraggly goatee. "I know I gave some stuff to the cops, but I might not have kept anything else."

"Sure, fine." Luke waved that away. "Anything you possibly remember from that night?"

"Shit, man. That was a long time ago." He kept his hands in his pockets, but his posture was too tight.

Luke leaned back, tried to make himself relax and hoped it would make Leo follow suit. "Sure. I know it's a long-shot. But how often has a hit-and-run happened right in front of your shop?" And the guy couldn't be so blasted he wouldn't be able to run his business.

His shoulders scrunched upward, really showing how uncomfortable he was starting to feel. "I told the cops all I saw at the time. Then I let it fall out of my head."

Luke nodded, but he knew his gaze had gotten a bit steely. "Right. You know, I talked to the detective. He says you changed your story later."

Leo was definitely nervous now. The hands came out of the pockets, and he lifted them, palm-out toward Luke as if to ward off an attack. "I don't remember what I did and didn't say, man."

Luke was losing him, but he couldn't help the irritation that was fast rolling into anger. "I bet you do, Leo. What made you change your story? Or who?"

There. Fear. Those beady eyes flashed away from Luke's face and back. "I don't want to talk about it anymore, man. Enjoy your sandwich." Leo turned on his heel, almost plowed into a couple of customers about to leave his shop. The black eyes lit upon Luke's face one last time.

Luke curled his fingers into a fist on the table and gritted his teeth. He snatched the sandwich, not even really hungry. What a waste.

He stalked around the corner and slowed.

Or was it?

They knew Leo had changed his story and thought they knew why. Someone definitely had this guy scared. But who was it? And how much reach did that someone have that he'd still be afraid ten years later?

Luke shifted the wrapped sandwich back and forth between his hands as he walked, absently making his way to the stoplight ahead. He didn't realize he was heading for the campus until he was halfway through the crosswalk.

He made his way past the parking lot to a path that wound around and through the grounds. He had no real destination in mind as he walked, but the pure nostalgia and the solitude did something to his mood that nothing short of getting home could do.

Maybe it was being removed from the world that was too much like his own, but missing the most essential parts. Now that he wasn't with this not-quite-right-Erin, not reminded that his best friend was gone, he could actually take a deep breath. He had not noticed the slow suffocation of depression and desperation—a terrible mix, really.

What assailed him now were pleasant memories, and he settled into the nostalgia, let it take him on a little ride as he wandered through the dappled shade of the trees. He remembered walking the paths this exact time of year, familiarizing himself with its twists and turns, excited and hopeful about what the next four years would bring him.

Jordan had been particularly light at that point, not yet sucked into the mire of engineering classes and the hours of homework that bogged him down. They'd gone on jogs together, back when they were still into the track and field theme, and Luke hadn't yet gotten interested in weight lifting. It had been his best sport through high school, so he hadn't been ready to abandon it yet.

He remembered that one tree with large, low branches that they could lounge or climb around in like little kids, its limbs lazily reaching to spread across a swath of grass so wide, a dozen students could relax in its shade.

He realized that's where he was heading without having consciously decided to. Some of the students were already utilizing the umbrella of leaves to relax or study. One guy sat in the lowest branch, strumming a guitar and muttering song lyrics under his breath.

It struck Luke as contrived, like he was overly focused on it but secretly waiting for someone to ask what he was singing so he could perform. Luke rolled his eyes, remembering doing something similar back in the day.

He found a spot in the shade to eat his sandwich and bask in the peace that came from having no demands, burdens, or complications. He could even pretend life was normal, and this was simply a random visit to his alma mater.

After he finished his sandwich, he leaned back against the sloped lawn and shut his eyes for a moment. He didn't even mind the bumbling guitar player or the chatter and laughter of the nearby students.

Once, he had lain in almost the exact same spot, Erin stretched out beside him with her head on his chest. It was picturesque. A scene cut from a chick flick. His hand traced lightly up and down her arm as he started to doze. Every time he'd drift off, his hand would stop, and she'd wiggle to wake him up enough to keep doing it.

"Hey, professor. You mind? This is our spot."

Luke started, blinking rapidly. He'd begun to doze off just like in that reverie. He ached for that moment again as it vanished like smoke on the wind.

He sat up, grabbed his sandwich trash, and left the "spot" to the douchey college kids. He looked at his phone for the first time as he walked, wondering if Erin had finished up with her fiancé yet or not.

The word made him automatically curl his lip in disgust. She hadn't confirmed anything about him, but he just knew something wasn't right. She carried around too much tension and stress for him to believe that guy was the one for her. There was no way she was struggling under the weight of all those burdens if her fiancé was supporting her like he should.

A voice in his head reminded him that the man had been out of town and Luke's own presence was complicating her emotions. He gritted his teeth and told himself that his jealousy was not the reason he doubted Erin's relationship.

Because he could remove himself from that equation entirely. After all, this version of himself shouldn't even be here. And it was obvious the Luke and Erin from this reality didn't belong together. But it sure as hell didn't seem like she should be with this Nathan guy either.

Luke slowed, realizing that the peace he'd found here had turned to smoke. Especially as his eyes lit upon the tree Erin had shown him the other day, the one scarred permanently by Jordan's death. He didn't feel the stirring of grief the way she had. Maybe he was still grappling with how surreal everything was, how distance from the "wrong" Erin had made it all seem more like a dream than something he was living in.

If only it was one long nightmare he was going to wake from eventually.

Something—maybe that uncanny and inexplicable intuition people had—made him look up and toward the sandwich shop. Leo, the owner, was standing close to the window, his eyes trained in Luke's direction. His expression was hard to place, especially from this distance.

It made Luke want to take another shot at talking to him, determination setting his jaw. He wouldn't mince words this time, wouldn't try to be subtle. He marched to the stoplight to cross back over.

Everything shifted when he was about halfway through the walk. That was when he heard the engine rev, caught the movement in his periphery, and made out the startled shout from a nearby pedestrian.

The car was black with tinted windows. Definitely strategic. Nothing very obvious about its body, and it took him long enough to realize that the missing markings depicting its make and model were intentional as it sped in his direction.

He called upon every muscle in his body, every ounce of training from his cross country days. But he was more than ten years older, less trim, and certainly out of practice.

Is this what Jordan had experienced? Or had he been caught completely unawares?

Panic gripped his gut so hard, the phrase "shit his pants" felt like it could become more than just a figure of speech.

All he could think as the car gunned for him was how he was never going to hold his Erin again.

24

Fancy Fiancé

ERIN

Dim and overly swanky. That was Erin's first thought every time they went to this place. She'd overlooked her first impression in the past because Nathan liked it and seemed to relish that the owners owed his father favors and, therefore, gave him special treatment.

This time, she really noticed how smarmy it made her feel. Or maybe it was just that she felt awful in general. Like everything was all wrong. As if she was the one in the wrong universe, not Luke.

But was it just that his presence had thrown her off-kilter, and she was just reeling from that? Because this world *was* where she belonged.

When Nathan smiled at her from their table, she made an effort to put some real enthusiasm behind her own. She'd shove everything else from her mind and work to just enjoy this. Try to right herself, a slightly warped puzzle piece that did still belong with the whole. It had fit once. It could again.

Nathan stood and leaned to kiss her cheek. He was used to

wearing a tie so often, even in his more casual button-down, he put a hand to his chest to hold it out of habit.

"You're a sight for sore eyes. All I've been looking at for the last week were sour suits."

Which would have been a sweet sentiment, but he didn't even look at her as he sat, instead lifting his hand to the bartender with two fingers raised.

The bartender nodded but threw a subtle glance at the restaurant manager when Nathan was no longer looking.

Erin had never noticed it before, but there was an irritated tension bouncing between all the employees.

"Service is slow today," Nathan muttered, his eyes going to the phone on the table beside him as a number of text alerts popped up on the screen.

"Other than sour executives, how was your trip?" Erin asked, trying not to be annoyed at his divided attention.

Nathan frowned, picking up his phone. "Busy. I don't think I had time to focus on anything but business the entire time. Luckily, I've been there more than enough times to get the sight-seeing part out of the way. Didn't feel like I missed out on anything." He spoke while typing furiously.

Is this how it usually went? She honestly couldn't remember if he ever gave her his full attention or not during their dates. Maybe it had just never bothered her before.

"You must have been busy too. You didn't call or text much." There was no hurt or censure in his tone. It was just matter-of-fact.

She pulled her folded hands from the table as a server set a glass of wine in front of her. "Um, my dad left town for part of the week, so I did have more on my plate."

And another man on my mind, her conscience added unbidden.

She gave a tight smile despite the guilt that swelled inside her.

"Mmm," he said, nodding, oblivious to her inner monologue.

He set his phone down and looked at her for the first time since she'd sat down. His brow wrinkled, then he glanced around, like he was making sure no one else was paying attention. "What are you wearing?"

She looked down at herself, not even aware of what she'd chosen for the day's attire. Lightweight linen pants and a fitted t-shirt. Admittedly much more casual than he was used to. Hell, than she was used to. But she'd been with Luke. There was no need to dress to impress.

"I forgot to change."

He expected her to sound sheepish, she supposed, but she didn't have the energy to be sufficiently self-conscious about it. Or maybe she just no longer cared.

His phone screen lit up again, this time with a call, drawing his attention before he could respond. His brows went up. "It's my father."

She waved her hand to give him the go-ahead, taking a sip of her wine. Out of the corner of her eye, she caught the ashen look that fell over Nathan's face and the way his gaze darted to her and away. He turned a little in his chair, his voice getting lower as his father's grew in volume.

Nathan glanced at her again, and he probably knew she could at least hear his father's voice.

Through clenched teeth: "I can't talk about this now. Yes. I can. I will. *I will.*" He hung up, staring at the phone for a moment. He looked stricken, borderline panicked.

"Is everything okay?" She pushed their wine glasses to the side, leaning forward to touch his arm. She'd never seen him quite so shaken before.

He flinched. "Um. Yes. My dad wants to see me right now. I was hoping it could wait until after this." He struggled to look directly at her. As if ashamed. "But he's impatient. And it does seem like something we can't put off."

She offered a reassuring smile. "I understand. Business comes first." Which sounded horrible, but it had always been true with her family as well as her relationship.

Engagement, she reminded herself.

He grimaced. "Yeah." Pause. "Yeah."

He pushed up from the table, looking a bit like he didn't know where he was or what he'd been doing. It was the most unbalanced she'd ever seen him in the two years she'd known him.

It was enough to make her feel a little shaky herself. "Nathan—"

"It's fine," he said softly, his hand splayed out to stay her, as if he knew she'd been about to stand. "Order whatever you want. I'll take care of it."

He walked toward the exit without even kissing her goodbye. She'd all but disappeared in the wake of whatever had upset him.

It was more than business. Something he couldn't share with her. But he probably should have. They were engaged, weren't they? Isn't that what people in a life-long commitment were supposed to do?

It would be different when they were married. They would live together, and so everything would *have* to be shared. That was the more permanent attachment. After all, engagements could still end.

So could marriages.

She shook her head against that pessimistic voice. Against that fear. That he would leave. That *she* would quit. But that's not what Baylors did. She could almost hear her father's voice when she thought it. They may not always be happy, but dammit, Baylors stuck with what they'd committed to.

Every time she'd tried to give up some sport or activity, it's what her father had drilled into her head. Follow-through, duty to the end.

She reached for her wine, sipped, and found she no longer had a taste for it and set it back down.

She grabbed her purse and headed for the door, contemplating the pale look to Nathan's face when he left. She barely registered the significant glances passed between the employees of the restaurant. Perhaps because she didn't really care what they may have been thinking.

As soon as she was outside in the glaring sun, her phone rang. She answered as she put her sunglasses on, not even bothering to check who was calling.

"Erin?"

An unfamiliar female voice jolted her distracted mind to attention.

"Yes?"

"This is Tara Pearson. Luke's sister."

The fact that Tara was calling her made Erin's stomach hit the ground. Her mouth was suddenly a barren desert.

"Are you there?" Tara's voice was quiet, like she was afraid to wake someone sleeping nearby.

"What's wrong?" Funny how experiencing it once could make her so in tune with the *tone*. In her mind, she was back at school, getting that phone call that changed everything. *Ruined* everything.

Tara took a breath. "It's Luke."

Aware of the sun beating down on her head, her keys biting into the skin of her palm, she took a shaky breath. "Is he okay?"

"He's fine now."

"What happened?" She couldn't keep the sharpness from her tone, a whip cracking on the air.

Why was Tara taking so long to just say it? What was it that was so bad?

"A car ran him down earlier today." Tara's voice was flat, like she was trying to keep it from hitting Erin like a ton of bricks..

But it did, and she thought she might actually throw up. She swallowed several times to beat the feeling back. "What? How? Who? Is he okay? Where is he?"

Before she could get any other hysterical questions out, Tara interrupted.

"The driver took off right away, and they haven't gotten the information yet. The car didn't hit him, though not for lack of trying. He's fine. Just scraped up from when he jumped out of the way." She stopped, and Erin heard what sounded like a sliding glass door opening and shutting.

Tara spoke at a more normal volume. "He didn't want me to call you. To tell you. He was afraid it would upset you."

Of course. Erin dug her thumb into her stomach where the pain seared her from the inside. "Is he at your place?" Her own voice was more subdued.

"Yes. I insisted he stay, but he wants me to drive him back to the guesthouse later."

"I'll save you the trip."

She didn't give Tara time to respond before she clicked off, an unholy and, admittedly, misdirected rage boiling inside of her. She wanted to throttle someone. Right now, it was whoever she got to first. But what she really wanted was to find who'd done this and make them pay. For what they'd done to Luke and maybe even for Jordan. Because, dammit, she was still pissed about that, too.

She slammed into her car, threw her purse at the floor on the passenger side, and peeled out of the parking lot.

What were the stages of grief? Wasn't anger the first one? No, second. So, she'd never gotten far in that process. Big surprise there.

What had she just been thinking inside the restaurant? When Baylors committed, they stuck with it. And wasn't anger just the easiest way to deal with things?

She took the long way to Tara's to work off the anger or at least get it to a simmer instead of brimming over. They didn't deserve it, that was for sure.

Tara's house looked the same as it had before, but this time Erin felt more self-assured walking to that door. No longer questioning the insanity that lay before her. Somehow she had gotten to this place of acceptance, and she wasn't even sure when that had happened.

Maybe it was the fact that Luke had almost lost his life today. And could very well still be in danger. Did someone have it out for him? Was it a fluke? A warning? A miss?

She shuddered, raising her hand to knock. Her anger was doused by the very real fear for Luke's life.

He answered the door himself. He grimaced as soon as he saw her and hollered petulantly at his older sister. Erin almost laughed. But then she saw Luke's attempt at hiding his wince and the stiffness with which he walked.

"Luke." She followed him into the living room.

"I'm just going to get my shoes on. Then we can go."

She decided not to press just yet. She waited in silence as he laced his shoes up, noting the scrapes across his knuckles, saw the wound on his cheek. He stood and a lock of dark hair fell onto his forehead, and for a second, he looked like the high school boy she'd been half in love with. She expected the boyish grin, the one he always gave her when he was teasing her.

She had glimpsed it a few times since he'd been here, haunting her with faded memories, with what could have been. She ached for that, for the thing she'd never had. And now she wanted it.

The weight of her engagement ring was heavy on her hand as they walked to the door.

25

Lock and Key

LUKE

There must have been something on Erin's mind. She ran her thumb across her bottom lip, her blue eyes narrowed onto some distant landscape.

It wasn't as if she were quite checked out or oblivious to Luke's presence. He was quite sure she was hyper aware of him. Her whole body was pulled taut, and she was turned slightly in his direction. But her mind was working something through.

He had no energy to figure her out and was in no mood to dig.

Instead, he rested his head against the seat as the blaze of the sunset warmed his chest.

His body ached, his cuts stung. He'd refused the hospital, though someone had called an ambulance to the scene. They'd cleared him of any possibility of serious injury. Road abrasions were the only bodily damage he'd sustained. Though he admitted his reflexes had not been as sharp as he would have liked, he'd moved fairly quickly to jump out of the path of the speeding vehicle he was sure meant to run him down. And so he ached from the effort, realizing how far removed he was from his sprinting days.

So who was it that had it out for him? Whoever wanted to keep Jordan's case unsolved? Seemed most likely. But there was always the professor's disappearance to keep in mind, though he wasn't sure he had much connection there. The two cases didn't seem related either. But they knew so little about either that it was possible.

Then there was the question of his presence here. Was that related to either case? Or was that entirely separate? So was the near hit and run related to that? None of the above? All?

He didn't have the mental capacity to try and figure it out. It was all so intellectually and emotionally exhausting, and he was utterly spent. It made him not want to figure it out at all. Just get home, *real home*, and sleep for a hundred years. He could convince himself this was all a dream, leave it all unresolved, and move on with his life. Marry Erin and figure out how to make it so that he never had to leave her presence, never stop touching her for the rest of his life.

Move his office into hers. Handcuff himself to her. She'd go crazy. So would he, but right now, he didn't care.

"Do you feel okay?" Erin's question cut into his fantasy, soft and tentative.

It was so disappointing to hear his favorite voice without the comfort of familiarity. The cautious question was just another reminder of the missing intimacy.

"I mean, I *feel* like I was hit by a car. Even though I wasn't."

She didn't smile. In fact, she lost all color in her face.

"It was epic, really," he said, trying his best to dredge up his usual playful tone. "Like a movie scene the way I leaped out of the way and rolled onto the pavement. Even the tires screeched as it rounded the corner."

"Please stop."

He did, feeling suddenly like the air had been sucked from the car. Of course, his intention was to lighten the mood, thinking only how she must have been upset by his brush with death. But, again, he forgot what describing a near-hit and run would bring her mind to.

Even if she hadn't been there when Jordan had died, no doubt she'd pictured it over and over, just as he'd done. The problem was that she'd lived through the gruesome after effects. Investigations, grief, drawn-out family drama that continued as a constant reminder that her brother was gone forever, and no one was paying the price for it but her own family.

His tone was subdued. "I'm sorry." It was all he could manage, and they rode on in silence.

It wasn't long before they arrived at her parents'. She avoided the front drive, opting instead for the side drive that was mostly hidden unless you knew what you were looking for. This led to a little spot next to the guesthouse and the side entrance that opened into the laundry/mudroom.

Neither spoke as he unlocked the door and let her enter first, then followed, shuffling in. He tried his damnedest to move like he wasn't in pain, like he wasn't aware of every muscle he'd called on, every bruise he'd gotten in his fall.

He wasn't sure why he bothered. There wasn't much of his dignity left, not after getting mugged, having to take a pity job and a pity place to stay, dive out of the way of a speeding car, and now he was feeling old and infirm. At least he knew what to change for exercise. He was definitely going to start some more cardio and add in stuff for increased flexibility. Erin had always wanted him to try yoga.

"No yoga for me. Unless you're doing yoga to me," he'd always say with a wicked grin.

Sometimes she'd laugh, or she'd roll her eyes, depending on her mood. Either reaction suited him just fine.

He looked at her now as he went for a glass of water. She perched on the edge of the couch, definitely not relaxed, twisting her engagement ring as if she were trying to unscrew her finger. Still debating something.

"How was drinks?" He worked to make his tone as neutral as he could. It ended up sounding robotic.

She looked at him as if he'd asked if she'd ever killed someone. But she recovered quickly. "Um. Short. His father called, so he had to leave not long after I arrived."

He watched her brows knit. She took a breath as if to speak again. But she didn't.

"Was that unusual?" he prompted.

"Not necessarily," she said slowly. "But he was thrown off by it. I'm pretty sure his dad was upset with him about something. I assume it was work-related."

"He works for his dad too." Wasn't really a question. "And jumps at every request. Match made in heaven."

She glared at him. "Don't be an asshole."

He laughed darkly but held up his hands. Not in surrender or apology. He *was* being an asshole.

She shot to her feet. "It's not like I betrayed you or something. You asked."

"I sure did." He tossed back the water he'd poured for himself, wished it was a shot of whiskey to burn the caustic words out of his mouth before he could do more damage. He just needed to quit while he was behind. "Listen, it's been a day. I should probably go to bed."

He slammed the glass down and pushed away from the sink. He moved past her, working to ignore the way her eyes had gone round and vulnerable. He kept his gaze lasered toward the bedroom door. Sleep really did sound good if he thought about it hard enough.

"Luke."

Against his better judgment, he turned and found her right there in front of him, face tilted up, her expression opening like a flower. Imploring, uncertain, wanting. His breath caught, and he tensed against the onslaught of physical and emotional yearning. It was so fierce, it nearly knocked him to his knees.

Because he was weak. God, he was so weak.

She lowered her eyes slowly, her fingers touching the backs of his hands at his sides. He concentrated so hard on not moving. He should have stopped her, should have walked away. Anything. But his desire to gather her in his arms, press his face into her hair, her neck, was a call so strong that his body screamed in agony.

Her breathing was deliberately slow and deep like she was focused on keeping it smooth. But he saw her pulse jumping at her throat. Erratic, just like his own heartbeat.

She brought her gaze back to his, her hands slowly tracing up his arms as she lifted her chin, lips parted slightly. Those damn lipstick lips.

And he lost it. Before he could even form a coherent thought, their mouths met, taking from each other with voracity. She crushed her body against him, melting like she wanted to become part of him. A key into its lock, sliding home. Her hands—God, they were everywhere. *She* was everywhere, everything, his air, the missing part of him, the balm to his wounds. Every part of him sighed in relief, finally able to touch her the way he had been craving.

Her hands fisted into his hair; her mouth was almost carnivorous in its hunger for his. He growled as she tugged a little at his hair, and he caught on fire, gathered her up and carried her to the couch where they tumbled together, never breaking contact. He never wanted, didn't think he could stand, to be disconnected from her again. She pulled at his shirt impatiently, and he sat up to yank it over his head—injuries be damned—and they gulped at the air for the split second they separated for him to complete the task.

They crashed back together, and he pulled her on top him in an effort to draw her closer. He wanted so much so badly, and he was sure it would never be enough. His hands were at her hips, gripping tightly before they made a trail up, just as hungry as his mouth. But he made himself slow down, wanting to savor the feel of her. Her skin was smooth and warm under his palms, and he could practically wrap his hands, thumb to thumb and fingertip to fingertip, at her waist.

He mentally stumbled, broke away, breath coming fast and hard. He'd felt her ribs, which was jarring. He remembered the way she often pressed her fist to her stomach like it pained her, was reminded that she was thinner, more stressed, more anxious than his Erin.

His Erin.

Searing pain lanced through his chest, sharp and violent, more brutal than anything he'd experienced that day. If he'd been standing, his knees would have buckled from the torment of it.

What had he almost done?

She didn't seem to notice the change, or maybe she was too

far down that road to stop herself. He caught her hands in his, felt the unfamiliar shape of her engagement ring against his palm, and knew they couldn't keep going. He smelled the faintest hint of wine on her breath as it fanned across his face.

"What are you doing?" she panted, her cheeks flush with desire and from their frenzied activity. Her hands clenched into fists inside his.

"Erin, I *want*. . . " He shut his eyes, mentally wrestling his physical response to her into submission. "But I can't. I can't do this."

I won't do this.

"Why?" There was real hurt there, tears in her voice.

He opened his eyes, and she looked away, dragging her hands from his grip as if that would lessen her embarrassment. No, it was rejection. But even that wasn't quite right. It was more painful than that. Maybe because she'd been pursuing acceptance from those around her for so long, this was a more crushing blow than simple rejection.

"You have no idea how hard this is," he said, letting the full force of his emotion show in his words. This was not a time for protecting his own dignity. Because, even as he said it, his hands reached unconsciously, wanted to touch her. *Erin.* He shut his eyes again briefly. "But think about it. This counts as being unfaithful."

"No." She shook her head. "Because I'm her. I'm Erin Baylor, the love of your life, the woman you're supposed to marry."

He could tell she was saying it to convince herself just as much as him because she knew what she said wasn't really true.

But he rebutted anyway. "But you're not. I'm sorry. You're

not."

"If it mattered that much, if *she* mattered that much, why haven't you married her yet?"

Fair question, even if it was asked in bitter anger. He had dragged his feet, content to just be where they were. Maybe a little afraid of the expectation that came along with it, especially in the Baylor family. But he knew now; he would marry her the second he got back. *If* he got back.

If he got back.

He decided not to rise to her bait. "You tell me how you would feel if your fiancé slept with another woman just because her name was Erin."

"That's not the same thing." Her chin quivered, the mark of half-defeat.

He took her hand gently, and he counted it as a win that she didn't yank it back. "But it is. You might look like her and sound like her—hell, you even smell like her. But you don't exactly think like her. You don't quite act like her. I could never forgive myself for betraying her like that. For using the excuse that you're *almost* her just to make myself feel better. I would always know it was a lie."

He pressed her hand to his lips when she turned away again. Because he wanted to soothe the sting of rejection, the agony of the sadness, the harshness of her realization that he was right. She might have been hurt now, but she would feel it, too. If not now, definitely soon. And so would her fiancé.

Great reminder, that. Nothing could crush the remnants of his desire more thoroughly. Maybe it would strike something in her too.

"And no matter my feelings about the guy or my doubts about your relationship," he said, "this would never be right as long as you were engaged to somebody else. I never want to be that kind of man."

A weak sob broke out of her, and she fell against his chest. He wrapped his arms around her and let her cry, lying back so that they were pressed together on the couch. This, he could do. Still a bit of a precarious situation, and he knew that it was definitely not something easily forgiven—holding another woman while she cried. But this seemed a much more palatable transgression.

26

Speculation

ERIN

The rejection didn't fade. She just grew used to its weight. It was overly warm, uncomfortable, itchy—like a wool sweater on a summer day. But she understood, even as she fought the logic in his response.

She would be livid if she were on the other end. This other Erin, *his* Erin, wasn't her. She was jealous just thinking about it. And it was herself she was jealous of!

Which made no sense.

Nothing did. Even outside of the parallel universe thing, her life had ceased to make sense. Before this, her path had been clear, albeit wrong.

That's one thing she was sure of now.

Work for her father, wasting away under the pressure and scrutiny. Marry the perfect man, get the big house, fancy cars. But what was after that? What was she working toward?

Filling that hole inside her? Because nothing had thus far. How had she been doing this for ten years? Jordan's death had maimed her, and, stupidly, she'd never addressed the injury.

Luke's arms were warm around her, steady. This was so different, such a feeling of safety and belonging. She had never known it existed until this moment.

Her heart squeezed that she couldn't keep it. Even if he never got to go home, how could they justify anything, like he said, in case he did go back? Was there a statute of limitations?

And what did they do in the meantime?

She twisted her engagement ring around her finger as she so often did these days. She knew one thing she needed to do, regardless of what happened with Luke. He had been right about that too. No matter what, she was not doing right by Nathan, and he deserved the truth, and a break-up for the right reasons.

It was time for her to start being honest with everyone. Especially herself.

"Are you okay?" Luke asked softly. His breath tickled in her hair.

She waited a beat, two. "No." Honesty, right? "But I will be. I think. Someday."

That was as honest as she could get. The future seemed too hard, too murky to even guess at for the moment. The present was painful too, though. Screw that "live in the moment" adage. Everything was agony. Past, present, future. Her chest tightened with a renewed desire to cry. But she didn't let it win. Wouldn't let despair have the last word.

He sighed. "This sucks."

She laughed, though it sounded halfway like a sob. Definitely not okay yet.

He gave her a gentle squeeze, which made her want to cry more. But she took a deep, steadying breath. She pulled back enough to see his face. They were close enough to kiss, still so intimately positioned, and she worked to keep her mind focused on something other than their proximity. It helped when her eyes lit upon the scrape across his right cheekbone, a kiss from the pavement in his haste to keep himself alive that day.

She pressed a hand to his bare chest to push herself back more, to inspect his body. It was purely academic now—a nurse checking for wounds. She sat up, her hands tracing lightly over his torso.

"All superficial," he assured her in a mellow tone. "Mostly my arms and hands."

She lifted his arms in turn. The faint beginnings of bruises painting his skin, the scrape at his left elbow, his knuckles on that hand, all told her the story and gave her the image of him diving and rolling. Just like in a movie, as he'd said. And it played out in her mind like a film. The slow motion realization that a car was coming for him, the fast-twitch muscles engaging just in time for him to jump out of the way.

It was playing in his mind too, she could see. Or maybe that was his effort to distract himself from the fact that she was touching him. Which she ceased.

"I don't even remember what I did, what exactly happened. Except the thought that I'd never. . . " He looked at her now, focused, intense. "How I'd never hold my Erin again."

He sat up himself, maybe to break their connection further, because he was turned away from her now. "Then I was rolling. I couldn't stop myself. I think I hit the curb, actually. That's what stopped me. And then there were these people screaming, someone was standing over me, shouting things at me. He said he was calling 9-1-1."

She was grateful he was alive. But she couldn't help thinking, wishing so badly this had been Jordan's story. That he hadn't been caught off guard, so oblivious. She still didn't understand that, how he hadn't heard the car and gotten out of the way. Was it just that he'd been tired, and it was dark? Luke had been alert enough to jump out of the way.

Unless this hadn't been intended to take him out. Maybe it had served as a warning.

Luke turned toward her now. "What is it? What are you thinking?"

He hadn't even been looking at her, but he'd known, sensed that her wheels were turning. He'd done it before—anticipated her in a way others never did. From familiarity, intimacy with who she was at her core, even if it wasn't truly her in this timeline.

"I was just wondering how you were able to get out of the way in time. . . and Jordan wasn't."

His blue eyes narrowed, not understanding initially. When it dawned on him, he pulled back slightly. "You don't think they meant to kill me?"

"I don't *think* anything. I'm just speculating."

"It definitely felt like they were trying to kill me." He turned, maybe hiding some emotion as he reached down to snatch his shirt from the floor and put it back on.

She used the line of thinking as a distraction from the way his bare chest brushed against her arm, or how the chiseled muscles bunched and shifted as he moved.

"I'm sure it did," she said. "And maybe they were. But I'm just wondering if it could also have been a warning."

He scooted away from her and stood, walking to the kitchen for another drink of water. Some of the stiffness he'd moved with earlier was gone. "A warning from whom and about what?"

She opened her mouth to respond with *Jordan's murder, of course*, but they both were connected, at least loosely, with the disappearance of the professor now. The motive there had seemed like it was associated with the parallel universe situation, and the timing was uncanny. It wasn't official, and she didn't know where Detective Brant stood with the investigation, but they did have to assume it was a possibility.

Which meant that there were three potential links here that could point to someone wanting to either bump Luke off or warn him away from something.

Luke gave her his half-smirk, a smug gleam in his eye. "You look like your hamster might blow a gasket. Don't worry, I was there not that long ago. Speculating can give you more than just a headache. Now we have too many possibilities."

She pursed her lips. "Okay, so maybe we can try to narrow it down to 'likelies.'"

He lifted one shoulder, winced. "Fine. Lay 'em on me."

She shifted to sit on the edge of the couch, tossed a throw pillow on the floor in front of her and pointed at it. "First, come here."

He gave her a childish, obstinate look, squaring his stance.

"Innocent shoulder rub, I promise." She held up her hands.

He took another gulp of water, then set it down to sit in front of her. "Go easy on me. I'm kind of hurting."

"Don't be a baby," she teased, moving her thumbs slowly in circles over his muscles.

It only took him a minute to relax into her hands.

"Don't fall asleep on me. This is an important conversation."

"Mm."

"Near-death experience, remember?"

He straightened a little bit. "Sure, sure."

"Okay, so logically speaking, because of the hit-and-run, it seems most likely related to my brother's death."

He tilted his head back and forth like he was waffling. "I can see that, given the common thread. Not to mention I'd been grilling Sandwich Shop Guy right before that."

She let her mind wander, settling into the comfort of Luke's presence and the normalcy of what they were doing. The conversation felt so removed from real life, like they were discussing the plot of a movie. It was nice to let herself think and talk it through so naturally.

"So," she continued, "either he's still being watched by whoever is keeping this investigation stalled out, or he works for whoever did it."

He leaned forward, and she stilled as he craned his neck to look at her. "You know, actually, he had this weird look on his face when I went to cross the street. I couldn't figure out what it was. But now that you say that, I feel like he might have known what was going to happen."

The abstract discussion came into sharp focus in her mind. "Did you tell the police? Wait, did you talk to Detective Brant?"

"I talked to the police, yes. The detective, no." His eyes went speculatively to the ceiling. "It didn't occur to me that it could be related at the time. I wasn't making any connections to anything, really. I think I was still running on adrenaline."

"So we should call Brant." She was ready to jump up to call him right that minute. "If Sandwich Shop Guy is connected, he needs to be taken in again."

"Hold on a minute. This is just speculation. I could be wrong about Sandwich Shop Guy. It was just a look on his face. The only link we actually have here to Jordan's death is the commonality of the hit-and-run."

She pursed her lips, skeptical.

"We don't want to scare off Sandwich Shop Guy or, worse, put him in danger."

That definitely wasn't something she wanted.

"Besides, remove that connection, and we aren't left with much. But it seems pretty suspicious with the timing and the professor's sudden disappearance."

She didn't like it or want it to be the case, but she'd obviously thought the same herself. She wanted this fresh lead to be real and connected to her brother though. It might finally give them a trajectory.

"But why would anyone feel the need to take you out, or even warn you away? You talked to him for, what, five minutes?"

"Fair question. But until we know more about what, or possibly who, brought me to this alternate timeline, we can't rule it out. If someone sent me here on purpose and means to keep me here, why wouldn't they try to warn me off of trying to figure out a way back?"

She shrugged. "All you did was ask a professor a question. Hardly seems dangerous."

"I'm guessing it's not like hitting a button on a remote, so if anything jeopardizes the effort it took to get me here, it might be motivation enough to make someone take pretty extreme measures. The professor is already in danger over it."

She balked. "That's speculation."

"Isn't that what we're doing here?" He smirked, but it was dark and humorless.

She took a deep breath, recognizing the logic in his perspective, even if it was frustrating. Even if she wanted there to be a clear path. Of course, it couldn't be so easy. And it wasn't as though this were a sign pointing straight to the perpetrator, even if they could make a direct link to Jordan's death.

She tried to allow the professor line of thinking to germinate. Grudgingly, with an edge in her voice, she asked, "Why would someone intentionally send you here? What purpose could that serve?"

He shifted, pushing himself up from the floor to sit beside her on the couch. "Let's table that conversation. All we'll find there is more questions and frustration. We have no way of figuring out motivation with that."

She shook her head, waving her hands as if to erase their words from the air. "Okay. Since we can't investigate *that* any further, can we just assume it's related to Jordan and go from there?"

"We have nothing to go on with that either." He must have seen something in her face because he took a deep breath. But his tone was more humoring than anything. "Fine. Let's focus there. So, essentially the same street corner, though the car came from the opposite direction, right?"

She nodded, nibbling the inside of her cheek, not even caring that it was an annoying habit he'd pointed out so many times. "Was there anything distinctive about the car?"

He snorted. "I was a little busy trying to stay alive."

Unnecessarily snippy, and she could tell he knew it. He rolled his shoulders and took another deep breath.

"From what the police gathered from witnesses, it was a black sedan of some sort." He shrugged.

She got the sense that maybe he was more bothered by the whole thing than he'd let on. Was it just the fear that he'd almost died? Or something else?

"Not helpful, I know."

"I get it. Committing details to memory wasn't high on your priority list." She put her hand on his arm. "Maybe I can use my connection with Detective Brant to find out more information. Getting him involved might help get things moving on that investigation too."

Luke didn't answer. He just stared at her hand on him.

"I should probably go to bed," he said finally.

She nodded, but neither of them moved. "Are you going to be okay?"

He smirked. "Trading that question today."

"We're both struggling."

The silence filled the room, and they sat in it for what felt like a long time. No way to assuage each other's pain. But they could understand it, if given the chance.

"Tell me," she said, her voice soft.

His intake of breath was sharp. She thought it would just pour from him, whatever was hurting more than the physical aspect of his ordeal that day. But he didn't say anything.

Instead he lifted his eyes to look at her, seeming to memorize her face. Or maybe looking for the differences again. She didn't feel as self-conscious as she thought she would.

He lightly brushed her hair back from her face, wincing as if in pain, then traced a finger down her cheek to her chin to tilt her face up. Slowly, hesitatingly, he drew close to her and brushed his lips ever so slightly against hers.

Something told her the moment was fragile, and so she barely moved, mentally locking down her muscles. Every cell in her body fought against her, calling to crash into his.

How the roles reversed. This must have been what he'd been feeling those first few days—wanting someone he couldn't have because she belonged to someone else. The fact that he held back when he was *used* to being close to her was unfathomable. This was new territory for her, and the pull was so intense, she felt like her body would split in half from the warring parts of herself.

He pulled back, his sigh, long and agonized, a testament to the effort it took.

"Good night, Erin." His voice was barely audible, but maybe because the air buzzed so loudly with the tension, the need that almost drowned out everything else.

She felt a strong desire to fight him on it. To push for more. Her heart was more in control than her head. It was less out of regard for herself, this other her. Because hadn't she denied what she'd wanted for as long as she could remember?

But Luke had drawn a line. And out of respect for him, she wouldn't cross it.

So she ached. And she could tell he did, too. She could tell it would never not hurt. The want, the denial, the what-could-have-been. Hell, what *should* have been. Jordan's death had robbed her of so much.

Time stretched another moment while neither moved.

Then: "Good night, Luke."

She squeezed his hand and headed for the door.

27

A Casual Swim

LUKE

He left the bedroom window open all night. It faced a manicured part of the Baylors' yard that was rarely seen or used. Still, they made sure to pay someone to keep it clean and in-check, which he honestly thought was a waste.

He listened to the birds tittering in the trees with murderous animosity coursing through him. He lay tangled in the down comforter, half-uncovered with his hand flat against his stomach and his eyes trained at the ceiling fan that lazily looped around.

He couldn't shake his anger. It was the kind that simmered under his skin. So he'd opted not to go in to work, at least for the morning. He planned to swim some laps in the Baylors' pool. Or go for a marathon run. Anything to direct the negative energy that pulsed through him in hot waves.

If he was really being honest though, his mad was really just a form of sad. But if he sat with that thought too long, the motivation to move, to *breathe*, disappeared.

Something happened yesterday, beyond his life flashing

before his eyes. Such a stupid euphemism. That was not what he'd experienced. There was no highlight reel of his greatest—or even his worst—moments.

It was simply the flash of Erin's face. From that trip they took to the gulf coast, when the sun had kissed freckles across her nose, and her hair had that wavy look to it from the salt water. No makeup as she glanced back at him, the sunset just behind her. The smile on her face was private, just for him, a secret beckoning to be discovered.

That was what had nearly killed him. To hell with the driver of the car—intended murder or not. His heart, his memories, sought to do him in with a slower, more tortuous death.

Because he had no idea if he'd ever get back to her. And no matter how hard he pretended, the Erin here would never quite be the same. There was an irrevocable shift in who she was and the way she saw the world. It didn't matter how much time passed, or how hard she worked to get back to herself, the core of who she was would always be something different after losing her brother.

And this, he realized, was like mourning a death too. It hadn't occurred to him before, and maybe he hadn't really accepted that he might not get back, that he could lose his Erin and their life forever.

He'd struggled to truly understand what losing Jordan had done to Erin, to her family. That loss would never really slide home until he'd been stuck in this timeline long enough.

But this was what had finally gotten him. Well and truly knocked him to his metaphorical and literal knees.

After Erin left the night before, he'd taken a cold shower to douse any craving he'd felt for her, then turned it ridiculously hot to loosen his tensed muscles. Afterward, he'd just collapsed to the floor and crawled his way to bed. At first, it seemed like a stress response after his ordeal. But the way he felt upon waking proved it was more.

And the pain was so unbearable, it had morphed into a rage beyond anything he could comprehend.

He watched the slow swoop of the fan as it revolved once more before deciding he needed to get out of bed and burn off some of his fury. He opted for the pool, reasoning that the cool water might lower his emotional temperature as much as the physical.

He found a pair of swim shorts in the impeccably, and largely empty, dresser in the bedroom. They fit well enough.

He dove into the water with abandon and pounded out lap after lap. He didn't bother counting. It was merely the drive to reduce the anguish that seemed stamped into his bones like a brand.

He wasn't sure how long he had even been going, though he was starting to feel the fatigue settle in, when he caught a glimpse of a feminine figure standing at the edge of the pool. He nearly collided with the wall, scraping his arm against the rough concrete, and came up sputtering.

Gloria Baylor had the soured look of someone who was too sober for their own preference. Her lounge wear communicated her intimate acquaintance with money, a billowing pair of linen pants topped by a silk tank. A sheer kimono fluttered in the light breeze.

"It's been a number of years, Lucas, but I'd recognized that overly wide stroke anywhere. Watching you all those summers keeps those things in my memory." The imperious look she gave him was accentuated by the thin, manicured eyebrow she raised.

Gloria had been an expert swimmer, even slated for the Olympics in her early years. So, of course, she always had something to say about his form.

"Mrs. Baylor" He coughed, wiping the water from his face. "Good morning."

In her hand was a champagne glass that sparkled in the sunlight. So a mimosa, which was at least socially acceptable for this time of morning. Erin hadn't given much indication about what her drinking looked like on a day-to-day basis, but he'd imagine she wasn't constantly as inebriated as she'd been the last time he'd seen her.

She lifted her chin a fraction. Spending too much time with this timeline's Hank, Luke thought.

"You're swimming like you're outrunning a shark."

"A demon, more like." He said it almost under his breath, but he could tell she'd caught it.

"Why don't you join me for a drink? Sounds like you might need it." She didn't give him the chance to respond. Her kimono billowed out behind her as she turned on her heel to head inside.

So he launched himself up out of the pool and snatched the towel off one of the lounge chairs where he'd tossed it earlier and began to dry off. He made his way toward the open French doors Gloria had disappeared through, rubbing his hair with the towel.

He didn't dare step in without being invited, especially not when he was still dripping. The house had a museum-like feel to it when he glanced in—not at all the way it felt back home. It wasn't a funhouse by any means, but it was definitely warmer than the vibe he was getting here.

From the shadowed recesses Gloria emerged, a second

mimosa held lightly between her fingers. She was slim, like her daughter, though not quite as tall. They both had that athletic build that lent itself to speed and grace.

Gloria raised her brow again, giving Luke the once-over. "Well, you certainly aren't a teenage boy any more. And you don't look like the derelict my husband seems to think you are."

He took the glass she offered, though he didn't actually want it. "Um. Thanks?"

She waved a slender hand. "I just mean that I would have a hard time believing you have the kind of problems he claims you do."

Luke decided to be wise instead of answering "ditto." He took a sip of the unwanted mimosa instead. Girly brunch drink. He'd rather just have the O.J. straight up.

But as he took in her appearance, trying not to make it seem like he was giving her such an appraisal, he could actually see the marks of her problem. Her face was more weathered, like she was constantly dehydrated. Her hair was noticeably thinner as well.

"I suppose you're no longer dripping," Gloria said. "Feel free to come inside." She turned from him again to retreat into the living room, dim and cool with its minimalist beach feel.

He wondered as he stepped in whether she was bothered by his presence. If her struggle came from a need to bury her feelings about the loss of her son, surely Luke being there would be the reminder of what was and what could have been.

"What are you doing with yourself these days?" she asked, as if this were a high school reunion or something.

He hovered awkwardly around the edges of the room as she settled onto a tufted chaise across from him. "Nothing terribly important."

That was as safe an answer as he could think of.

What could he say? That he was investigating her son's murder? Trying to find a way back to an alternate reality? Doing administrative busywork for her daughter to pay the bills while he loafed in their guesthouse?

"I understand you've struggled a bit since Jordan passed."

He tried not to let his surprise show at her easy mention of his name. "Haven't we all?"

She smirked, more catlike than with humor, and he wondered just how much trouble he could get himself into without much effort.

Luke thought back to the conversation he'd had with his sister, when he'd asked about the accident and what had happened to the Luke here. "I blamed myself for what happened."

Gloria looked away at that, her breath hitching for a second. "Part of me did, too," she admitted softly. "I've been thinking about that a lot. And that conversation we had."

He stilled. Obviously he knew nothing of a conversation they might have had, but dread coiled in his stomach.

"I regret a lot of things in my life. But lately I've come to understand the kinds of burdens I've put on the people around me." She paused, staring hard at something to her left. Finally, she looked at him, then stood. "Luke, I said some awful things, put blame on you where it didn't belong. We all could have done something, anything differently. Who knows if any of it would have made a difference?"

Even though this wasn't his story, and would only ever be a small part of his life if he had his way, he felt the anger come alive at her admission. Anger for his other self, and what kind of pain she'd caused a young man. How had this ruined his life, besides driving him so far away from Erin that nothing would ever put them in the same orbit?

He couldn't think like that. Who knew if he would have ended up with her anyway? That was a heavy grief between them. And a constant reminder to each other of what they'd lost.

But the trajectory of his life, the struggle with addiction, might not have been there if not for. . .

"I understand if you don't forgive me."

Luke looked at Gloria again. The shimmer of tears were in her eyes, and that gut clench hit him as it always did when a woman he loved cried. Because, of course, he loved her. In his world, she was his best friend's mother, his second mom, the woman who'd brought the love of his life into the world.

But he was still angry. He moved across the room for some space, to clear his head of the wild and paradoxical emotions warring inside of him.

On the floating mantle above the fireplace sat only a couple of pictures. One of Jordan—his high school photo. Luke knew that some day, seeing it would be the gut punch it must have been to the rest of them.

The other one was more recent, and it did knock the breath out of him. It was of Erin standing with a blond man. Her left hand was placed against his chest at the perfect angle for her engagement ring to catch the light.

So, this was the fiancé. Good looking guy, sure. Hard to gauge much else. Something tickled in the back of his mind though. Familiarity. Couldn't place why. But maybe the guy just had one of those faces.

Gloria came up beside him, her eyes on the picture. "You don't owe me an explanation, but is part of the reason for your mad laps. . . this?"

He turned to look at her, and she met his gaze full-on. No shame there, though he hadn't doubted her apology. But Baylors didn't dwell in their weaknesses, and they certainly didn't grovel.

"It was always obvious that you cared for her, you know. We all knew it."

That was news to him. Although he shouldn't be surprised. Jordan had admitted as much the night he'd given his permission. Hank and Gloria had taken it in stride, no real change in their behavior toward him when he and Erin had made it official at the end of that summer. He'd always supposed it was because he'd practically grown up in their house. Why would they act differently?

"I don't know if it would have worked with what happened," Luke said, drawing his mind back to this moment, what he knew of this world. "It doesn't matter any more."

"Doesn't it?"

This response reminded him more of the Gloria he knew. Her answers, her advice were hard-won. Mostly because she liked to only give the slightest hint and make them work for the rest. Which made him view even this weakened, underestimated Gloria with some modicum of respect. What wealth of knowledge had Erin overlooked because she saw her mother as needing to be cared for instead of as someone to speak into her life? Would either be struggling as they were?

"The past doesn't," he finally answered.

She seemed to understand. "So what about right now?"

He sighed, his anger now gone. He felt tired. Trapped. Homesick to the bone.

"There are a lot of roadblocks right now." Which was as honest as he could be at the moment. And it was accurate enough, though it felt more insurmountable than that. If he never got back, God forbid—and his stomach lurched at the very thought—could he overcome them? Erin could break it off with this fiancé, but how could they move forward after that, after everything?

He could and would love any incarnation of Erin. But she would never be the *right* Erin. And that was hard. Painful. Could he ever move past that fact? Would she ever feel secure that he wasn't thinking about the other version? He never wanted to do that to her.

"I'm sorry, Mrs. Baylor. I'm not great company today. It's been a difficult. . . " How long had it been? ". . . week."

She tossed back an unladylike gulp of mimosa as if in toast to his words. "Take care, Luke. Use the guesthouse as long as you need."

He didn't want to need it for another minute. He handed her his half-empty glass and made his way back outside, the brightness of the sun burning his eyes as if to confirm that this place was just a level of Hell designed especially for him.

Part of Luke didn't care to find answers about Jordan's death. Not part, he admitted. Right now, he didn't give a shit about anything that was happening in this world.

With a determined set to his shoulders, he marched back to the guest house, stripping the swim shorts as soon as he got to the bathroom. He took a quick shower and called an Uber, which arrived while his hair was still dripping.

28

Answers

LUKE

His driver tried to strike up a friendly conversation as they drove, but Luke's mood shut it down pretty quickly with his one-word answers. He couldn't spare the brain power to feel bad.

The Uber dropped him at the bar downtown where he'd started off this nightmare, and he barely acknowledged the driver's farewell. Poor guy made a valiant effort there, but Luke just couldn't reciprocate.

He looked up at the sign, assured that the bar was, indeed, the same as in his world. He strode toward the door, but it was locked. He checked the hours of operation. Too early, then. He wasn't sure what he'd find inside anyway. Some kind of time vortex or wormhole or something? Besides, it wasn't here that he'd been transported.

He chewed his thumb for a minute, looking around. He needed to find something, anything, that might be amiss. Maybe he should retrace his steps.

He glanced in either direction before jogging across the

street. Keeping his mind focused on every detail of each building he passed, he made his way the couple of blocks he'd walked that night.

But wait. The homeless guy.

Luke skidded to a halt and turned back. The corner was empty. Too early for anyone to be there. No chance for begging money from passersby when there wasn't enough activity.

Could it have been that guy?

Luke felt twitchy just thinking about it, remembering how the man had followed him and appeared just when Luke was about to head home.

He continued his walk, his senses more alert for the noises and sights around him, paranoia making him jittery. Soon, the parking lot of his office building came into view, and his eagerness to get there and look around overtook his nerves.

As before, cars were lined up, shining under the summer sun, unassuming and so utterly normal-looking. He cut across the pavement just as he'd done that night, though he had to dodge more cars since it was the middle of a work day.

He glared at the unfamiliar name above his usual parking space, hating that it wasn't his own. Another reminder that he was in the wrong freaking place.

He circled the lot, not really knowing what he was looking for, but the desperation demanded he scrutinize every detail anyway. Two, three, four loops later, and his stream of cuss words had led him nowhere.

He gave a guttural roar before squatting down to grip his head in his hands. How was he supposed to get back if every lead he had was a dead end, literally and figuratively?

His phone buzzed from within his pocket, and he automatically reached for it.

You coming in??

Erin. Of course.

She hadn't said anything until now. Maybe knowing he'd needed the space. But that could only go for so long, he supposed. There were pressing matters at work. And since this investigation into Jordan's death and his near hit-and-run yesterday had hit a wall, he supposed he might as well concentrate his frustrated energy on *something*.

Be there in about ten, he typed back.

He admitted, even if only to himself, that he didn't want to face her. He hated how rejected she was, how barely in control of himself he'd been.

But the only way forward was to move. So he stood up and set his jaw, then his mind. He turned toward Baylor Industries and began walking, determination more out of self-will than anything.

By the time he got there, he'd wrestled his emotions down to manageable. Erin's office door was closed when he arrived, and he could tell as he passed that Hank was in there with her. Best not to disturb *that* meeting.

Probably better in the long run as his mind flipped gears again. He flung the chair away from his temporary desk and slid in, using the momentum to glide right back into place at the computer. He glanced at Erin's shut door again as he wiggled the mouse to wake the computer and log in.

There was a list of to-dos on the desk beside the keyboard, which he ignored for the moment. Busywork that would be done in an hour's time, he was sure.

First he pulled up a search engine. His fingers hovered over the keys for half a second. Hank and Gloria were not really the traditional type, but Hank's mother had been raised in the south. Her southern belle drawl was unmistakable every time he'd interacted with her. And because of her upbringing, the woman was as traditional as they came.

His eyes flickered to the closed door again. He didn't want Erin to know what he was searching for, and he definitely didn't want to draw Hank's attention either.

Nana Baylor was as reliable as she was polite. It only took a quick search of the Baylor name in conjunction with "engagement." No one did newspaper announcements of engagements and weddings any more. Not anyone he knew, anyway. But Nana insisted on tradition.

The day they'd told her he'd proposed, she immediately started putting together an announcement for the paper. And because of her age, and the inevitable loneliness that came after losing a spouse and a number of friends, they let her have her way.

And sure enough, she came through for him. Some of it was curiosity, some of it was his jealousy, and some was that odd inkling of recognition he'd experienced looking at the picture. But he needed to know this guy's name. And he wanted to know a host of other things.

Nathan Dunn. Clean-cut, chiseled jaw, blond hair combed just right.

He did a quick search of the name and had immediate results. He was a consultant at his father's firm. So a marriage between heirs of two empires. Classic nepotism meets blue blood politics.

But here is where he paused. Because the name was connected with another one, and it was one he definitely recognized.

Bruce Dunn was known for many things, namely his foray into local politics with an effort to push for the big leagues. But most importantly for the family scandals that came to light during his bid for governor.

The scandal he remembered best was that his son crashed his car while under the influence his senior year of college. He'd already been kicked out of a previous school for something similar, though he couldn't remember what. Come to think of it, he remembered that, because of it, he'd gotten an earful from his mother as if he were out partying every weekend during his own senior year, though he'd been swamped with classes plus an internship and seeing Erin when he could.

Crashed his car while drunk. Luke's nerves began to tingle.

Someone with a lot of money and power was stalling out an investigation into the killing of an innocent college student by what appeared to have been a drunk driver. Like maybe someone with a multi-million dollar consulting business and political ties?

Did Bruce have another son? Or was Nathan the only one? Either way, a sick feeling snaked in his gut. It meant a possible tie between Erin's fiancé's family and her brother's murder.

Luke couldn't find anything about another son, or even other children for Bruce Dunn. The sick feeling grew until he thought he'd throw up.

Kicked out of his first college. Could it have been Luke's own alma mater? Is that what else had triggered his memory? *Had he seen this guy before?*

He did another search and found an out-of-state university listed as where Nathan Dunn had graduated. But his anxiety didn't abate. How many people transferred schools if their first choice wasn't working out?

Not to mention that the Dunns were local. The first and obvious choice would be the school nearby. Though it was small, it had a great reputation.

Now he felt like maybe he was onto something. The sick feeling mingled with anticipation, and he wondered if this is what detectives went through when they had caught a lead that was snowballing. Morbid eagerness to get to the answer.

He clicked through some other links, desperately in search of Nathan Dunn's face, but in his earlier years. Was he familiar only because of the family scandal? Or was it something more? Had he gone to Luke's school, been in the same program? Or did he know Jordan somehow? What was the connection?

He clicked through page after page, digging deeper. Most people never went past the first page or two of search results. He went dozens deep. And hit pay-dirt.

It was a connection that came at him from left-field. One he never would have made. An old high school dance photo, connected to an old social media page. After all, didn't they say nothing on the internet could truly be erased?

Nathan was thinner with long hair that swooped over his forehead and partly into his eyes. The smile was unmistakable, a mild but recognizable under bite.

But it was the girl that shocked Luke. Her chestnut hair had that overly curled look popular back then, the skirt of her formal dress falling in tucked up waves. He remembered Erin's having a similar style.

Oh, Kelly, he thought. Jordan's college girlfriend, who later became his wife in Luke's timeline.

She'd dated Nathan Dunn. Had he really been drunk when

he'd run Jordan down? Or was it more? Revenge for stealing his high school sweetheart?

There was no doubt now.

Oh, God. Had he *known* who Erin was? Was it a sick game to him? To marry the sister of the man he killed—intentionally or not?

At least Luke knew Erin was safe for now, tucked up in her office. Was she still in a meeting with her father? Should Luke interrupt to tell her? Should he tell Hank too?

He looked up, but the door to her office stood open and no one was inside.

He shot out of his seat, craning his neck to look across the mass of cubicles as a lightning bolt of fear shot through him.

"Shit, shit, shit," he muttered as he jogged to her office, just to make sure it was truly empty. "Where's Erin?" he asked the nearest person.

"I think she headed for the elevator. Whatever she talked about with Mr. Baylor had them both pretty heated."

He registered the woman's face—roundish with glasses, an eagerness in her eyes that showed her appetite for the gossip she'd just shared.

"Do you know where she went?" He worked hard to keep the demand from his tone.

She still seemed taken aback. "I'm not sure. . . "

"I think she said she needed to discuss something with Nathan." Hank Baylor's cool voice betrayed very little emotion. But it made a shiver run rampant down Luke's spine as he spun to face the older man.

"What?"

Hank's eyes narrowed at Luke's barely contained hysterical tone. "I imagine she's about to ruin that man's day. She's on a tear about doing what's right for her and no one else."

So that explained Hank's demeanor. His little girl finally stood up to him, and he was not taking it well. For anyone who didn't know him well enough, he seemed no more than unimpressed. But this was beyond even anger. Hank Baylor had been rejected, put in his place for once, and he was livid. Good for her.

But, crap if Luke's pride distracted him from what the bigger picture—and huge problem—was.

"Where?" he demanded.

Hank lifted his head and raised a brow. It was like he was looking at a curious, but disgusting bug. "Nathan's office, most likely. What's this about?"

Did he have time to explain?

"I think she's in danger."

"From who? Nathan?" Hank scoffed.

"I need your car keys, Hank."

"Excuse me?" Hank turned his body slightly away as if Luke had already reached for them.

"Life or death, Hank." He'd give him three seconds to decide before he'd dial an Uber on his way out the door. He'd steal a car if he had to.

Something in his eyes must have been convincing because Hank slowly reached into his blazer and pulled out a set of keys.

Luke snatched them from his hand and took off at a sprint. "You should call Detective Brant and have him meet me there," he called over his shoulder. He didn't bother making sure Hank complied. All he cared about was getting to Erin as fast as he could.

While he rode the elevator down, cursing himself for not taking the stairs, he pulled up Nathan's office on his phone to find the address. He assumed it was at his father's consulting firm, the name of which he recalled from his earlier research about the guy.

He bolted from the elevator as soon as the door opened, almost knocking a man over who was waiting to get on.

"Sorry!" he called, pushing his way outside. He spotted Hank's Jaguar almost immediately, thanking the gods of parallel timelines that Hank's taste in cars seemed universal.

29

Nepotism

ERIN

She was riding the high telling her dad off had given her. Erin had spent at least the last ten years kowtowing to her father's every whim, even submitting to his authority on what she had been doing for the company instead of taking on the role she'd gone to school for and had planned to take up as soon as she'd proven her worth.

Though there certainly was an element of nepotism at play—she had been guaranteed a job at Baylor Industries upon graduation—her father never would have let her into an upper position she hadn't earned. She'd started at the bottom. And then he'd subtly bullied her into jobs she'd hated. And she'd never even noticed.

Because she'd been too focused on trying not to rock the boat after her brother had died. After all, it was Jordan and Erin *together* who were meant to take over Baylor. Her father had been preparing them for it since they were young. But he'd had no contingency if something happened to one of them.

Of course, no one could have predicted losing Jordan. But

what if one of them had decided to do something else? It had never even been a thought for either of them, and especially for her once Jordan was gone. Who else would have taken over Baylor, if not her?

And after all this time, and her tireless efforts, she realized she didn't want any of it.

She wasn't sure what she wanted yet, but it sure as hell wasn't anything she currently possessed. And so, she'd told Hank Baylor she was out. And he'd been stunned, sputtered even. At a loss for words, probably for one of the first times in his life.

She'd even left him standing there in her office, mouth slightly agape, riding that high right out to the elevator and then her car. While she had that heady feeling and the confidence, she needed to call things off with Nathan.

She'd seen Luke had come in, absorbed in whatever he was doing at his desk, more engrossed than she'd ever seen him while doing the admin work she always unloaded on him. And because it had nothing and everything to do with him, she snuck past him to do this without his input or help.

Her knuckles were white on the steering wheel, her heart was beating hard, yet simultaneously, she felt like she was floating. She was probably driving a little too fast. Probably too worked up to do this right. But she was so afraid of losing her nerve.

She whipped into the parking lot, swung around into the nearest empty space, coming in a little too quickly for someone who was walking across the parking spot. The woman gave her the stink eye, and Erin mouthed an apology before pulling all the way forward in a more cautious manner.

Taking her time gathering her things, she focused on deep

and slow breaths. For once, the anxiety and anticipation didn't make her stomach ache. It was doing flips all right. But there wasn't even a phantom stab, which made her feel like she had finally done the right thing for herself.

She got out of the car, finally feeling more calm, more focused and assured. The lobby of the building was large, clean, minimalist. A waiting area with luxurious leather seats sat in one corner and a sweeping, large desk curved in front of her where two receptionists with headsets were engrossed in their computer screens. Both beamed at her as soon as she approached.

"Ms. Baylor," the brunette—Ingrid—said. Her smile seemed more forced than usual. "Is Mr. Dunn expecting you?"

Erin tried not to let her own smile stiffen. "No, I don't imagine he is."

The receptionist slowly reached for her phone. "Let me just check. . . "

Erin's smile disappeared. That was definitely odd. Not that she made a habit of dropping by unexpectedly, but it had never been an issue, even if it meant she'd have to wait in his office until he was available.

She was too impatient for whatever nonsense this was, so she went straight to the elevator. She needed to get the difficult conversation over with. The craving to get her full freedom propelled her forward, even as the Ingrid stood and called after her.

She got on the elevator and pressed the *close* button four times for good measure, and the doors slid shut in the receptionist's irritated face. Erin smirked and leaned back against the wall as she rode up.

On the third floor, she stepped out, glancing at the executive assistant's desk. The phone there was ringing, but no one was in sight. Erin assumed it was the downstairs receptionist trying to pull the assistant in to stop her.

Despite no one being around, she speed-walked to Nathan's office just in case someone made it back and thwarted her plans. She glanced down the hall in both directions before slipping into his office as quietly as possible.

It was empty, the richly furnished office impeccably clean, as always. She didn't sit right away but opted to wander around for a few minutes, her eyes roving the space with more scrutiny than usual.

She rubbed the leaf of a plant on the book shelf between her fingers. The rest of the shelf was filled with classic antique tomes, most of which she knew Nathan had never read, and caught herself nibbling her lip.

The more she thought about it as she walked down the row of bookshelves, the more the receptionist's behavior bothered her. Had Nathan warned them that she wasn't to be allowed up? What reason would there be for that? He shouldn't have any clue what the reason was for her visit, let alone that she would come by. And avoiding her during the day would only lead to a confrontation later on.

She supposed she should have waited until the work day was finished, but here she was, casually looking through everything in the room as if it would tell her what was going on, while the eagerness to get the conversation over with buzzed under her skin.

It wasn't long until the door opened and Nathan came in. By the look on his face, she knew he'd been prepared to find her there. The question was whether someone had retrieved him to meet her or if he'd been coming back to his office anyway. It shouldn't have mattered much, but for some reason it did.

Because she felt it. A change in the atmosphere. A tension that was unfamiliar and hard to characterize, and she worried he knew what this was about.

Nathan moved into the room with a deliberate slowness, his eyes locked on her like she was a mountain lion deciding whether he would be a good snack.

Despite the fact that she stood by the floor-to-ceiling bookcase against the far wall, she did feel poised for a fight of sorts. But mostly because of that feeling.

He went to his desk, but didn't sit, his fingertips brushing the lacquered surface. It was obvious he was trying to be casual, but he definitely wasn't relaxed.

"Erin. What brings you by?" he asked.

No endearments. No hug, no kiss. Did he suspect what was up? How was that possible? He'd been the distracted one the day before, leaving their date early. And she hadn't even hit her realization by that point.

His fingers tapped silently on the top of his desk. Why was he nervous?

"I wanted to talk to you about something," she said slowly, feeling the need to be cautious, though not to spare his feelings. Some part of her warned that something else was going on, something hanging in the air like too much perfume.

Danger.

Not from him, exactly, though she couldn't explain why or understand what it meant. It had to be her mind playing tricks, trying to dissuade her from what she was going to do and the discomfort that would follow.

Still, a tingle cascaded down her spine, and her pulse picked up. Her eyes slid to the door as she analyzed whether she could make it there before he did. Then she appraised him to see if he seemed like he'd try to stop her.

The notion was absurd. Had she really cultivated such a need to please everyone that she couldn't even do this one thing for herself?

"Is it so important you needed to come now?" Nathan asked. "We could get dinner later." He looked at the door too, but more like he expected someone else to come through it.

Yes, later, her mind chanted.

But she'd come for a reason, and she reminded herself that she was just losing her nerve. It had to be now.

"I need to get this off my chest," she said, as much for herself as him.

She moved toward the desk, though it was more to get closer to the door than him, just to ease her irrational impulse.

He sighed and sat, but he still didn't relax.

She sat too because that was the normal thing to do. Maybe it would help him loosen up, help soften the blow. She didn't want this to seem like a power play. It would be such a *Baylor* thing to lord it over him, to drive the point home with haughty self-righteousness. And she wanted to be something else for once.

With a composure that was entirely manufactured, she pulled her engagement ring off and set it on the desk.

Nathan's gaze followed her movements, taking in the ring as it wobbled where she'd put it. It didn't seem to register. Or maybe it did, but he didn't seem hurt or surprised. Which should have bothered her more than it did.

A resignation settled into his features. And something else. That unnameable thing again.

He took a breath and raised his eyes to her. "Because of your brother?"

Her brows crashed down over her eyes at the confusing turn of conversation. "My brother?"

Ah, there it was. Plain in his eyes was fear. Perhaps his surprise made his guard slip to reveal what was really there. But she was even more thrown by that.

Her chest tightened with her own fear, her uncertainty, and her inability to comprehend what was happening. She wasn't sure why she should be afraid, but her mind told her it was appropriate.

That danger she'd sensed before wasn't imagined, wasn't her own mind sabotaging her efforts. Nathan's words reverberated in her head, trying to knock some kind of understanding in her jumbled thoughts.

"What about my brother, Nathan?" Her words cracked on the air like a whip as her stomach clenched. She shot to her feet, which was probably the wrong choice, but her emotions dictated she move

He stood too, his hands extending toward her. He seemed unsure what he should be doing, his eyes going wide.

She wondered, too. Did he want to restrain her? To calm her?

"It really was an accident, I swear it was," he stammered, a stumbling attempt at backpedaling.

This couldn't be real.

"What did you do?" She sucked in a breath, needing a second, needing more air, needing this to be a dream. "Nathan, *what did you do?*"

She was going to hyperventilate. Or maybe strangle him.

His hands still hung suspended between them, and he shook

his head. "I didn't. . . "

The door opened behind her, and she twisted to see who would come in.

30

Bad Daddy

ERIN

She knew there was a wild look in her eyes, but Bruce looked more resigned than surprised, his lips thinning.

It didn't calm her. In fact, she felt the air in the room shift again. Someone else's fear mingling with her own. No, not fear. Sheer panic.

She looked at Nathan. He was a trapped animal, frozen by the sight of his father. Which told her who was really in charge here. She knew Bruce was a bit of a master manipulator and that Nathan jumped whenever he said to. But she didn't realize it could go this far.

Oh, God, how far had it gone?

"Erin, how lovely to see you," Bruce said conversationally. "It's unfortunate we have to get into this here, but I can't control everything." He looked at Nathan, and his eyes grew flinty.

She was sure her heart stopped for just a moment.

Bruce looked down at the engagement ring on the desk and frowned. "Has he confessed, then?"

Terror held her words hostage. She hadn't gotten that far in her thought process, though it must have been some sort of protection mechanism because it had all been right there, even if he hadn't said the words. But none of it had seemed to compute until the word *confess* finally triggered the zip of connection in her mind.

She shifted her gaze to Nathan, her fear disintegrating for a moment as all the pieces clicked together to form the picture. His face turned down in shame and guilt, and an ungodly fury came over her.

"You? You're the reason my brother is dead?" God, she felt sick. "And you *knew*? You knew you killed my brother, and you. . . " She shivered, revulsion pulsing through every cell in her body.

Because he'd touched her, been intimate with her, been privy to her thoughts—even sometimes her grief. That thought made her the most nauseated. That he could listen to her cry about the fact that Jordan was gone, and he'd been the one who'd taken him from her.

God, she wanted to throttle him, to scream and rage, to rip this building down to its foundation with her bare hands.

"It was odd," his father said, almost disinterested.

Her eyes snapped to Bruce, and the violence that called for action leaked right out of her.

"His obsession with your family, with you." Bruce shook his head, walking forward casually, and stopped to stand between her and the door.

Watching him froze the blood in her veins.

"You knew all this time," she said, trying to keep the anger in her voice to hide that she had returned to enough rationality to realize his move was deliberate.

Because she knew now what threat she'd sensed before. Not Nathan. No, the way he was looking at his father now told her they were both in real danger from Bruce.

"My son often makes messes that I have to clean up," Bruce answered.

Nathan flinched when his father turned a baleful eye on him.

"Mr. Dunn, there's a man down here making a scene, demanding to see you."

Erin jumped at the sound of the administrative assistant's voice over the intercom.

Bruce smiled and flicked a hand at his son.

Nathan snapped to attention. When he spoke, his voice was surprisingly even, his eyes never leaving his father's face. "Thank you, Ingrid. Send him up."

Bruce looked at Erin. "I would imagine that's the old friend you've been spending so much time with lately."

The cold look in his eyes rooted Erin to the spot. She wasn't sure if he meant to make her feel guilty or to draw Nathan's attention to her. It occurred to her that he possibly just wanted her to know he was aware of what she'd been up to.

Which was chilling to think about. There was little doubt in her mind that he'd been the one to orchestrate Luke's brush with death. And that also meant he was the one stalling out the investigation into her brother's case.

Anger flared at the thought that all this time she'd been trying to get his approval. At least she understood now why he'd never warmed to her. It had nothing to do with her at all. It was all because of Nathan, his obsession, and how it had put the cover up of Jordan's death in jeopardy.

She shivered and shut her eyes against an onslaught of realization. This was who destroyed her family, ruined her happiness. She'd been about to marry her brother's killer and have been tied forever to the man who'd covered it up.

Bruce laughed, sending a chill up her spine.

"I can see it all on your face," he said, still grinning when she opened her eyes. "The disgust. It's only what I've been dealing with all this time. The screw up you almost married is the one I've spent too much time trying to fix."

His words settled over her and brought a new wave of understanding. Even some phantom sense of sympathy. It had never been quite so obvious before that Bruce felt that way about his son, but it did clarify Nathan's workaholism, his attempts to win his father's favor, the way he never quite relaxed in his presence. It didn't sound much like his efforts had mattered though.

What a sick, twisted way to live life.

And she realized too that she had been no better, but she recoiled from the thought that there was anything even remotely similar about their situations or their decisions.

The door opened behind Bruce, and he grabbed Luke by the cuff of his shirt and dragged him inside before he could react. He shoved him toward Erin and Nathan, sending him staggering.

"Welcome to the party, Lucas," Bruce said with a sneer.

He reached inside of his blazer, pulling a gun from an inner pocket, but he apparently didn't feel the need to point it directly at them. Too confident in himself and his handle over the whole situation.

It was bizarre to have Nathan lumped in with them as Bruce's victim, but she realized as she thought it that it was true.

It didn't change the fact that he was the reason her brother was gone, but she could see how things had gotten so out of control for him.

Luke was staring at her, asking a question with his eyes. He didn't seem surprised by this situation, but his concern for her was obvious.

"I'm okay," she said softly.

"For now," Bruce amended.

31

Stray

LUKE

Luke looked at Bruce, scrambling for something, anything to distract him, to stall.

"I came to tell Erin about her brother and her fiancé, but it seems like someone beat me to the punch." He grimaced. "Hadn't quite put together the dad angle, though. Other than covering up the hit-and-run, of course. Because, duh."

True enough. He'd come blazing across town, thinking only Nathan was the dangerous one. While covering up a mistake as big as his son's certainly put him in the untrustworthy category, Luke had never considered Bruce to be some sort of mastermind.

Not that he'd had much time to think through every angle. It was fairly rash of him to come without the police anyway. But all he'd thought about was Erin's safety.

Bruce scoffed. "You gotta be careful when you're asking questions, son. Never know who's on the payroll."

Luke's eyes tightened, thinking of Leo and his sandwich shop. "Or owes you his payroll."

Bruce smiled, and it was genuinely filled with mirth.

Luke swallowed back the rise of bile in his throat.

"So the fiancée and her lover," Bruce began, gesturing between Erin and Luke with his gun, "have come to break off her engagement together. Because she certainly would need more of his support."

He raised a brow at Erin as if that were a hint about something. Like maybe he *knew* what exactly had been going on between the two of them.

That boiled Luke's blood.

Luke followed Erin's gaze as it shifted to Nathan, but his face had turned to stone, as if he knew what was going on too. Or maybe because he knew what was coming next.

Bruce continued: "But, aw, poor Nathan. He was always a fragile thing." He tsked.

Nathan's eyes flashed to his father's face, and Luke hoped, mentally urged Nathan to actually do something with that reaction he'd seen there. Maybe he'd stand up. Do what was right.

Resignation dragged Nathan's shoulders into a slump, and he looked away.

Luke felt the disgust infuse his thoughts as he realized Nathan was going to take it all lying down, like an abused puppy with no hope for freedom. Had he been so victimized by his father's put-downs and schemes that he couldn't do something about it, even when his life depended on it?

"So it's to be a murder-suicide then?" Luke asked, hoping the words would provoke Nathan.

Bruce turned his attention to Luke, raising the gun. "Let's see here. Where shall we put you?" He narrowed his eyes, clicking his teeth together. "Maybe you all were just sitting.

I'll give Nathan a little dignity before he dies. He didn't blubber or beg. He pulled the gun straight from the drawer and—" Bruce imitated firing two rounds, one for each of them.

Erin flinching both times, and Luke caught the movement in his periphery. Dread solidified in his stomach as Bruce smiled once again, so confident in his plan.

But there had to be holes, had to be a way to get the upper hand.

"You really think they won't figure you out?" Luke asked, grasping. "Your assistant knows you're in here. Your money and power keep a lot of people in their place, but this seems like a stretch."

Bruce considered him with narrowed eyes. "That's a good point, Lucas. One I did think about. But I appreciate the reminder."

Before they could even begin to guess what his plan was, he pushed the barrel against the soft muscle between his pointer finger and thumb and squeezed a round off.

Erin, Nathan, and Luke all ducked toward the ground as if he'd fired a wild shot at them. Erin made eye contact with Luke, and her gaze reflected his exact feelings. They were dealing with a legit psychopath, and their efforts were probably wasted.

"I did try to wrest the gun from my poor, desperate son's hands before he took his own life, you know."

Luke's eyes went wider as Bruce gestured with his wounded hand like he'd spilled paint on it and wasn't bleeding profusely.

The insane man stepped forward and shoved the gun against Erin's temple, making Luke's gut clench.

"You need to come sit over here now." Bruce tipped his head toward a chair.

She straightened slowly and walked over to the chair he

indicated, sitting obediently.

"You, next to her."

Luke did as instructed, his eyes on the bleeding wound on the older man's hand, hoping, praying that the cavalry swooped in soon. This was getting bad fast.

"Nathan, have a seat at your desk."

Erin's ex-fiancé stared at his father with a look of such incredulity that it seemed more fitting to a comedy sketch than the horror film they were stuck in.

Bruce strode forward and pushed the barrel into Nathan's forehead, gritting his teeth. "Sit. Down."

It was the first time he'd shown any sign of disruption to his mood, and Luke thought, *finally*.

Nathan winced, but he moved to sit as his father bid and lowered his head like the coward he was.

Bruce came to stand behind him, his lip curling back. His rage came bubbling to the surface again. Aggravated by his self-inflicted wound and his son's weakness, no doubt.

"I would appreciate a little cooperation after everything I've done for you." He ground the words out between his teeth, his manic gaze blazing down on the back of Nathan's head. "Every time you screwed up, I fixed it as if it had never happened. Gave you this job, your cushy life."

Nathan didn't move his head, but his eyes lifted to Erin's. Luke clenched his whole body, watching her for a reaction, which she kept from showing as Nathan locked an intense stare onto her.

Whatever he was trying to communicate was lost on Luke, but even as he fought the jealousy and urge to guard Erin from her brother's killer, he wondered if there was more backbone in Nathan than he'd thought.

"Lucky for you, I'm even going to do this part for you," Bruce continued, positioning himself where the gun sat convincingly at a height Nathan might have held it if he were to shoot Erin and Luke.

Something in Nathan's eyes shifted, softened. He was trying to communicate something that Erin seemed incapable of comprehending because her head tilted just a fraction.

But Luke's hands tightened on the armrests of his chair, the anticipation sending thrills of electricity through him.

"I'm sorry," Nathan finally said, and Bruce stiffened.

Color had drained from Bruce's face already, and Luke could tell he'd regretted firing that shot into his hand so soon. It was unlikely to be as convincing as a defensive wound, as if he had jumped in to stop the death right after the double murder but during the suicide attempt.

But Luke sensed it—that the apology encompassed more than just what Bruce blamed him for. Being a screw-up, yes; but even beyond killing Erin's brother, as well. And Bruce must have too.

None of them anticipated the move, though.

Nathan grabbed the gun from his father's grip, and a shot blasted out of the barrel.

32

Bullet

ERIN

Erin dove to her left with no regard for dignity or the fact that she was in a dress. She was sure she'd ripped the fitted skirt in her bid for safety as a second shot ripped through the air, but it was the last thing on her mind.

Her heartbeat hammered in her ears, the panic was such a loud wave inside her head, she was unable to hear any other sound for several minutes. She simply cowered on the floor until she realized the room had gone still. She lifted her head and looked over to where Luke was sprawled to her right. But it dawned on her that he was positioned oddly. Not like he'd jumped out of his chair as she had. More like he'd fallen.

And there was. . . blood.

Her mouth went dry as a desert, and she tried to focus her mind on what was happening in the room around them. She couldn't see Nathan or his father, and she couldn't hear them either as she strained past the roar of her own pulse in her head.

She army-crawled along the floor the two feet to Luke's side.

His eyes were panic-wide and locked on her face. A blossom of blood painted the left side of his chest and across his shoulder, but she couldn't tell where the bullet had hit him. She leaned over him as horror pulsed through her. She prayed it was his shoulder as the blood seeped into the bodice of her already ruined dress.

"Luke," she whispered. "Where are you hit?"

He didn't seem capable of focusing on her, his gaze trained somewhere behind her. It took her a moment to realize it was because he was looking at someone.

She jerked around to see Nathan standing over them. The gun was hanging loosely at his side, and his expression was eerily blank. Terror jolted through her, but she realized how quiet and still everything was. And Nathan wasn't moving.

Where was Bruce?

He was the murdering maniac they should be most worried about, who'd shot himself in the hand to make sure he looked innocent. But Nathan was the one who'd killed her brother ten years ago.

Her eyes jumped back and forth between his face and the gun in his hand.

"My father is dead," he said flatly.

Even his soft words made her flinch. Luke moaned, and her attention went back to his ashen face.

"We need to call 9-1-1." Her voice was quiet. If she spoke softly, maybe, just maybe, he would help her.

She was so afraid that he wouldn't, that his plans didn't deviate much from his father's, even if he'd seemed an unwilling participant, even if he'd taken the gun from Bruce's hand.

She didn't really know him, after all.

She would never find out if her fears would be realized.

The door to his office burst open, chips of wood spraying like shrapnel into the room. Uniformed police officers flowed into the room like liquid, and her ears began to ring as they shouted at Nathan to drop the gun and get on the floor.

Simply locking eyes with Luke was all she could manage as chaos unfolded around her. This time, she could tell he wasn't focused on anything, that he was losing consciousness as quickly as his blood.

Had he lost too much? Would he ever wake up? Why hadn't she looked for a wound?

She thought all of these things in the breath between seconds as hands dragged her away from Luke.

She could have applied pressure. That's what they always did on TV, wasn't it? Should she have ripped his shirt back to find it? Or would feeling around until she found it have worked?

"Wait," she whispered as they led her out of the room. "Wait," she said again, the weight of her inaction a heavy boulder in her gut.

* * *

The word surgery still echoed in Erin's mind. Her father had come and gone with a change of clothes for her. He'd said little, but she knew now Luke had told him to call Detective Brant, that the phone call had probably saved their lives.

She dragged her finger across her bottom lip, staring absently at Luke, unconscious in the bed before her. His brow was wrinkled, and she wondered what he was dreaming about that he couldn't even relax in sleep.

Detective Brant had been by to say that Nathan had readily confessed to the shooting of his father and the hit and run that killed her brother. She asked if the sentence would be lessened in the case of Bruce's death, given that it was done in self-defense.

"He didn't claim self-defense." Brant's eyebrows pulled together as he looked at her.

"It most definitely was," she replied mildly. "I'm sure we wouldn't be alive right now if it weren't for him." She recounted all that she'd seen, that he'd fought his father for the gun, that it had gone off and the stray bullet was the one the surgeons had worked to remove from a spot right above Luke's heart.

Her voice hitched on that last part. "Lucky" was the word she'd heard numerous times over the last couple of hours, as she'd sat in the fluorescent lighting that gave her no real concept of time. She'd spent some time scrubbing the blood from under her fingernails, wiping the smear of it from her neck. She wasn't even sure how it had gotten there.

But she wasn't sure about a lot of details. She barely remembered what had happened from the moment they'd pulled her away from Luke. Her ears had been ringing, her hands shaking. Had she thrown up? "Shock" someone had said.

Now that the dust had settled, why didn't she feel better? Why wasn't she relieved? The man who'd killed her brother—that ragged, painful question had finally been answered—was behind bars. Shouldn't she feel some kind of release of pressure?

Maybe it would come later, when it really sank in. Would this fix anything though? Would it make her mother better? Heal her relationship with her father?

She realized, somewhere in the back of her mind, she'd

expected things to miraculously feel right inside of her. That justice would be the thing to stop her grief and heal her heart.

But she saw now that it was a process that only she'd had the control over all this time.

Luke groaned, and her gaze snapped into focus. She scooted her chair close to his bed and slid her hand into his.

"Water?" he croaked.

She grabbed the cup from the nearby nightstand and stuck the straw into his mouth.

Without opening his eyes, he thanked her with a smile. "I feel like shit."

"Getting shot and having emergency surgery might do that to you," she answered, unable to hold her own smile back.

"Surgery?" He grunted. "That explains the cotton in my mouth." He smacked his lips. "Wait, did you say 'shot'?"

"You don't remember that part?" She leaned closer.

"Hmmm. Not really. Kinda."

For no reason she could explain, his response made her chest tighten and tears spring to her eyes. She brushed a stray lock of his dark hair from his forehead and trailed that finger down the side of his face.

A nurse bustled in, followed by a cheery doctor. "Mr. Pearson, welcome back!"

Erin pulled back and released his hand to give the nurse space to work. They went over post-op information with him and checked his vitals. Eventually, she slipped out into the hall because the frenetic activity was overstimulating to her already frayed nerves.

It had been way too much that day. On top of too much for over a week. Is that all the time Luke had been here? It felt too long and not long enough.

Wasn't it his presence that had led her to her self-realization? He'd been the one who'd found out about Nathan, too. His presence in that room had saved her life.

She owed him so much.

When the nurse and doctor left the room, she quietly came back in. He seemed to be resting, and she almost left, her chest constricting.

But then he smiled, his eyes still closed. "Getting shot is exhausting."

"I imagine so," she murmured, moving closer.

He reached out, and she took his hand.

"At least they give me the good stuff for the pain," he mumbled, tugging her lightly, weakly. It took her a moment to realize he wanted her to lie down on the bed beside him.

Despite his rejection only—what? The day before?—she obliged because he was wounded, because he'd done so much for her, and because she was still too heartsick to turn away comfort.

She curled herself against him on the edge of the bed, feeling like she could fall off at any moment. And still, she dozed, even with the nurses who came in to check vitals. They blessedly left her alone, and she drifted into a deep enough sleep that when they shook her violently awake, she was as disoriented as if she'd be in a coma.

"Where is he?"

Erin lifted her head from the pillow, blinking against the bleariness of sleep, trying to orient her mind.

"Where is he?" the nurse said again.

"Who?" Erin asked, bewildered.

"Luke Pearson. The patient."

Erin sat up, completely awake, panic sending her stomach

into her throat. She was sprawled out in the bed, alone.

33

Disappear Here

LUKE

Pain was what woke Luke this time. He felt worse upon waking than he had right after his surgery, merely groggy and sluggish from the aftereffects of anesthesia. His shoulder was on fire, agony radiating down his arm, even into his fingers.

He was also lying flat, on top of the covers, cold and alone.

Squinting, he looked around the room. All of the machines and equipment that had been blinking or beeping earlier were turned off and stored against the wall, nothing hooked into any part of him. Which was odd.

Given his pain level, there should have been more meds pumping into him. Or at least someone ready to give him something.

He winced as he pushed himself to a seated position to find the remote that would adjust his bed and give him the call button, both of which he took care of in short order. He needed more pillows. Hadn't his arm been propped up before?

And Erin. Where was she? Waking up completely miserable had been softened by her willingness to snuggle with him in the bed earlier. Misery was an understatement now. And what a blow it was to find she was gone.

The door to his room stood open, and a nurse poked her head around to look at Luke, her mildly perplexed expression turning to alarm.

"What are you doing in here?" she demanded, marching into the room.

Luke blinked. "I beg your pardon?" The words came slowly on a rasp.

The nurse looked him over. "What happened to you? Where's your chart? Who are you? What room are you supposed to be in?"

Luke grimaced. "I can only answer part of that. But before I do, can you get me some water and pain meds or something? I'm dying here."

"Dying?" The nurse scoffed. She took in his gown, his wrapped shoulder in the sling. "Hmm."

"Please."

"I have to call a doctor in here." She backed up to the door slowly, her eyes still on Luke.

"And maybe find Erin. The woman who was here earlier. She'd be helpful right about now." He couldn't help the irritation showing in his voice now.

The nurse disappeared.

Pain. Agony. Just from moving, sitting himself up. He started inhaling through his nose and exhaling heavily out of his mouth, imagining he looked like a fish out of water.

He gritted his teeth, about ready to get out of the damn bed and find his meds himself when the nurse returned with a doctor in tow.

Thick lenses magnified already large brown eyes in the

middle-aged woman's face. Her mouth turned down, the confusion mild, like she was trying to figure out how she'd gotten a stain on her shirt rather than who Luke was.

"Sir, can you tell me your name?" The doctor pulled out her flashlight and checked Luke's pupils, unruffled as Luke continued his breathing routine and exhaled in her face.

"Luke Pearson," he managed through his teeth.

The doctor nodded, giving his body a thorough once-over, avoiding his shoulder. She saved that for last. "Lean back and try to relax. Anything else you can tell me about yourself?"

Luke clenched his jaw as the doctor investigated his surgery site. "Pisces. Favorite color is blue. I love Italian more than any other type of food, especially lasagna."

The doctor paused to look at him, her exasperation at Luke's caustic tone mild but evident by her raised eyebrow.

"Oh, did you want something specific?" he asked. He hissed when she probed around his wound.

The doctor looked at the nurse. "Surgery. Recent. 24 hours or less." The brown eyes shifted to Luke's agonized expression. "Heather, go get us some ibuprofen until I get some more info. Any medication allergies?"

Luke jerked his head to indicate the negative.

"Was this surgery done here?" the doctor asked.

"Why the hell do you think I'm here, in one of *your* hospital gowns, with my arm wrapped up?"

The doctor frowned. "We have no record of anyone in this room. Did you happen to wander here by accident?"

"I was asleep until about ten minutes ago, so your guess is as good as mine. Can't you check your system for my name?"

The nurse returned with a tiny cup of pills.

Luke grabbed the cup and tossed them back, chugging the

water she handed to him next.

"There's no one in the system under his name," the nurse said as she took the cups back.

The doctor huffed. "He's dehydrated. Get an IV going. We'll sort this out once we get his physical needs taken care of. I'm going to do some investigating. Mr. Pearson, was this a scheduled surgery or an emergency?"

"I was shot," Luke said dryly.

The doctor gave him a grim look. "Emergency, then. Excuse me."

"That should hit your system soon enough," the nurse said. She turned to pull out one of the poles and hung up a bag of fluid, setting out needles and supplies for starting Luke's IV again.

She examined Luke's arm, probing lightly over the spot where the previous one had been. "Hm" was all she said before placing the needle again. She seemed to struggle with the process, likely since Luke was dehydrated.

He couldn't have cared less about that since his pain level was more manageable and exhaustion settled into his bones.

"How'd you get shot?" the nurse asked, trying to sound casual, but he could tell she was wary. No doubt most patients that came in with gunshot wounds wouldn't often be the most savory of characters.

"My best friend's murderer."

The nurse's eyes shot up to Luke's, her eyebrow raised.

"He's in jail now," he reassured her.

She turned back to what she was doing. "Who was it you had asked for earlier?"

"Erin Baylor." He grunted as he repositioned himself. The nurse helped him pull the blankets over his legs. "She was with me when I fell asleep," he continued. "She could clear all this up. I honestly don't know what happened between then and now. I know I didn't get up and walk out of my room."

"I'll see if I can find anything out about that. Maybe check security to see how you got moved without anyone letting us know."

He didn't reply as the nurse helped a little bit more with how he was laying, asked if he was comfortable, checked his IV, did the oximeter on his finger, wrote notes on a scrap of paper.

When she finished and left him alone, Luke laid his head back and tried to relax, but as much as his body begged for sleep, his mind reeled.

The bed had been made like it was prepped and ready for a new patient. Not like he'd been in it the whole time and somehow had taken off the blankets. The place was an icebox and dark. He wouldn't have taken them off. The door had stood open, and the nurse was genuinely surprised to find him there. No record of anyone in this room.

The view out the window was the same, so Luke didn't think he, however improbable in the first place, walked here in his sleep. And he just knew Erin wouldn't have left without telling him, leaving a message—something.

Oh God. What if. . .

But he hadn't had that intense ear pressure and ringing like before. The last thing he remembered was Erin's body heat next to him, the two of them practically melded to each other on the bed.

But he had been deeply enough asleep that he hadn't even noticed when the nurses came in for checks.

Had he been so knocked out that he didn't feel the transfer to a different universe? Was it possible that he'd gone home and not realized it?

The hope surged inside of him, much more powerful of a pain reliever than any meds they could give him. He opened his eyes to the ceiling, smiling until he sensed the presence of someone in the room.

He lifted his head to look, fully expecting to see *his* Erin standing there.

It was a pair of stone-faced men, and his gut dropped to the floor. How they'd entered the room without him hearing, he wasn't sure, but he knew their presence could not be good—in any universe.

"Luke Pearson," one said. He was slightly taller, thinner on top.

But they looked remarkably similar and insanely *un*remarkable in appearance. So average, one would have a hard time describing them to a sketch artist.

He had a distinct feeling this was *not* the right universe. His heart sank, panic tingling into his fingers, ramping his heart rate up.

"You've been somewhere you don't belong." The first one spoke again.

Luke tried to work around his dry throat. It seemed a vain hope, but he dared to say it anyway: "Please tell me you can get me home."

Neither of them answered.

And Luke decided he'd rather get shot again.

Epilogue

THE RIGHT ERIN

It was late and getting later by the minute, though each of those minutes felt like seconds for her. The first few days had dragged, weighed down by the questions and uncertainty and all the waiting.

But the last few nights, Erin sat alone and wired, obsessing over all the details that didn't add up, and felt herself creeping farther into the realm of insomnia.

It wasn't a conscious choice to stay up all night. She didn't even feel the time as it passed. She simply blinked, and the night was gone.

Because grown men didn't just disappear.

She stared at the two water glasses on the table. Both were empty. One had been hers; the other had been Kelly's. Her family members were all taking turns sitting up with her as late as they could stand, and tonight had been her sister-in-law's shift. But being pregnant and perpetually exhausted, Kelly hadn't lasted much past midnight.

There was a thud on the front porch like a footstep, but Erin didn't move. She'd imagined his tread on the steps so many times that this felt like another mental mirage designed to trick her into checking for him.

A second thud pulled her out of her trance, and she turned with the first inkling of hope flowering inside of her. Still, she tried to talk herself out of it, out of the compulsion to see *just in case.*

Her hope won out after a moment, and she flung herself from the couch to run for the door, yanking it open so fast it blew her loose hair away from her face as she peered into the darkness.

She didn't react at first because she'd convinced herself it had been wasted effort, that he wouldn't be there, that the figure she saw moving up the steps was her imagination again.

Because grown men didn't just disappear and return home as if nothing happened.

The figure didn't break stride, moving forward with an urgency she didn't yet feel because it hadn't slid home that this might be real.

"Luke?" she whispered, almost afraid to believe, to let her voice take volume in case it was just her mind tormenting her.

But then hands, *his* hands, the exact shape and texture her body remembered from millions of caresses before this, slid around her waist, and he was pulling her against him.

She melted, her bones and muscles becoming useless in the wake of the relief that flushed through her. She molded herself to him as a little sob clawed up her throat. Her fingers ached as she gripped so tightly, clinging because she wanted to feel every part of him, to make sure he was whole. His sigh in response made it seem as if he could hear her thoughts. Or maybe because he felt the same way.

"Where have you been?" She couldn't bring herself to detach from him, so the words came against his shoulder, still half-choked by her emotion.

He moved his hands up into her hair and tipped her face back. Shadow shrouded him from behind, but the light spilling tentatively out the front door illuminated his face. His expression was pinched, lines carved into his skin by pain.

But before she could ask, he caught her mouth with his. There was a hunger and a desperation behind his kiss that she didn't understand.

He walked her backwards into the house, keeping them blessedly connected. She gasped for air when he finally broke away to shut the door.

"Luke—"

"We need to pack. We need to leave tonight. Go some-where—anywhere. First flight out." His words tumbled out, the urgency in his voice like a punch to her gut. "Marry me right now."

She blinked, thrown. "What?"

Marry him? That had always been the plan, the dream, sure. She'd been ready for a long time. But this was out of left field, and she didn't like not understanding, not having the whole picture.

He had yet to release his hold on her, which suited her fine, even with the confusion and all of her questions. But with their bodies still connected, she felt the buzz of his anxiety, and it made the apprehension wind in her belly.

"We'll go on our honeymoon—a month-long European vacation," he said, backing them farther into the house. "I don't care. But we have to go. Tonight."

The prospect sent a thrill of excitement through her—a spon-taneous trip with him, no distractions, no family obligations. But she still didn't understand it. He'd been dragging his feet about the wedding all this time, and *now* he wanted to get married? After disappearing without a trace a week before?

"Wait," she said, her voice tightening with the demand for answers she had yet to let loose, that she hadn't figured out how to put into words. The questions tumbled into each other in her mind, vying for first place.

"Erin, we are in danger. We need to go *now*."

That sent a tingle of fear down her spine as she stared at him, the intensity pulling his expression tight.

Grown men didn't just disappear of their own volition.

"Danger from whom?" she asked, though she wasn't sure she was ready for that answer.

She had no idea what he could have gotten involved with, and she didn't want to think what that might say about him, about her, about their life together.

He shook his head, frustration pulling his mouth down. "I don't have that answer. But we cannot stay here. Not until I know we'll be safe."

His answer sent another jolt of fear through her, and she jerked out of his arms. If he hadn't disappeared for days, she would have thought it was one of his elaborate practical jokes.

When she saw the color drawn from his face, she looked at the arm he'd suddenly clutched against his abdomen. Had she hurt him?

"What happened?" she asked, her hands lifting to reach for him against her will.

"I was shot."

His words hit the air between them with an impact that made her flinch.

"What do you mean you were shot?"

"Erin, I know you have questions. But please. I need you to trust me."

She searched his face again—earnest, stone-cold sober, and desperate. She wrapped her arms around herself. Luke Pearson was the love of her life, the one she'd built a life with, the only man she wanted.

If he asked her to trust him. . . she would.

"Okay," she said, unable to put much strength into the word. But she forced the conviction, put as much confidence as she could muster. Fake it 'til you make it. "Okay. Let's do it. I'll rearrange some things—"

"On the way," he interrupted, starting toward their bedroom. "Better yet, after we've landed in Europe."

She trailed after him, nodding, though she didn't release the self-hug. It was the only thing holding her together.

She watched him pull their luggage out of the closet with the frantic energy he'd arrived with. The questions she wanted to ask percolated in her mind, assembling into manageable lists for when there was time for him to explain.

She let the only pertinent one bubble to the surface. "Where should we go? Paris? London?"

"I don't care," he said, tossing the first suitcase up onto the bed with a grimace, and she looked at his arm again as he pressed it against his body. Then he abruptly turned to gather her against him again like he needed another hit of connection to get through whatever came next. "I don't care as long as I'm with you," he murmured into her hair.

She squeezed him hard, building a stronger resolve, taking comfort in the very real feeling of his arms around her. She'd prayed for his return, cried in grief and desperation, had been sick with worry every day that he'd been gone.

Because grown men didn't just disappear and come back alive.

But he had. Miraculously, he was here again, holding her with a new fierceness that seared her heart. And so she released him and set to work packing with an intensity that matched his.

If they were together, that was all that mattered. She didn't need to know. Not yet. Luke was a good man. She could trust him.

He'd disappeared, but he'd come back to her.

Acknowledgments

There are so many amazing people in my life who support me in many different ways. I could get philosophical, run long, write poems—nay, epics—about the people who love me. But none of us have that kind of time. And you all would probably get annoyed as I dragged it all out.

I should start with my parents, especially my mom. Obviously they get the credit for bringing me into existence and raising me to be the literary genius I am. Though that was sort of happenstance and not a conscious effort. Ha. Mom, you get extra credit for taking my kids so often so I can have alone time, a.k.a. writing time.

My husband deserves a huge shout out for being the biggest support, the most excited and encouraging person, and the one who has let me take my writing as seriously as I want. Even when it was a hobby, you made sure I had time for it. Thank you, my love. Forever and ever.

To my friends, who have been crazy awesome. You all make my life a joy, filled with laughter and trauma dumps, parties and girls' trips. And so many of you have bought and read my books, inspired conversations, characters, and scenes.

Alyssa, you always get a special shout out for being the best best friend who ever best friended. Love you forever!

To my critique partners and beta readers: Megan, Dairis, Julie, Meredith, Danielle, Penny, my Quill & Cup family, the writing community—you all are so amazing! Cheyenne, Lucy, and Mandy—my Llama Ladies, you are the group I needed in my inner circle. Love you all! If you haven't discovered the beauty of the writing community on Instagram, you are seriously missing out.

I could never do justice to what you all mean to me and what you have done to help me get here! THANK YOU will have to hold the biggest meaning in the smallest package.

About the Author

Tracey Barski lives in Colorado with her husband and their two children. When she's not writing or wrangling tiny humans, she works as an editor and proofreader. For fun, she likes to pretend to be 80 years old, crocheting and watching Hallmark movies. She can also be found reading or singing loudly to any song she knows the words to. Find her on Instagram and Facebook, as well as at traceybarski.com, to find out about her upcoming books!

You can connect with me on:
- https://www.traceybarski.com
- https://www.facebook.com/authortraceybarski
- https://www.instagram.com/authortraceybarski

Also by Tracey Barski

The Alternate End of Cassidy Marchand
What happens when you're pulled into an
alternate version of your life?

Cassidy Marchand is abandoned, on the run, and out of money. She's just gotten arrested for stealing, but that's the least of her worries. When she wakes up, everything seems normal—at first. She soon discovers she has entered an alternate reality where she encounters devoted and loyal friends she's never met, meets the golden-boy doctor she's engaged to, and finds out the father who deserted her in her own world actually stuck around to raise her alternate self. The biggest hitch? Alternate-reality Cassidy is not only dead, she's been murdered.

Dealing with the complicated mess of her own emotions and the grief of those around her is nightmarish enough, but there's still a killer on the loose. Will Cassidy become a victim for a second time? When someone else gets taken by the killer, Cassidy can't justify her desire to run away from the heartache and the danger, and finds herself running headlong into an alternate end she hadn't bargained for.

Resurrecting Cassidy Marchand

What happens when you're pulled into an alternate version of your life—again?

Cassidy Marchand thought the alternate reality thing was done. Of course, it's a little unsatisfying not to know exactly what sent her sliding through dimensions, but she's glad to be alive. Surviving a serial killer tended to give perspective.

But then the father who abandoned her as a child and the mother who died when she was eight walk into her hospital room, and she realizes she must be in the wrong universe. Again.

Now she's navigating this new family dynamic while dealing with the case against her would-be killer and investigating just what the hell was happening to her. But things get complicated fast as her search lands her in danger, her childhood dream falls apart, and her past catches up with her.

Cassidy has to decide if she's going to do what she's good at and run from it all or finally stand up and take charge of her life.

Cassidy Marchand Unraveled
What happens when you're pulled into an alternate version of your life?

Cassidy Marchand has finally taken a stand in directing the way her life goes. Finding the device that enables her to jump when *she* wants seems to be the break she's been waiting for. She throws herself into the search for answers, determined to make sense of everything she's been through.

Even if that means putting herself and everything she's building in danger.

More questions than answers seem to pile up, and she's coming to realize that sliding dimensions is truly as unnatural as it sounds. The toll it's taking on her mind and her body force her to reevaluate her priorities, causing her to pivot her focus.

But even as she adjusts, the things she turns her attention to start falling one by one like dominoes.

When she's faced with a decision that could ultimately take everything that remains, she makes the only choice she thinks is left. But it might just be the one thing that tears her apart.